To Sue,

I hope that you enjoy escaping into the world of Nero, Its been a pleasure to finally meet you, Val x

by Valden Bush
2021

Butterworth Books is a different breed of publishing house. It's a home for Indies, for independent authors who take great pride in their work and produce top quality books for readers who deserve the best. Professional editing, professional cover design, professional proof reading, professional book production—you get the idea. As Individual as the Indie authors we're proud to work with, we're Butterworths and we're *different*.

Authors currently publishing with us:

E.V. Bancroft
Valden Bush
Helena Harte
Karen Klyne
AJ Mason
James Merrick
Robyn Nyx
Simon Smalley

For more information visit www.butterworthbooks.co.uk

This trade paperback original is published by
Butterworth Books, Nottingham, England

Cataloging information
ISBN: 978-1-915009-01-2
CREDITS
Editors: Nicci Robinson
Cover Design: Nicci Robinson, Global Wordsmiths
Production Design: Global Wordsmiths

Acknowledgements

My writing journey has been both fun and full of learning "the craft." Without a doubt, this has been due to Victoria Villaseñor and Nicci Robinson. Four years ago, in response in my innocent question "How do I write a book?" Victoria suggested I go away and write. So, there it was...my starting point.

After several writing retreats and workshops with Global Wordsmiths (run by Victoria and Nicci, aka Brey Willows and Robyn Nyx), and extensive development editing with Nicci, Nero has finally become something real. Each step along the way has had their support, suggestions, help, and unending supply of humour. That they have seen something in my efforts continues to surprise me, and thank you seems somehow inadequate. But I know I would not have done it without them. I'm also thankful that Nicci selected my short stories for inclusion in the Lesfic Eclectic series. They gave me confidence in myself when readers wrote to tell me of their enjoyment of the words I had written.

My personal support bubble of fellow soon-to-be authors has been inspiring. Thank you, Gill, Isa, and Anne for giving me a safe space in which to make my numerous mistakes, for holding me up when I was down, and generally just being there for me. I've really been grateful for those hours we spent writing on Zoom, often silent but supporting each other.

Finally, I couldn't have done anything without my wife, who has always encouraged me to follow my heart and fed me all the way. I love you.

Dedication

To G

For always encouraging me
to spread my wings and fly.

CHAPTER ONE

THE TWO MOONS reflected on the highly polished boot and into her eyes. Stele had to look away. *Where am I?* She tried to focus beyond the boot, but that pink Gandon slime that Shimo, her drinking buddy, all but forced down her throat had messed with her vision. In addition, she couldn't feel any part of her body.

"Stele Hosun."

The deep timbre of the woman's voice sounded like the bell that had rung on Nero when Stele was banished. The bet over that last drink had tipped Stele into this state. Naveh! Shimo lived in Alton's bars, mostly the Strip outside the Defense Force base, and bet on anything and everything, making enough credit to drink her way through each sun cycle. Stele had lost to her yet again.

Why is my face so wet? She could smell her own sick and there was also the aroma of something like glit, the medicinal wash her mother would wipe her face with when she was sick as a child. Maybe she was in the med center? She couldn't remember much about last dark, other than she'd bumped into Shimo and had been losing bets and drinking as penance.

Stele managed to look up from the boot. The thick blue material of the woman's trousers looked expensive, and she smelled of pilton fruit. Why was everything reminiscent of home? She hadn't seen a single pilton fruit on Alton these last three moon cycles. Pilton fruit only grew at home on Nero, and she'd never be allowed there again. Banished for life as if she was nothing. Nothing on Nero, and nothing here on Alton.

"I'll take another Gandon wine, thank you." The black nothingness of being unconscious beckoned her into its arms.

"I don't think so."

Stele showed her wrist and the credit counter. "I have credit...well, I think I do. I should have enough for another few bottles."

"I'm sure you do, but this isn't a bar."

Valden Bush

"Oh, Naveh! Have I asked a planet guard to get me a drink? I'm sorry. What's my fine this time?"

"You're not in the drunk holding bays, and I'm not a planet guard. And if you'd let me speak, I'll tell you exactly who I am. Are you going to be quiet and listen?"

Stele couldn't comprehend what had happened to her. The thought ran through her mind that maybe she'd been kidnapped. If so, no-one would miss her at all.

"You won't get any ransom for me. I'm worthless. No one on this, or any other, planet will pay you a single credit."

"Just be quiet and listen. Have you ever heard of Kian Ray?" she asked.

Stele opened her eyes at the name. Ray's story had been a cautionary tale for as long as she could remember. *"You'll end up just like Kian Ray,"* had been a constant refrain. "Kian Ray was a Neroian with impure eyes. She could not complete the rite of passage, was violent, and loved women." *Like me.* "She was banished once she reached maturity, and her records were expunged."

"Do you know what happened after that?"

"No. Should I?" Stele moved up and rested on her elbows. It was about all the movement she could muster. She focused on the woman interrogating her: athletic build, navy blue dress uniform, and stern face. She'd probably been strikingly handsome as a young woman and when Stele looked into her eyes, she could see a look that mirrored something inside herself.

"I was originally from Nero, as you'd be able to tell if you were sober and thinking straight. I'm Kian Ray, now Colonel of the Alton Defense Force."

Stele's mind began to clear, and with that came the pain that always accompanied several moon cycles of alcohol abuse. She looked at the woman and knew Kian was telling the truth. Her purple eyes reflecting the rarest of Neroian rock had black lines spread across them like a starburst. The owners of purple eyes were usually members of the Neroian Ruling Council, but because the black lines were considered a genetic abnormality, she would not have been able to complete the rite of passage and would have been banished as soon as she came of age. But how was she a Colonel?

"Naveh! The rumors weren't wrong." Kian pointed at Stele's face.

"I never thought I'd see eyes as black as yours. Nero must have been astounded by you."

Fully black eyes had never happened on Nero before, and thus Stele had been labeled as an abomination. "Creff! You're just like all the rest..." Her rage festered just below the surface like a volcano about to blow. She clenched her fists and wanted to pound Kian Ray with her frustration.

"No." Kian rested her hands on Stele's shoulders. "I'm nothing like the rest. Please stay calm. I used to get angry like you, and right now, I want to knock some sense into you. You're on a journey that will end with you dead on the Strip. If you can sober up, there's a job for you in the ADF that comes with pay and accommodation."

"I'm trouble." Stele echoed the words she'd heard for years whenever anyone spoke of her. "I'm seriously not worth your time or money."

"I once thought of myself as you do. But becoming part of the ADF changed everything for me. It'll do the same for you...if you let it. But you have to want it." Kian took hold of Stele's wrists and pulled her up to her knees. "If you agree, I'll spend the next moon cycle removing all trace of alcohol from your system and getting you ready for selection."

Stele shook her head. "Why would you help me?" No one had ever given her any assistance without wanting something in return, usually something she didn't want to give.

"The ADF did the same for me when I arrived. You're like me, an outsider on our own planet, but you'll find that you're not an outsider here. The ADF is open to all and accepts recruits from any nation of the Federation if they can pass the selection. Almost all banished Neroians have joined the Force."

"I have no skills." Stele pulled her arms from Kian's grasp. "I have nothing to offer you or the Force."

"Everyone has something to offer...but they need to be sober."

Stele shrugged and laughed, though the action drew attention to her aching body. "That's me out. I need another drink." She didn't need one more failure to add to her already long list, like being banished from Nero for being different. Her thoughts drifted to the unexpected pain of saying goodbye to Ariane. Stele shook them off and tried to get to her feet but stumbled back into a heap on the ground. "I can't move. I can't think straight. And everything hurts."

Kian raised her eyebrow and smiled. "You've nothing to lose if I help

you out. Let's get you cleaned up and fed. We can take it from there."
Stele said nothing. Kian was right. She no longer had *anything* to lose.
"Sergeant Drax." Kian waved beyond Stele. "Your help, please."
Stele felt strong hands reach underneath her body and lift her both gently and slowly as if she were a valuable Neroian gem sculpture. Her head drooped backwards, and she shut her eyes. *Just a little sleep.*

***

Stele had been drifting in and out of consciousness but couldn't quite hold onto being awake for long. She was trying to rise from a deep sleep and grapple with a new morn, but something was off-kilter. Her head was banging and felt like it was attached to the rest of her body with metal rods that vibrated, making her body taut and pained. She tried opening her eyes, but they didn't want to work. Her mouth tasted like she'd been chewing on sun-hardened decko dung. She tried to open her eyes again and this time succeeded. The white ceiling above her was studded with foreign-looking fitments but Neroian clear gems emitted a powerful light. She didn't know where she was but remembered she'd silently agreed to Kian's offer of food and a shower. She'd needed that, sure, but what she needed more was a drink to take her right back into a thoughtless oblivion.

Stele carefully and slowly raised herself onto one elbow to try and take in her surroundings. She saw herself mirrored in the reflective wall beside her, her pale face and black eyes staring back. The center of them was black, as black as the planet…as black as her soul? At least that's what they'd have her believe. The color of their eyes categorized everyone on Nero and black simply wasn't acceptable as a color. And Stele had no starburst to mitigate the darkness. She'd been a pariah since birth; the Ruling Council believed that she was the result of a birth defect and the only person on the planet who was wholly abnormal.

She lived all her life knowing she was going to be banished, because she wouldn't be able to complete the rite of passage and get her full powers and thus reach her potential. There was no black shard in the Coliseum to allow her to connect. There had been quite a few members of the population with black starbursts on their colored eyes in the past who also couldn't complete the rite of passage because the shards that were the color of their eyes held no power for them. They were banished too.

"Impure," was a taunt she'd heard all her life.

"Stele Hosun."

Stele heard the voice before she saw where it was coming from. A barrage of Alton language came at her, and she understood the woman wanted her out of bed.

"Um…" was all she could make her decko dung mouth say. She slowly raised herself onto one elbow again to look at the woman. It was the sergeant, whatever her name was. She reminded Stele of a trepple, a rectangular vegetable with a bitter taste that was prevalent on Nero.

She came closer. "Up, now."

"I need a drink."

"No." She pinched her nose and motioned toward an open doorway. "I am not putting up with your smell or disobedience. Get in there."

Her attitude was an unpleasant reminder of too many people in Stele's life. Back on Nero, Jasper Sloan had made a grandstanding speech to the Ruling Council about Stele Hosun and her infamous life. Her parents, both on the Council, were shamed. The speech was broadcast across Nero and was the final straw for her. Stele wanted to kill Sloan with her bare hands. She'd been in danger of making herself into a murderer, and it frightened her. Now here she was on a new planet having similar dark thoughts about someone else.

She flopped back onto the bed, closed her eyes, and imagined a measure of Weston Green slipping down her throat. There was a tug at her cover, and Sergeant Trepple-face ripped it from her bed. Stele was naked underneath and made a snatch for the cover, but the sergeant made her way to the door with it. Stele managed to grab a corner of the cover, and the sergeant's momentum pulled her out of bed, leaving her uncomfortably vulnerable.

Stele caught a whiff of her own scent: a sticky, dried sweat mixed with sour Gandon wine and the chemical smell of glit. No wonder the sergeant wanted her to shower. Her head throbbed savagely, and her body hurt like she'd been run over by stampeding decko escaping the hunt. The effort of standing up straight was almost too much. "Okay, I'll go and get clean," she said as she was almost through the doorway, moving fast to hide her exposed body.

"Back here in ten crons." Sergeant Trepple-face pointed to where she was standing.

Valden Bush

Rage enfolded her like a favorite cloak, and she drew from its strength. She roared and pounded on the partition between the two shower units until she'd vented the steam of her anger. She settled and looked at the near stranger in the mirror, almost a younger version of her father. She was flushed, and her lips were thin. She was angry, yes, but she could see straight through that anger. Her skin was dark around her black eyes, and she looked thinner. A lot thinner. Too much alcohol for three moon cycles with little food resulted in this skeleton-like person looking back at her. She had gained that imperious look her father often had, as if there was a smell under his nose. On Nero, she was strong in body and mind. But now? Thin equaled weak, but there was no way she would be like her father. Always taking the line of least resistance and never standing up for anything or anyone. In particular, never standing up for his daughter. She had always known herself as strong. *When did I become such a failure?* Her thoughts were interrupted when she saw a movement behind her.

Trepple-face appeared with a pile of army fatigues in her arms and pointed to a shower. There were no boots or shoes. Obviously Trepple-face didn't trust that Stele wouldn't skip out on her, so she wasn't giving her any. The only word Stele could make out was ten crons. Trepple-face caught sight of the partition. She was silent, her face had gone red, and she grabbed Stele's hands. She lifted them, looking at them carefully.

"Five crons." She shook her head, turned on her heels, and left the room.

Returning to her room after a refreshing vibe shower, Stele found the sergeant waiting. She stared at Stele standing in bare feet, looked her up and down, and checked she was wearing the clothing correctly. The sergeant took her along the corridor to a food hall which was deserted and sent her to collect a tray of food from the counter. She wasn't hungry and would rather have had a drink. But the sergeant sat opposite and stared at Stele until she started eating the least offensive-looking offering of brown slop with a small biscuit floating on top. Stele pushed it aside after one unpleasant spoonful of the congealed, half-cold liquid and tried the second bowl of green puree, which turned out to be sweet and fruity. Stele took a sip of tak. It wasn't alcoholic, but it was better than nothing, and she'd always liked how the blue liquid left a stain on her tongue.

The minute she finished, the sergeant bustled her out of the food hall and back to her room. She sat on the bed and a moment later, Kian appeared in the doorway.

"Good morn, Sergeant Drax," Kian said. "And hello to you, Stele."

Drax pulled Stele to a standing position and brushed her off as if she were dirty and disheveled. Drax spoke to Kian at length and grabbed Stele's bruised hands to show her. Stele was angry again. She was not going to do this with this trepple-faced Sergeant Drax; she would quit before submitting, she was not going to do what they wanted. She'd had enough of this sort of treatment on Nero. She didn't need it here. She clenched her fists.

"Stele, stop it," Kian said. "I can feel you exploding from over here. Please, can we talk as two outcasts together? Come, let us sit." She sat on Stele's unmade bed and patted the space beside her. "How are you feeling after some sleep and food?"

Stele swallowed against the ball of anger for the moment. She'd listen to what Kian had to say. She sat and rested her fists in her lap.

"I understand how you're feeling. You've a lot of anger inside you. But we can help you channel that anger positively and get you fit and healthy. You just have to consent."

Stele said nothing. Could she survive this place with these people? Kian was the first person ever to take an interest in her. Stele still wasn't sure of her motives. Why would she care? Did that even matter? Kian was offering Stele a new life, and it wasn't like she had anywhere else to be.

"Why don't you stay here for a moon cycle? It's not that long in the scheme of things, and it'll give us a little time to get that Gandon wine out of your system."

Stele laughed. "I don't think I have enough credits for any length of stay here."

"This isn't a credits thing. Will you agree to follow my plan?"

"Okay. Like you said before, I've nothing to lose." Stele turned and looked into Kian's purple-black starburst eyes, still searching for Kian's motive in helping her. "I always let people down, so don't expect much."

"This time will be like nothing you've known before. Complete it, and you'll not let me down. You'll spend the first half moon cycle with Sergeant Drax. She'll shout a lot and push you physically harder than you've ever been pushed before. If you strike her, we'll both hit you back twice as hard, and that's a promise. If you feel tempted to quit, tell me, and I'll listen. You'll be with us both a lot in the second half moon cycle, and we'll continue to work on your fitness, do some testing, and start to build up your knowledge of Alton." She looked down at Stele's bare feet. "Sergeant Drax will get you some boots, shoes, and more fatigues. There's a locker inset into that wall for any belongings you may have. This room will be yours while you're here. You're in a wing of the medical facility. You won't be able to leave without my permission. Your treatment bed will monitor your body and dose you for the alcohol. It'll take the full moon cycle to clean your system fully. Good luck."

Kian left the room with a quick salute to Drax. Drax turned to Stele and smirked, clearly looking forward to drilling Stele.

"You're mine."

Drax ordered Stele to make her bed. She left the room and came back with a bucket of cleaner and a cloth and said she expected the floor to be clean by the time she returned. Stele followed her instructions. Drax returned with clothing and boots and dropped them in front of Stele. After she'd put the boots on, Drax started shouting at her. She pointed to the bed and showed Stele how she should have made it. Drax pointed to the floor and the marks left by the cloth and her boot prints. She quickly demonstrated how she wanted Stele to polish the floor.

"Re-do," Drax said.

Stele took a deep breath and quelled her rising anger. *It's just a test.* She nodded. She knelt down, and her head started to ache, and nausea wracked her stomach. But she ignored it all and set about polishing the floor again, determined that Drax wouldn't find fault this time. Drax came back and nodded. She hardly looked at the room and indicated that Stele should follow her.

She entered an empty training room. "This will be your work. You will start now. Run. From here to there and back again." Drax shouted, "Faster!"

Stele did as instructed and returned.

"There to here. Faster!"

Stele started a second run with Drax chasing and shouting at her. Stele continued to run with Drax pushing her until her lungs were on fire and she dropped to the ground. Drax let her rest briefly and gave her a flask of tak. She pushed Stele into a circuit around the room with different exercises designed to increase her strength and flexibility. Every time she slowed, Drax got in her face, pushing and shouting at her. Stele worked out her rage on the ropes, trying to control her instinct to explode like a misfiring rocket. Kian's words repeated in her head like a mantra: *If you strike her, we'll both hit you back twice as hard.*

Finally, Drax held up her hand to indicate the end of the session. "Follow me," she said. She led Stele back to her room, showed her the recycler for her clothes, and pointed to the vibe showers. "Clean yourself up. Be back here in ten crons."

Stele let the strong vibrations surround her body and enjoyed the feeling as well as the rest from Drax's shouting, albeit a temporary one.

Drax returned to take Stele to eat again and stayed to watch her consume everything on her tray. The training had made her so hungry, Stele even ate the brown soup. Drax escorted Stele back to her room.

Drax pointed to Stele's bed. "Get some rest. You're going to need it."

Stele stripped off her fatigues and boots and climbed under the cover, asleep before she was barely horizontal.

***

The klaxon alarm sounded at full volume, and Stele jumped out of bed with a shout, her heart vibrating like the hammers in the mines below Nero. She clenched her fists, ready to attack. Someone grabbed hold of her fist.

"No!"

Stele recognized Drax's shout since she'd heard enough of it in the last sun cycle. She slowly became more aware of her surroundings and saw a small woman in fatigues holding a trumpet and looking at her, laughing. Drax snorted and said something to the trumpeter, who slowly appraised Stele from her feet to her eyes. The small woman's gaze lingered at Stele's breasts. She'd never seen someone look at her with such...*lust*. Was that what it was? Like the woman wanted to taste her. Stele loved females and everything about them, but she'd never done anything about it. More to the point, she'd never had the opportunity. The trumpeter began to leave but turned at the door, took another look at Stele, and said something to Drax which Stele didn't catch.

Drax shook her head, turned back to Stele, and motioned to the woman as she left. "She wants you. Do you want her?"

Stele's body flushed with heat. Could it be that simple? The trumpeter was attractive, but Stele was still exhausted from the last sun cycle's exertions. A glass of Gandon wine might help. "Maybe later when I'm healthy."

Drax raised her eyebrow and shrugged. "Your loss. Now, shower and back here in ten crons ready for morn-meal."

And so the sun cycle progressed similarly to the sun cycle before. She made her bed, correctly first time. The floor cleaning was a different story. Drax's inspection of her second attempt was too detailed for Stele. Drax was looking for errors where there were none. Stele stood, a satisfying two hands or so higher than Drax. "There was nothing wrong with this floor the first time. You're just playing games with me."

"Yes. Because I can, and I'll enjoy doing it. On your knees now, and make it shine."

Stele rolled her neck, stretched out her hands, and repeated Kian's words in her head. *If you strike her, we'll both hit you back twice as hard.* She crouched to the floor and began her task again.

Once the floor passed inspection, the sun cycle was exercise, drink, repeat, over and over. Food was a welcome change, even though it tasted like the droppings of a decko. After dark-meal Kian came into in the dining hall and motioned to Stele to follow her.

"Sergeant Drax tells me that you're trouble. Should I believe her?"

Stele shrugged. "*I* told you I was trouble, but I haven't battered the Sergeant…although I've thought about it." *Many times.* "I can't change in one dark."

Kian smiled as if Drax's behavior would have warranted Stele's rage.

"As long as you keep trying, I'll be happy." Kian pointed to the monitors next to Stele's bed. "Your medical treatment seems to be going well, and you're already a lot healthier. How do you feel?"

Bruised, battered, and desperate for a drink. "Better than I thought I would." Stele sat on the edge of her bed.

"Good. Well, as you know Alton is a mix of people from other worlds, and there is no common language. But most new residents and travelers tend to have an Information-Module-Interface, aka a Mesh, fitted to their brains. It will allow you to communicate in any of the common languages, find information about Alton and the Federation, and the worlds that are a part of it. If you agree, I'll authorize you to have the most basic Mesh installed. The basic model is easy to use, and you'll be happy with it after just a few hours."

"I don't have the money to pay for any of this, and I don't want debts." Stele didn't want to owe anybody anything that could be used as leverage. She'd seen it with other people, and she wanted no part of it. "I've never had debts before, and I won't start now. How can I pay for all of it?"

"When you have work, you can pay me back for the Mesh. But for now, understand that I'm willing to take the risk on you, and I trust you."

Trust. That was an alien word that even the Mesh wouldn't translate. No one had ever trusted her, and she'd never trusted anyone. How could she have earned Kian's trust when she barely knew Stele? "It won't make me obedient or do something to my brain, will it? I don't want to be controlled."

"That's a fair question, but I'm a violent person according to Nero's criteria, and a Mesh hasn't controlled me, even when I could've done with being less aggressive. As an officer in the Defense Force, I've had numerous free military upgrades that allow me defense, security, and strategic abilities. And should you join, they'll be available to you too. I recommend you go for it."

If it had worked for Kian, it should work for her. Kian had shown her nothing but respect and kindness. Maybe this was a good way to test that trust thing. "Okay. What do I have to do?"

"Stay here and the medical team will come for you," Kian said.

Stele nodded, leaned back, closed her eyes, and waited.

CHAPTER TWO

STELE LAY ON her bed, savoring the relaxation she desperately needed. She began to doze, and her thoughts soon turned to Ariane.

Ariane. Knowing she'd never see Ariane again hurt worse than any physical beating she'd endured. There was a darkness and a yearning when she thought of leaving Ariane behind. They'd been best friends nearly all their lives, and Ariane was the only person on Nero who understood Stele's difference. Ariane didn't judge Stele for being what Neroians considered to be an outsider. She'd been the only person who had ever seen through Stele's furious façade…until Kian, who seemed to have that ability too.

Neroians expected Stele to be irritable, loud, mean-spirited, and violent. Ever since her childhood she'd been told there was something wrong with her eyes and other children had ignored or bullied her. She'd spent her life listening to insults like "black-eyed barbarian" and threats to banish her. Stele began to believe the words hurled at her like missiles. But rather than bow to the shame and the shuns, Stele became the person they expected her to be, embraced it even. She was bored in lessons, bored in work, and created problems wherever she went. They expected violence— she gave it to them.

The color of her eyes had made her a misfit in her own world and eventually the planet's government had made good on their threat. She'd said goodbye to Ariane in her hideaway deep underground on Nero that last sun cycle. Stele had spent her last few crons sitting on her usual seat on a rocky outcrop in an underground cavern at the side of an undiscovered gem nest. The colors of gems embedded in its circular walls comforted and calmed her. Stele had found this spot when she was a child running away from trouble, from other children, from the terror her young life had quickly become. She went there when the pressure in her life made her head pound. The explosive rage inside left her almost as soon as she caressed the hard surfaces of the precious stones. Over the years she had railed against the rules, her parents, the education, and the culture that tried to make her fit into their social mores. She couldn't accept them. And of course, the more she'd rebelled, the less chance she had of becoming a functioning part of the population.

Stele replayed her last moments with Ariane like a vid-story in her head.

"I knew I'd find you down here. Though why you love this dark and wet space is beyond me," Ariane said.

"You know you enjoyed the challenge of finding me." Stele stood up to greet her. When she saw Ariane smile, Stele's mood lightened, and her stomach fluttered with warmth.

"How long before you leave?"

Ariane's question had never before been voiced. Stele had never wanted the conversation between them, and neither, it seemed, had Ariane. She moved closer, and Stele could smell the fragrance of flarnic that would always remind her both of Ariane and the rock forests of Nero.

"I'm going in front of the Council at sunset. I'll probably be off the planet by dark-meal."

"I hoped it would never come to this, Stele."

Stele's legs gave way, so she rested her head on the wall to steady herself. Ariane put her hand on her arm. The heat of Ariane's body warmed Stele from the inside, and her hand on Stele's arm gave her strength. Those hands that were always flowing were now still.

"I'm not sure how I'm going to cope without you being here," Ariane said. "You've been with me all my life, my rebellious friend, but I won't miss getting into trouble with you." Ariane gave Stele a playful shove. "I'll be like an angel in comparison. I suppose they'll say I've grown up. The times of being banned from leaving our homes for moon cycles have long gone."

Devastation lingered in Stele's stomach like a load of rocks. "I hoped I'd get a reprieve, that my parents might intervene. I wanted to wake up this morn, and it would all be a bad dream." Stele sighed and knocked her head against the cold, hard wall of the cavern. "But it's meant to be. I've always been a misfit, and this was a foregone conclusion." Stele pushed away from the wall and pressed her forehead to Ariane's. "I want you to know that you'll always be in my thoughts." Stele swallowed hard when Ariane began to cry. She used her thumbs to brush Ariane's tears away. "Come sit with me for a while. The Ruling Council won't be happy that you're meeting me, but it's good to have a short, private time to say good-bye."

Stele drew Ariane down beside her and kept her arms around her. They were silent but for Ariane's gentle sobs. Stele was reminded of the countless times they'd done this for each other during their lives, and it always seemed to strengthen the bond between them.

Ariane looked up at Stele, her eyes searching for something.

"How do you feel about leaving?"

Stele stayed silent for a moment while she contemplated. Only Ariane ever asked how she felt about anything. "It's strange, but I'm a lot of things. I'm sad. And I'm angry—"

"Obviously." Ariane poked Stele in the chest and grinned.

Stele smiled. Naveh, she was going to miss Ariane. "But there's a small part of me that's hopeful I can find a place on Alton where I won't be a freak, where I can fit in."

Ariane raised her head against her chest. "I dreamed that the Ruling Council would find some reason for your beautiful eyes. I know that Naveh gives us our lives based on the gems. I've been lucky as a singer and musician."

"Do you mean lucky that you aren't destined for the Ruling Council? Most people with purple eyes end up on the Council," said Stele. Ariane's purple eyes always meant something else for Stele though. Her friendship and acceptance of Stele's differences made her heart race, and Ariane's purple eyes that sucked her in when Stele looked at them was something that she would take away and treasure forever.

Naveh granted eye colors to the population, and it was related to the commonality of the gems. Ariane's parents, both with purple eyes, were unusually talented musicians and sat on the Ruling Council representing the green-eyed population. Ariane would never be on the Ruling Council because she was such a talent as a singer and composer and had been giving concerts even before her rite of passage.

"Ha! No, I'm lucky because my rite of passage gave me extra skills in composition, and it allows me to write and sing the music I have in my head, as well you know. You've never stopped joking about me and the Council."

If I didn't joke, I'd cry. Stele laughed. "If you had clear eyes, you'd have little ambition. You probably wouldn't think about composition and be happy to keep banging away at the drums or whatever."

They sat silent for some time, enjoying the last moments of closeness.

"I'll have to go, Ariane. I've no choice. There's nothing much I'll miss about Nero…but I'll miss you." She put her hand over Ariane's. She'd never been any closer to her than this. Stele wanted to kiss her but didn't know what Ariane thought and didn't want to make a mistake. She couldn't face Ariane being angry with her during their last moments. If they couldn't part as lovers, they must part as friends.

So she did nothing.

"I've two pieces of black Nero rock that look like our tears." Stele pulled the rocks from her pocket. "I want us both to keep one to remind us of our time together. I found them on the ground over there." Stele pointed at a large alcove in the rock that looked as if it had been mined out. She gave one to Ariane and slipped its twin back into her pocket. "When you feel lonely or you need strength, just hold it in your hand and think of me. I'll do the same."

"Up. Up. Up."

Stele looked up at Drax's blotchy red face. The painful dream of Ariane melted away, and she leapt to stand beside her bed before Drax could punish her for not responding fast enough.

Stele's Mesh had been implanted and she'd been told to sleep afterwards. The medical bed seemed to have done its job, as she'd slept for the first time rather than falling unconscious, and her headache was gone. Her whole body ached, but that was due to the physical exertion Drax was pushing her through. She wasn't sure she was up to more running and circuits.

"You need to learn how to work your Mesh. You'll use it to learn about the Federation until mid-meal, we'll exercise for the rest of the sun cycle, and then you'll study with the Mesh again. I'll be asking you questions, so you need to pay attention." Drax leaned closer to Stele. "You're still mine. I *will* punish you for the wrong answers."

Stele smiled, which seemed to annoy Drax more than when she got angry. "That's amazing. I can understand every word you're saying." She'd rather enjoyed making things difficult for Drax by feigning ignorance of many of her words. That game was now over, but Stele was sure there would be more.

"It's working as it should. If you look straight ahead, your Mesh will give you a menu for the things that are available to you. Move your eyes slowly to access the functions until you get used to it. You'll soon speed up and make the movements automatically. Colonel Ray has limited your communicator for now and will discuss contacting people other than the two of us later. You'll only see me and Colonel Ray on the address menu. The Colonel has set up a credit for you and will pay for your account balance until you're earning the means to do so yourself." Drax shoved Stele's shoulder. "So, Hosun, task one is to send me a polite message."

"Okay." Stele smiled and did as she'd been bid.

"Not funny: be polite. Task two is to locate the headquarters of the Federation."

Stele looked straight ahead at the menu and moved her eyes to the search function. She started with Fed and the search engine finished the word Federation to give her options. She chose headquarters and was presented detail about the headquarters, the first part being about them being on Alton.

"Alton."

"Correct. Okay, Hosun, that was quick. I think you've got the hang of it. I expect you to be able to answer questions on the first three learning units by the end of the sun cycle. Send me a message if you get stuck. I'll come and collect you for mid-meal. In the meantime, stay here and no wandering. I expect you to study."

The following sun cycles continued in much the same pattern. Drax continued to haunt Stele and punish her for real and imaginary errors or mistakes, and there was nothing Stele could do but accept it. She'd got her head twisted trying to work out how she could give Drax a little payback, but now she figured Drax was just doing what Kian had instructed her to do…and Stele was beginning to believe in Kian. Kian had promised that Stele would be free and gainfully employed in the future, and she could say good-bye to Trepple-face forever. She'd like to say good-bye with her fist, but thus far she'd managed to control most of her outbursts and hadn't struck out at Drax once. And maybe Drax had other issues that meant she was on Stele's case nearly all the time. Come to think of it, Drax reminded her a lot of Jasper Sloan back on Nero. Jasper Sloan, the blue-eyed healer who had renounced her on a worldwide broadcast as an abomination. Stele's mother YahYah was his boss and the Chief Healer in the Ruling Council. Jasper had always been jealous of her mother. Maybe he'd given Drax some lessons.

***

Stele was pronounced clean by the medical staff after half a moon cycle under Drax's control. She was in better shape than she'd ever been, and while she hadn't enjoyed getting there, she did like the results of Drax's physical training. Her head was in a better place too, and though that was unfamiliar, she liked it.

Kian arrived for their regular meeting. She'd told Stele at the previous one that discussing her future would be the main agenda item.

"I think that the Defense Force would be a good fit for you. They'll find something you're good at, and you'll be able to shine. You'll finally have something to look forward to each morn," Kian said.

Stele bit her lip. Kian's confidence in her buoyed her, and she fought against the comforting feeling. All of this was sure to disappear sometime soon. Yes, Kian had been an outcast too, but Stele didn't know why that meant Kian had to rescue every other outcast that came her way. "I haven't got any other offers. I'll give the tests a go. But…"

Stele knew from the heat in her face that she'd gone red. She looked at the floor. *Creff! This is difficult.*

"What's the problem, Stele?"

She sighed and looked up. "I'm worried about the tests."

"You've nothing to fear from them. They're all straightforward and will allow the ADF to work out your strengths and weaknesses."

"What about my weakness for…for women? Is that one of the tests? It was a big thing on Nero, and it was so bad that even if I'd managed to complete the rite of passage, I don't think I could have got a reasonable job, whatever color my eyes."

"Ah, I understand your worry. Did you ever meet Kallie Tremontain on Nero? I expect she was on the Ruling Council."

"Yes, she was the Chief Peacekeeper. We had several talks…well, more like I was given several lectures on my conduct," said Stele.

Kian winced and sucked in a breath quickly. "Kallie and I are the same age, and we were good friends when we were young. We did everything together, and over time, I understood I had a thing for her. I couldn't take my eyes off her, and she gave me funny feelings in my stomach. Because we were so close, I thought she felt the same. She was soft, gentle, open, and happy until the morn her parents interrupted us in each other's arms. We'd done nothing, but I was already soiled goods and, if I also loved women, I was dangerous."

"What happened?" Stele asked.

Kian turned away but not before Stele saw the beginnings of tears.

"Her parents were on the Ruling Council and decided that she would be removed from daily life on Nero and receive remedial learning. I was banned from being anywhere near her or the family, and it was rigidly enforced. I never saw her again. But Alton is nothing like Nero. It's an open world, and so is the ADF. They'll not test you on it. Indeed, they'll not even ask you about it."

Her heart ached, as it did only when she thought of Ariane. She had such a bright future on Nero, any link with Stele would have created problems for her. Since Ariane's rite of passage, her already excellent musical abilities had increased. Her voice, which had bewitched Stele since they were children, had now become something ethereal and unique. Ariane had a future that was assured as long as she didn't do anything that would jeopardize it…as long as she didn't fraternize with Stele.

"Where've you gone?" Kian clicked her fingers in front of Stele's face. "Were you thinking about Nero? It looked painful. Was it a girl? Did you have one?"

"I was thinking of my childhood friend, Ariane. I always wanted her to be more, so much more, but I don't think she's into women. She knew I was, but we never talked about it. She has everything going for her on Nero. I've relived our good-bye time and time again since I got here, and the pain never lessens. Part of me wishes I'd had the courage to have kissed her…but if I had…if she'd responded, I would've lost so much more than I did. It's probably for the best that she never knew how much I liked her, or I might've ruined her life on Nero. But Naveh, it's so hard."

Kian nodded and looked thoughtful. "I left someone behind too. I understand. I wish I could help you with Ariane but contact between Nero and the rest of the Federation worlds is minimal," said Kian.

"I know there's little contact, but how did that happen?"

"Nero has always been an artistic world where most of the population create sculpture, jewelry, art, and music, as you know. According to legend, after the Federation settled in this planetary system, Nero was occupied by pacifists who wanted as little as possible to do with the other worlds. They believed them to be aggressive and inclined to warfare. It's remained isolationist and therefore, the chance of you and Ariane meeting up is minimal," said Kian. She stood up and went over to the window, spending a cron in silence before turning around.

"So, moving forward. Everyone who applies to enter the ADF is tested to see what they are good at, which jobs suit them, and their potential. On the other hand, the ADF needs to be sure they need you. Sergeant Drax and I need to put you through the various scenarios which will be involved during a sun cycle at the testing center. Are you happy to do the testing? You can decide whether the ADF is for you."

"I may find I can do something. More likely I've missed my calling and should be a crakah jack serving drinks all day." Although Stele wondered how she could ever hold that position and not have a drink.

"I'll make a date for you to attend. I expect it'll be in the next few sun cycles, and we'll see that you are better than you think," Kian said.

***

"Report to Colonel Ray's office immediately," Drax said as Stele finished another grueling run.

"I'm hot and sweating. I need a shower and some clean clothes."

"Forget it." Drax shoved Stele toward the door. "Straight there. It's in the next building, ground floor, right-hand side. Room zero-six. Run."

Stele arrived at Kian's office hot, flustered, and out of breath.

"Stele, come through."

Stele followed the sound of the voice into the next room. A large and colorful painting of the planets of the Federation hung on the wall, demanding attention. She could smell the pilton fruit that seemed to be Kian's signature scent. Stele couldn't decide whether she hated or liked it, because it never failed to evoke memories of Nero.

"Goodness, Stele, didn't you think to shower and change before coming over? You smell like a snock on heat."

"Sorry. I understood it was an emergency, so I ran straight over." *Creff.* Drax had got her again. But why would she want Stele on the back foot at this meeting? Why was she still playing games? Maybe she was just jealous of all this attention from Kian.

"Never mind. My nose has been assaulted by worse. Sit, and we can discuss the results of your tests for the ADF. There's good and bad news depending on how you want to look at it."

Stele did as Kian instructed and sank into the seat. Of course she'd failed. Why had she even begun to hope that she'd be good at anything? "Let's have the bad news. Did they decide I was too aggressive and don't want me?"

"No, they do want you. But the bad news first. You're never going to be a diplomat: you scored low on tactfulness and sensitivity. You've also shown enormous leadership potential, so they don't want you to go into the Corps."

Kian smiled, and Stele swore she looked almost proud.

"So, the good news is that they want you to be an Officer Cadet." Kian pushed some papers across her desk toward Stele. "Your scores show that you're extremely bright with strong strategic understanding, and your spacial awareness is off the scale."

Stele shifted in her seat, a little uncomfortable being the focus of such praise. This was the first time she'd been told she was good at *anything*.

"So, the ADF will train you in ship warfare and defense. If you do well, you'll be fast-tracked for command. What do you think?"

Stele's eyes widened. This couldn't be happening. She shoved her hand into her pocket and grasped her tear-shaped black rock to ground herself. What would Ariane think of this? "Seriously? They're offering *me* a position like that. I haven't lasted longer than ten sun cycles working anywhere, and they're willing to make me an officer? And command? They must be mad. Colonel, what should I do?"

Kian stood, came around her desk, and leaned against it. "You've done better than even I expected. Accept this offer and start training with the next officer cohort."

"How long do I have to think about it?"

"Sleep on it. Let me know in a sun cycle." Kian put her hand on Stele's shoulder and squeezed firmly. "Don't waste this opportunity, Stele. You've used alcohol as a crutch through bad times. It took control of your mind, and you thought you were solving your troubles by ignoring them. But there's no quick fix. What happened to you should never have happened...

just as it should never have happened to me. But you have to move on. You have to take responsibility for the person you want to be for the rest of your life, not the person they tried to make you. Leave the drink behind, Stele, and there's no limit to what you'll achieve."

Stele wanted to reach up and put her hand on Kian's. The physical and mental comfort from such a simple gesture hit Stele hard. *This* was how her parents should've treated her. Ariane's tales of her own parents' support had always jabbed at Stele like a boot to the face. "I know you're right, and I *wanted* to lose myself when I first came to Alton. But I worry about leaving this facility and being tempted again. I'm not sure I have the self-control I need to stay on this path with you."

Kian nodded. "We're going to work on that. I've spoken to Sergeant Drax, and she's going to organize a few darks out with some of the troops. You're not to drink even though they will be. Neither the Sergeant nor I will be there to stop you, so you'll have to find the strength to resist within yourself." Kian released Stele's shoulder, gave her a light punch on the arm, and winked. "I understand there's a sexy trumpeter with her eye on you. That should take your mind off the wine."

The heat of a million nastons spread across her face. "But I wouldn't know what to do with a trumpeter. I've never…I like looking, but more… oh, creff."

Kian laughed loudly, and the sound reverberated around the office. "Go and enjoy yourself. Take your time. Don't let anyone push you to do something you don't want. And don't drink."

Kian stood, clearly signaling the end of the conversation. Stele got up from her seat and saluted Kian. *Naveh, what have I gotten myself into?*

CHAPTER THREE

AFTER DARK-MEAL, Stele attended an event set up by Sergeant Drax. Stele had no intention of failing the no-drinking test and satisfying Drax's expectations to the contrary. Her new friends joshed and joked with Stele as if she'd known them for longer than the one sun cycle. Stele turned down the Gandon wine that was offered and was relieved when she noted two of the others weren't drinking either. They obviously didn't believe drinking was an integral part of a social evening of fun, and she could be strong enough to resist, despite the nerves of being a newbie amongst them.

Drax introduced Limony, the trumpeter who'd witnessed Stele's abrupt wake-up call in the medical center, and she recalled the way Limony had looked at her when she was naked. She'd made Stele feel special and somehow like the centerpiece on a table of food that Limony wanted to devour.

Limony held out her hand. "Come sit with me for a while in the lounge, and we can have some tak and a chat."

Stele looked at Limony and couldn't help but compare her fair, straight hair and pale skin with Ariane's, who had the typical dark hair and dark skin of all Neroians. It was so stupid to consider comparing them: life going forward had no Ariane and Stele should, and would, get used to it. This looking backward would do her no good. Limony was pretty, and her petiteness brought out the protectiveness in Stele. She also made Stele aware of the fact that she had no experience in dealing with women.

"I'd love that. Lead on," said Stele.

They sat in a couple of comfortable chairs with their crakahs of tak.

"Drax says you're from Nero," Limony said. "There are a lot of Neroians here. Alton seems to be a home away from home for lots of you."

Stele settled into her chair and put her feet on a nearby table, feigning a confidence she didn't feel. "Yeah. We're all genetic mishaps with imperfect eyes."

"So what's wrong with yours? They look fine to me." Limony wiggled her eyebrows and smiled. "All the other Neroians I've seen have black lines through their eyes, though, mixed up with some other color."

"Well, they have starbursts. People with starburst eyes can't complete the rite of passage. Only those with pure eye colors matching the Shards in our Coliseum are allowed the rite of passage. The Shards are people-sized pieces of ancient gems that were found when Nero was first settled, and they give powerful skills to Neroians with the same color eyes. Starburst eyes mean a person is genetically impure, and the shard doesn't recognize them. Anyone unable to complete the rite is banished. I'm different in that I'm the only person ever to have pure black eyes, and as there isn't a black Shard, I was banished anyway."

Limony furrowed her brow. "You mean you were always going to be banished from the minute you were born? That's awful." She reached over and touched Stele's knee before sipping her drink. "So why do the banished Neroians all come here?"

Stele swallowed, the heat of Limony's hand matched the fire she was beginning to feel elsewhere. "Nero isn't part of the Federation. It's an associate member. They only joined so they could rid the planet of all its genetic anomalies. As you know, Alton allows anyone from anywhere to settle here and encourages people from all worlds to join the Defense Force. So it's ideal for Nero's Ruling Council. They pay a small sum of money and get rid of the misfits. Alton doesn't mind because Nero considers most of their misfits as aggressive or violent, which makes them ideal recruits for their Defense Force."

Limony nodded. "I've seen that you're aggressive."

Stele tensed and drew in a deep breath. "How do you know that? We've only just met…" She calmed herself and steadied her breathing. "Oh, my wakeup call…"

"Yes, I was busy remembering the tune and got distracted looking at your face. Drax wasn't wrong when she said you were my type though."

Stele shifted in her chair, unsettled by Limony's far from subtle approach. "Your type?"

"Yeah." Limony jutted her chin toward Stele. "Tall, dark, and handsome…and I get to break you in."

Limony stared at Stele until she could bear it no longer, and she shifted her attention to her feet. "I don't know what my type is…yet. I liked a girl on Nero. In fact, I still like her a lot. And I liked the look of several more but, well, they were all dark…"

"You never got to kiss any of them?"

"No." Stele thought of her last moments with Ariane. "I wanted to. But Nero is not…well, Nero doesn't…like girls kissing girls. So I never did."

Limony moved to the edge of her chair and placed her hand on Stele's thigh. "Have you thought about kissing me?"

"Yes. When you looked at me after the trumpet blowing, I wondered what it would be like to kiss you."

Limony raised her eyebrows and ran her tongue over her lips. "Do you still wonder?"

"Yes. I like you, and I think I want more than just a kiss, whatever that is."

"Whoa, hold on. One thing at a time. You should charm and romance your women, Stele, even if you don't intend being around for more than one dark. You have to make them feel like they're important to you. And that includes me. I may like the look of you and want to do all sorts of things with and to you, but you need to learn how to get a woman like me into your bed."

Stele took a drink and wished it were stronger. She could do with some courage. "So…teach me."

"Ha. I can't say I expected you to say that. Let's start with a hug, shall we?"

Stele stood, took Limony's hand, and pulled her up into her arms. The top of Limony's head reached Stele's shoulder, and she smelled of the fresh outdoors. Stele inhaled deeply. Holding Limony was good, and Stele lingered there for some time. Her black tear-drop rock pressed against her leg, but she didn't want to think of Ariane now. She shouldn't think of her. She had to move on with her life. Besides, Limony seemed like fun and that's what she needed right now.

Stele pulled away from Limony slightly. "Now that we're comfortable, will you teach me? I want to kiss you, and I want to do it properly."

Without words, Limony stood on her toes, put one hand on each side of Stele's head, and pulled her down to her mouth. Limony's lips were soft, and Stele found that a kiss was so much more than she had imagined. The intensity of feeling that came with the kiss gave her weak knees and shaking legs. The resulting ache in her stomach left her feeling as if she needed something more.

"I need to sit down." Stele dropped back into her chair.

"If that kiss is anything to go by, you're not going to need much in the way of lessons. We do need to go somewhere quiet though so that you can copy what I'm doing for the more…complicated moves."

"I'm sorry." Stele looked up to Limony. If only she had her own accommodation. "I only have my room in the med block."

"Don't worry." Limony held out her hand. "I have just the place."

Stele took Limony's hand and stood. They kissed again before going out into the Alton darkness.

***

Stele decided to go for the officer training; the decision gave her some control. She had few other options and certainly nothing with a future. Maybe it was a foregone conclusion, but all her life, the decisions had been made for her. This career was going to be *her* decision.

She would have to say good-bye to her new friends while she was off limits to everyone for a while. It was the first time in her life that Stele had been able to label a group of people as friends, and she felt both rewarded and strange at the same time. She was sad to lose Limony in particular. Limony had been fun and had taught Stele a lot; she couldn't help but think about what she and Ariane had missed. The contrast was that she really wanted kisses and closeness with Ariane, and as enjoyable as it was with Limony, it just wasn't the same. The depth of feeling was missing. There would be no further interaction with Limony, but at least there was no Sergeant Drax on her case every moment either. She could picture Sergeant Drax in her mind and fantasized that she was in charge of training the sergeant. What tortuous things could she devise? Actually, all she wanted to do was to face Drax in a fighting competition. Stele knew she would flatten Trepple-face. She sucked on her bottom lip and swung her fists in a few practice punches.

On arrival at the Academy, she was directed to her sleeping quarters to dump her bag. She picked one of the three beds, sat on it, and began to unpack. The door opened smartly and smashed against the wall behind it. A person entered the room, and they weren't a race Stele had come across before. They had a deep pink face with short blue hair that resembled electrical cabling. The bright blue eyes in the face were wide open and the person looked at her.

"I am Questa Quess from Pargent. Who are you?"

"I'm Stele Hosun from Nero. I've never heard of Pargent. Is it in the Federation?"

"No, it is a service world in the Allied Nations, which has a number of different planet systems, so it is much larger than the Federation." Questa's hair moved as they spoke.

"What does a service world do?"

Questa tilted their head to the side and frowned. "It provides services."

Stele laughed. "Of course. I can think of some, but I'm sure they're not the services that your world would want to provide." She laughed and considered that until her evening with Limony she had no idea what that meant. Now she both understood what sexual services could mean and was looking at this stranger thinking about what her lips would feel like.

Questa's hair cables changed color to green for a brief moment and returned to blue. "You would be surprised. Pargent does provide those services as well as a lot of others. We are a world of telepaths and provide many types of services throughout the galaxies. It is considered an honor for a Pargent to be accepted into the Alton Defense Force. I am to become a Communications Officer before specializing in something like contracts, diplomacy, or welfare."

"You can read my mind?" Stele grinned. "I should stop thinking about how attractive you are."

"No, and yes. Pargent are only allowed to use our telepathic abilities in clearly defined situations, and there are an enormous set of rules. You will always tell when we are using telepathy because our skellen, what you would call hair, turn green. I am still young and sometimes don't have control, so my hair will flash green when I do not succeed in controlling the telepathy. Pargent are also empathic, so I can tell that you like me, you are curious about me, and that you have one big question. In answer to that, I am neither."

Stele raised her eyebrows. This was new. "How can you be neither male nor female?"

"Because I am Pargent. That defines who we are and where we are from, and we mate with Pargent and no-one else." They turned and walked away. "I am taking the bed in the corner."

Valden Bush

Stele smiled. Questa's abruptness could easily be taken as rudeness, but Stele could tell there was no malice in their actions. She'd never met a Pargent before. Stele suspected it might simply be the way they were.

After waiting for Questa to continue the conversation, Stele ventured to talk about tak. It was an inane subject, and she wasn't sure why it had popped into her brain, but at least Questa engaged as they both unpacked their belongings.

Someone knocked on the door and walked in.

"The best tak in the Federation is from Alton," he said. "And you'll be spoiled while you're here. Be prepared to be underwhelmed in your travels though, I can tell you Weston tak is nothing like as good. I'm Domino Gratis from Weston, tak expert and hoping to be a weapons specialist."

Stele and Questa introduced themselves, and Domino asked the same questions as Stele had of Questa about being Pargent. Stele sat on the end of her bed and watched Domino. A male sharing her room. That would be something new for her. Kian had told her to expect it because the ADF bundled all troops into pods irrespective of gender or sexuality. But knowing it was likely and seeing a man who would be sleeping so close were two different things, and it unsettled her.

"This is what I call stirring up the recruits so that we rub off on each other," Domino said. "Weston, Nero, *and* Pargent. Male, female, and Pargent." He sat down on the end of his bed facing Stele. "I've always wanted to visit Nero. I know it won't happen because your people are just plain antisocial, but my family have been involved with Neroian gems since the worlds in the Federation were first settled. My family were responsible for the work that engineered light from Neroian clear gems many generations ago." He leaned back on the bed, hardly drawing breath. "I've not done any work on the gems myself, but my father and grandfather have been exploring and testing different gems all their lives in an effort to find other uses. My sister is in charge of using them to see if it's possible to produce high power outputs from them." He sat up and mimed using a weapon, complete with sound effects. "Me, I just want to shoot at things!"

Stele laughed. Questa and Domino seemed nice enough. Maybe this wouldn't be so bad after all.

The following cycles comprised a continual timetable of lessons, tests, and more lessons. Each set of lessons was accompanied by periods of hard

28

exercise, self-defense, and the use of the different personal weapons. Stele got used to spending several sun cycles doing hard exercise in zero gravity and facing a test at the end on a completely different subject.

After a particularly tough sun cycle's physical training, Stele was sleeping hard when a trumpet sounded. She and the others jumped out of bed. They stood to attention to find Drax shouting at them and Limony blowing her trumpet.

"I've been posted to take charge of discipline amongst the Officer Trainees and to encourage quicker reaction times to orders when they're given. I'm starting with your section. So, I expect you to stand to attention when I am speaking to you. Hosun, that includes you. That is not attention, lift your chin. Hosun, I told you that you are mine. You are still mine, and now I have all your friends too."

"Thank you, Musician Gillan. Dismissed."

Limony's eyes sparkled in Stele's direction, and Stele tried not to smile. Drax would be looking for her to react.

"You, your name?"

"Questa Quess."

Drax motioned to the ground. "Ten push-ups, now. Drop." Drax circled around them. "Questa Quess. Do you have more names, Questa Quess?"

"No," said Questa as they pushed up from number ten.

"Ten more." Drax placed her boot on Questa's back. "Move. You're too slow. Come on." She removed her foot and circled as Questa continued the exercises. "To me, you're just Quess." She squatted down and pushed at Questa's elbows. "Stop shaking, Quess. You remind me of a red Gandon jelly with blue slivers on top when you quake like that." Drax stood up. "What's your name?"

"Quess."

Stele had to help them. Questa clearly hadn't realized in their anxiety that they'd missed the word Sergeant following their name. Drax would be vindictive.

"Sergeant," Stele said.

"Okay. Ten push-ups, both of you. Come on, Hosun. You can do these in your sleep." Drax poked her toe into Questa's side. "So. You. Your name?"

"Quess, Sergeant."

"*Now* you're getting the message. This room, and each of you, will be spotless, just like the rest of this section. I expect to get the Commandants Cup at the end of your training. Continue with your morn. I will speak to you later about my detailed expectations." Drax strode to the door. "Hosun, a word outside. Put on your working jumpsuit first. Quickly."

"Yes, Sergeant."

Stele's anger bubbled in her gut, and she tried to quell it. She'd managed two moon cycles free of Drax, and now she was back. Drax seemed dangerous and could ruin Stele's career, though she still had no idea *why* Drax would want to do that. She ran her hand over the back of her neck. She'd have to be careful, particularly with Drax involving her friends in the one-sided battle. She was, for the first time in her life, managing to do well at something and enjoying her life. She would *not* get angry. Stele had survived Drax in her face while getting sober, she could—and would—survive this. She zipped up her jumpsuit emphatically, letting out some of her frustration in the action.

Once in the outer corridor, Drax handed Stele a message bubble. "This is from Colonel Ray. She says you must go outside and switch off your Mesh before accessing the message. This is important. Do it now. The Colonel will speak to you after dark-meal." Drax marched off quickly down the corridor and out of sight.

Stele looked at the message bubble with alarm and set off at speed for the park. What was this about? Had she done something wrong? On Nero she'd only ever survived a short time in any job, and this moment had been expected. She was going to be removed from officer training. If she hurried, she'd have a chance to listen without being late for daily briefing. Stele needed to know. She found a quiet spot between two rocks commemorating lives lost in some ancient battle and switched off her Mesh. Her hands were shaking so much she had difficulty working the message bubble. She held down the feeling of nausea as she pressed the small rubber nub on the bubble and looked straight ahead for iris recognition.

"Recipient confirmed. Message from 6901732 Ray, Colonel."

Stele grasped one of the rocks for support... *Ariane*. Stele smiled as Ariane stood before her virtually, alive and full-size.

"My dearest Stele, I expect you're standing there with your mouth open in surprise that I've managed to get a message to you. You can close it now."

"Your wonderful Colonel Ray knows someone in the Nero Distribution Company, and they managed to contact me so that I can message you. Everyone involved has taken a big risk, so we won't be able to do this often. I'm so excited I have the chance to talk to you. I've missed you so much, dear Stele. Life has been so difficult. I keep touching and looking at the black rock you gave me and thinking of you, but it's just not the same as having you here." Ariane's hands moved and the sound of tinkling gems in her voice was something she hadn't expected to hear again.

"I know we never talked about our relationship because we just…*were* all our lives. But now you're gone, I feel as if someone's thrown a blanket over my life. Colors are washed out, the sounds of living are muted, and I'm struggling to motivate myself to even get out of bed. You've always been a part of me, and without you here it's like I can't function properly. I need one of your hugs. Do you realize that we never kissed? Why was that? I hope I can message again. Your Ariane."

Stele squeezed her eyes shut, both to stop the tears and to keep the picture of Ariane in her mind for just a little longer. She had run through the park fearing what the message might hold, with no thought of Ariane. She was still shaking and so breathed out slowly. She could hear her heart beating. No, it was roaring, because Ariane missed her, wanted her close, wanted…a kiss. Stele moved as if she were in slow motion. Ariane missed her. *"Your Ariane,"* she said. She heard the band start playing at the morning flag ceremony and she came to with a start. Her heart bubbled and she had the heady feeling she got from a glass of Gandon wine drunk quickly. She switched her Mesh on and saw she needed to be in the morn briefing. If she ran, she might just make it. She skipped forward. *My Ariane.*

***

Stele responded to Kian's Mesh call and met her in the park after dark-meal. Stele stood to attention, saluted, and tried to look serious though her grin was difficult to hide.

"At ease, cadet. This will be classed as a mentor meeting in the logs. I am turning my Mesh to discreet and suggest you do that with yours." She nodded towards Stele's head and waited. "Our conversation will be unavailable to routine surveillance."

Stele felt slightly lightheaded, and heat rose to her face and neck. "I can't believe you organized a message for me. Thank you, a million times over." Stele hesitated. Showing gratitude to someone for their kindness was unfamiliar, to say the least. "You got me off the street, on my feet, and not just working, but in a real career. I daresay that I'm enjoying life." She wasn't used to that either. The specter of being banished had hung over her for so long that being out from under its shadow seemed so unreal. "And a wonderful message this morn from Ariane."

Kian patted Stele on the shoulder and smiled. "Is she all right?"

"She misses me as much as I miss her." Stele sighed, regret clawing for her attention. "I think we could've been together, you know…if I'd asked the right questions and not been so frightened."

Kian shook her head and grasped Stele's forearm gently. "If Nero allowed women to love women. If you hadn't been banished. If you'd been born with different colored eyes. Stele, there are too many ifs surrounding the situation." She released Stele's arm and gestured toward the dark sky littered with stars and constellations, knowing that Nero was out there somewhere. "That's the past. You need to look to your future and get a message back to your girl."

My girl. Stele liked the way that sounded. She liked the thought of having Ariane in the same way Limony had shown her she could truly *have* and be *with* a girl. "How did you fix it?"

"I have a contact in the Nero Distribution Company," Kian said.

"How?" She just couldn't see her mentor breaking the rules. "The Treemon have been the trustees of Nero's trade since Nero was settled. I thought that employees and their families were the only people allowed anywhere near Nero?"

"Indeed, but a crew member of the Treemon Vanguard cargo ship has been most helpful, shall we say. I think he could be even more helpful to us. He comes from an Alton family who are not close with the Treemons. They are gem sculptors but can't compete with Nero's brilliance. The whole family is poor. They've been trying to produce works of art without the use of the extra skills Neroians have." Kian shrugged and looked contemplative. "He's happy to do anything, legal or illegal, which will make him money."

Stele considered the possibilities. Could she be smuggled on board to meet Ariane? Could Ariane come to Alton? Could Stele get to Nero? If the ship ran between Nero and Alton, they could spend some real time together. But could she be looking toward the future, as Kian just told her to? Could her future include Ariane? The way her life had been, it would all go wrong and she wouldn't get to see Ariane. Even if they did meet, what future was that for either of them? It was all a little much to process. "I don't know what to say."

"Say it's a good thing," Kian said. "But we do this on my terms, and you don't try to do anything rash like use the Vanguard to visit Nero or get Ariane here without my prior knowledge. That would be way too risky and could cause untold problems to a great number of people who use this same conduit to contact family and friends." Kian moved to face Stele and narrowed her eyes. "You can't put Ariane's life at risk. This is why I haven't told you the name of the contact."

Stele clenched her jaw. So Kian didn't trust her yet. "I wouldn't do that." She swallowed against the desire to pound her fists into a rock. It was early. Trust had to be earned. It wasn't as if *she* fully trusted Kian yet either.

Kian laughed and shook her head. "You mean to tell me you weren't already trying to work out how you could get to *see* Ariane?"

Stele looked away from Kian's intense gaze. "That doesn't mean I was going to *do it.*"

Kian half-smiled and sat on a bench nearby. "Put together a reply message for Ariane straight away. The Vanguard will leave at two moons, and I need to pass it on with some others that I have." Kian tilted her head and looked at Stele. "Am I right you don't wish to send a message to your parents?"

Stele joined Kian on the bench and slowly shook her head. Time stood still as she remembered her mother and father doing nothing when she was banished. They were on the Ruling Council and yet, they said nothing. She had that familiar feeling that had accompanied her to Alton as if she was broken somewhere inside. *I need a drink.* Yes, trust had to be earned, but surely parental love came with no caveats. She'd been a trial to them but always hoped they still loved her. Doing nothing and saying nothing wasn't an option in her book. She flexed her arms and rolled one hand into a fist before punching it into the other. She stood quickly.

"Yes and no. I don't know what I think about my parents, and I don't want to contact them. I'll Mesh you when I have done my message for Ariane."

CHAPTER FOUR

"HELLO, MY DEAREST one. If you're like me when I got your bubble, you'll be crying right now."

Stele swallowed and wiped away the tears as she watched Ariane's next message. Her melodious voice reached across the galaxy and poured honey over the lyrical words.

"It's so hard being apart and not able to contact each other easily. I need to talk to you and tell you my thoughts in person. I can't tell you that things here are fine. I'm not fine. I've been told I'm going through a depression following my rite of passage, which is not unusual. I know I'll get better, but without you here, it's even more painful."

Stele closed her eyes briefly. She *wanted* to be there. She never *wanted* to leave Ariane. Ariane, whose hands were clasped together and no longer free in the breeze.

"Jasper Sloan seems to be everywhere. He's creating all sorts of problems for your parents. He's pushing his agenda against your mother for giving birth to a black-eyed child. He's jealous that she leads the Healer Order when he can be no more than her deputy. He hasn't gotten over letting his parents down by being a blue-eyed boy when they're both purple-eyed and on the Ruling Council. You'd think that having a purple-eyed starburst and banished older brother, he'd stop creating problems."

Stele tried to understand how Jasper, the youngest son of two members of the Ruling Council, could cause firstly herself, and now Ariane, so much heartache. He was loud, self-serving and could be poisonous. His parents were both studious experts in Neroian law and always worked to help people. His older brother, Sergeant Harlen Sloan, was a quiet unassuming man as an engineer and technical specialist in the ADF. Stele concentrated on the rest of Ariane's podcast.

"Jasper loves nothing better than pushing me around and saying things to me like 'How does it feel to be left behind by your black-eyed friend?' and 'You've got no-one to stick up for you anymore.' I hate him more than

I can say."

Stele watched Ariane's hands moving in increasingly small circles. Her anxiety was almost visible.

"I try to avoid him, but you know what it was like before you left. He always seems to know where I'm going to be and enjoys making things difficult."

Stele paused the message and clenched her jaw. Her hands balled into fists, and white-hot fury set her skin alight. She'd rip Jasper Sloan apart. She tried to steady her breathing. *Control yourself.* Her anger would serve no purpose here. She continued with Ariane's message.

"I've taken some time staying with friends and sitting in your favorite spot in the caverns so that he can't find me. I do miss you. Looking back, you've always given me a part of you that made me feel loved. It helped my confidence and gave me the feeling of being someone worthwhile. I need you here. But your black stone is all I have of you."

"Oh, Ariane, I'm so sorry." Stele said the words out loud despite Ariane not being able to hear. Ariane's voice moved higher and became more melodic.

"The good news is that I've found some guys who can give me some illicit bandwidth to talk to you direct. Jaz and Detter are responsible for the external comms links on Nero, but Jaz has a brother with starburst. I think you knew him. Anyway, he and I were reminiscing about our lives and the time I spent with you. He remembered. I told him I needed to talk to you, properly. I love these message bubbles, but it's not the same as us being able to talk to each other. Some sun cycles later he came to me at your nest and offered to help me talk to you one to one. He does this for a number of banished, as well as talking to his brother. We'll be able to speak to each other at last, although the messages will have to be short. Jaz will send a message bubble with the technical stuff. Sorry to be a little down and blue. Your Ariane."

Stele rubbed her eyes and closed them to take a moment in remembering Ariane's face and voice from the bubble. She could almost smell the flarnic that always accompanied Ariane. She saved the message so she could replay it over and over again. *My Ariane.*

Stele worried that Ariane wasn't coping well. Sure, the rite of passage could cause problems but obviously Stele not being there was causing Ariane trouble on Nero and adding to her depression. Stele sighed. She needed to see Ariane, to hold her and look into those dazzling purple eyes; and like any normal couple just be there for her. Naveh! This was so hard.

***

"Epsilon pod, ATTENTION."

Stele stood to attention staring straight ahead as Drax entered Epsilon pod. This was the third inspection Drax had given the whole cohort, and they hadn't got any easier. They were considered part of the training of the academy and designed to encourage teamwork, cleanliness, and pride in appearance of both self and living quarters. Never mind that once the team were commissioned, they would have robot cleaners and assistants and all kit, except ceremonial, would be recycled. The inspections were noted on a cadet's record, and in some cases would ensure that if a cadet were borderline in training and poor at inspection, they would fail. Drax had made Stele pod leader, and thus she was responsible for both herself and the others in her pod. Their faults became hers, and it was her job to check everything they did before inspection to ensure it was correct and help Questa and Domino get to a high standard.

Drax stood in front of her and looked her up and down.

"Hosun, follow me. I'll point out any errors your pod has made. They'll be noted on your Meshes, and I'll re-visit for a remedial inspection after dark-meal."

Stele went to move, but Drax indicated she should stay still.

"You are standing in the incorrect spot. You should be here," said Drax, indicating a spot just behind Stele. "Move."

Stele moved back.

"And the floor here by your bed is scuffed."

Stele could see nothing until Drax scuffed the floor with her shoe. Stele stiffened and desperately tried not to show any reaction to Drax. But Drax didn't need any encouragement.

"Give me twenty."

Stele dropped to the floor without hesitation. Once Stele had completed the punishment, Drax bent over Stele's ceremonial uniform laid out across the bed and screwed up her jacket.

"Hosun, your ceremonial kit is less than perfect. I expect better of you."

Stele couldn't think. She dared not move a muscle. This was so wrong.

How could Drax get away with this? Her old mantra of "because I can" didn't help. Stele followed as Drax turned towards Domino and Questa. Stele remained stiff and held herself together. Her anger threatened to rise in defense of her underlying feeling of helplessness. She carried on breathing evenly, trying to calm her raging storm. Underneath she was a seething mass, like an asteroid shower awaiting that moment when it would engulf any object in its path. Naveh! What she would do for a Gandon wine about now.

Drax found blue hair on Questa's uniform, which was impossible because the Pargent didn't have hair. Their skellen were permanent and didn't shed like hair. Drax put fingerprints on the toes of one of Domino's boots. Both had scuff marks on the floor by their beds, again courtesy of Drax.

"So, Hosun, the results for this inspection will be listed on your record as poor. Gratis and Quess, you will be listed on your records as average. I will return after dark-meal. Make sure everything is perfect." With that, Drax turned and swept out of the room.

Stele started to feel as if her world was unravelling and struggled to find the words to give to her friends. She looked from one to the other, open-mouthed and speechless, and ran from the room. She needed space. Her legs seemed to carry her without effort, as if they had anger as fuel. Stele ran without much thought until the guarded entrance to the base was ahead and she had run the turmoil out of her system. Footsteps sounded behind her as she slowed to a stop.

"I know Drax is trying to goad us into doing something wrong, and it is inexcusable but what is going on with you, Stele?" Questa said. "You are beginning to lose your temper about mundane things in training, and I know you are not sleeping well. I can tell things are muddled for you. Talk to me."

"Oh, Questa. I wish things were simple."

Stele put an arm around her smaller friend and silently guided them both towards the park and a seat that she could see in the distance. Questa rarely interrupted her silences, and Stele loved that about her friend. She needed that unquestioning support whilst her head was in such turmoil. Stele sat, and Questa joined her, moving in so that their thighs touched. The closeness calmed her.

"I started the course knowing that I had nothing better to do. I was growing into the training and enjoying the friendships. And, well, I'm good at it. I felt as if I'd achieved something. For once in my life, I'm not a failure. But since Drax arrived, the bottom has fallen out of my world. I've lost confidence in myself. I've wanted a drink several times, and it's making me want to walk away."

"Have you spoken to the colonel? This is the sort of thing she is there to help you fix," Questa said.

"No. I think she may be aware that I'm struggling. I don't want to whine about it. Life will get difficult in training, and we're expected to work through the things that cause us problems. If I'm going to be an officer, I should work out how to fix it myself. Otherwise I could lose my place in the ADF. Having a commission gives me options for the future, especially if I want to meet Ariane."

"All you say is correct, but I still think you should talk to the colonel. Drax has been mean to us and especially you. If you do not speak to the colonel, you will just need to handle it calmly, my friend. We are over halfway through training, and if she has nothing over you, you will have won," said Questa.

Questa was right. Stele would have to try and ensure that Drax didn't get her down. She wouldn't let Drax win.

***

Stele headed for the park after dark-meal and settled in between her usual two rocks. She received an alert on her Mesh and before she could move, a virtual Ariane hologram was in front of her. The figure was so clear it was as if she could put out her hand and touch her. Stele was speechless with surprise.

"Can you hear me, Stele?" Ariane asked. "Is the sound working? I can see you, but there's no sound."

"Sorry, I can hear you clearly," said Stele and laughed. "I was mesmerized by seeing you as usual. Didn't you notice my open mouth?"

Ariane was luminescent. Her Ariane, close enough to touch. Stele reached out into the night air.

Ariane smiled and clapped her hands before allowing them free movement in the air. "It's so good to be able to talk to you and to hear your reply."

Her melodic voice was both familiar and something that Stele missed terribly. "Yeah. Sometimes when life is difficult, talking it through with someone makes all the difference. You've had it bad."

"Yes, for a while there I was sad."

Stele understood this sadness, this ache. Their separation and loss of hope to ever be together had been gripping. "How are you feeling now? Do you still have the rite of passage depression? Creff. That must have been gutting."

"It's okay. I think being able to tell you and with this direct messaging going to happen, it's all getting better. Things looked black for a while. Oh, Stele, how I've missed you."

Ariane's eyes teared. Stele was so helpless and out of control of the situation, and there was nothing she could do except give her support in words. Maybe… She opened her arms. "Have one of my big hugs. It'll make the rest of the world go away, so there's only you and me." There was silence for a few moments as Stele looked into Ariane's beautiful eyes. "There is only you and me, isn't there? I don't want anyone else."

"I'm waiting for the day we can meet and I can kiss you. I know it's probably in my dreams because I'm sure I can never come to Alton. No one has ever managed to get off Nero except the banished. And even if I did manage it, Mumma and Poppa would suffer because the Ruling Council would punish them. But I'm not giving up on my dreams. I still want that kiss."

How would Ariane's soft and warm lips joined with hers feel? "I want that too. There's so much more that we can do to be close. We have to make it happen," said Stele. "I just want to be with you. I dream of us being together."

"So what's happening with you? How's the Academy training going?"

Stele didn't reply. She didn't want to worry Ariane about how she was feeling.

"So what's wrong? You can't always be tough, even heroes have their off days. Tell me."

Stele felt the heat rush to her face and couldn't look at Ariane. She wanted to be stoic but was failing.

"We need to be strong for each other. Times will get hard, and we need each other's support. I needed you in my dark times, and you obviously need me now. Tell me."

"Training is going well, and I have good friends in Questa and Domino," Stele said and Ariane nodded. "I was enjoying it, but Sergeant Drax, that woman from before I joined, arrived. She's enjoying making my life a misery, and I'm just losing my confidence. I'm getting depressed and cross with people, and I don't know how to fix it." Her desperation rang loud and clear for all to hear.

"Can't you talk to that Kian lady and get her to help? She's looking out for you, isn't she?" Ariane asked.

"Yeah, but I'm going to be an officer. I should know how to fix this myself." Stele stood and moved from foot to foot as if that would solve her problems.

"Why? Do officers know everything?"

Stele laughed at Ariane's attempt to brighten things. "Ha. No, of course not, but as officers we'll have people looking to us for leadership and support, and we need to be able to sort things. If I can't sort this, perhaps I shouldn't be an officer."

"Oh, Stele, don't be silly. I know deep in my heart that you're in the right place. You will be a good officer. Your worrying about this shows you care. This must be so hard if you can't fix it. I suppose you'll just have to ride it out and talk to me about how you're feeling. I'll hold you and take care of you over the airwaves."

Ariane's hologram opened her arms, and Stele closed her eyes briefly imagining the smell of flarnic as Ariane wrapped her gentle arms around her.

"Oh, Creff, there's Jaz. We're finished. Hugs and dreamy kisses," said Ariane.

So soon. It wasn't long enough, and Stele hadn't said anything of substance. She needed more time. There was never going to be enough time. "It was too short, but so good. Hugs and dreamy kisses to you, my Ariane."

Her Mesh went dark, and Stele sat between the rocks in silence enjoying the warmth and closeness of talking to Ariane. Her Mesh lit up.

"Stele, please help us. Domino and I are stuck working out our astro calculations for the morn."

She stood stiffly and took a deep inhalation of the night air. As much as she wanted it, there wasn't even a hint of flarnic. Life was continuing and she had a girl to think about. *My Ariane.*

Valden Bush

***

Stele sat in the bar nursing her tak with Domino and Questa. It had been a tough few sun cycles, and they'd all been struggling with their training. Drax had been on their case with her inspections. Despite Stele having insider knowledge from her pre-academy training, Drax still found fault with everything they did. And when they had first class kit and perfect rooms, Drax simply created an issue. *Because she can.* Despite discussing it with Ariane, Stele still hadn't found a way to deal with Drax.

"Come on, Stele. You've been clean the whole time you've been training," Domino said. "Don't you deserve a little down time?"

It was the third time he had invited her in his monologue about how difficult things on the course were. Drax was getting to all the cadets, but especially to their pod. Domino had already downed a couple of Plasoton aeros and wanted some drinking company. Drink wouldn't help anything, and it wouldn't solve the stresses of training or her feelings about Drax. But Drax was someone she was managing to deal with. She had ignored her with the help of Ariane's support, Questa's calm approach, and Domino's jokes and impersonations. She did need to let out a little of her angst and concern about the pressure of the training. Of course she was in control now, wasn't she? *I can handle it.* Two or three drinks would be easy enough, and she'd been working hard enough to justify them.

"Okay, okay. I'll just have a couple of Gandon wines as a treat."

"Stele, are you sure?" Questa's hair gently moved as they spoke. "You told me this could be dangerous."

Domino was ordering her drink using his Mesh before Stele answered. She shrugged and avoided Questa's questioning gaze.

"Two Gandon wines as ordered. Oh, goodness, the standard of officer cadets has gotten better in the last moon cycle or two. And how did you get here, Stele?"

"Hey, Shimo." Stele quickly sat up but didn't smile, not wanting to encourage her. She didn't need her old life coming back to haunt her now. She'd moved on, and her life was so much better because of it.

"You look happy and sober. I bet you met a woman who put you back on the straight and narrow. How sad. If you need anything, *anything* at all, you just let me know, and I'll be pleased to fulfil your wildest dreams. Or are you still full of love for the girl you left on Nero?" Shimo asked.

Shimo had spent most of their drinking time together when Stele first arrived on Alton making outrageous bets to finance her drinking and trying to get Stele into her bed. Stele didn't feel anything for her, not back then and certainly not now. *Now I know how beautiful being with a woman can be. And I've found Ariane again.* She didn't want to talk about Ariane with this woman; it would somehow sully her memory.

"I'm fine, thank you, Shimo." Stele gritted her teeth. Shimo would enjoy embarrassing her, and sure enough, she stood with her hand on her hip and a lascivious look on her face as she licked her bright red lips, staring at Stele. Domino laughed and nudged Stele as Shimo left the table.

Stele knew her face was red, and she buried it into her crakah. The pungent aroma of Gandon wine, with a hint of nuttiness and sweetness, raced into her nostrils. She'd forgotten how good it could taste. She took a long swig of the pink wine and savored it, like an elixir that exploded in her mouth. It was as if she had been running for hours and not had a tak, and the first drink was like greeting an old and familiar friend. She gulped down the contents of the glass before she put it on the table and grabbed the second one. She could do this. Questa put out their hand and rested it on Stele's arm stopping her from lifting the crakah.

"Let's go, Stele. I think we've all had enough," said Questa, despite not drinking themselves.

Stele was just beginning to enjoy herself. The wine gave her a warm feeling inside, and she put her other arm around Questa. Stele pushed aside Questa's hand, picked up the crakah, and downed the drink. She'd be fine with a couple of drinks, and Kian would be pleased that she'd mastered her addiction. Besides, it was helping her deal with her stress from the Academy and the nasty and vindictive Drax.

"Enough? I've only had one drink, and I'm feeling good. Who's up for another one? Should we go for something stronger? Let's have a Weston Green."

Stele ordered a double for both her and Domino, which Shimo quickly delivered. She moved in closer towards Stele, pursing her lips and pushing her majestic breasts out. Stele tried to move her chair back and began to wish she were anywhere but there. She now had a future, a career, and credit. Credit that Shimo would enjoy spending. What was she supposed to do to get rid of her? Stele had no idea. Shimo was pushed aside by another woman, who towered like a giant decko above Stele. She leaned into

Stele's face. Her breath was warm, and Stele could smell the smokiness of whatever the woman had just eaten. Her nose was crooked like she'd seen her fair share, and someone else's, of fights. Stele couldn't tear her attention away from the woman's nose, trying to work out what it would look like if it were straight. She was struggling to concentrate, and her brain didn't seem to be helping.

"Why are you flirting with my girlfriend?" asked the big woman.

Stele finally focused. She pushed her chair backward to get away from the breath and was on a non-return trip to the floor, taking the table and all its crakahs with her. Questa moved around her chair and helped her up.

"I have my own girlfriend; I don't want yours. You owe me a drink," said Stele as she pointed to her crakah on the floor. Her temper flared. Her stomach trembled and energy crackled in her hands. "You OWE ME a drink."

The big woman laughed in her face. That was the final straw. No-one ever cared about her and what she wanted. She'd deal with this herself. Stele tightened her hands into fists and swung at the big woman who put up her arm to block the blow as if she were swatting a small snape. She laughed.

"Making fun of me, are you?" Stele said, her anger rising to the point of explosion. All those moon cycles of Drax needling her and having to hold her feelings back rose to the surface. *I need this. I need to let it out.* She rushed forward with a roar and jumped at the woman, landing both feet on her chest. Stele fell backward onto the floor, but it felt so good to have let out her buried frustrations. Questa helped her up again, and Stele felt a warmth inside she wasn't familiar with. Was this real friendship? When someone stood by her side, no matter what? The only other person to do that had been Ariane. She swallowed hard and blinked away the threatening tears. She held onto Questa whose blue skellen flashed green, and Stele knew they understood.

Stele turned and saw a number of patrons of the bar helping the woman up. She was red-faced and shouting insults.

Domino laughed. "Come on, everyone. Let's all have another drink together, shall we? Nothing need be this serious. A drink can solve all our problems."

The big woman turned in his direction and swept his crakah off the table. She turned back and moved toward Stele. Stele felt like a flag in the wind and couldn't seem to control her movement. Her legs were only just keeping her upright, but she couldn't move.

Domino was out of his seat like one of his missiles firing from a ship. Stele felt him grab her arm and pull her forward. Questa had her other arm. "RUN. I'm right with you," he said.

They headed toward the door. The big woman and her friends gave chase, and they rushed through the front door of the bar in a jumbled mass. Stele tried to turn. She wanted, no needed, to lash out at that woman but she couldn't swing her arm with Questa hanging on it.

"We are going back to the pod now. Come on. We are all going now," said Questa.

Stele ran as best she could with her friends and headed toward a Defense Force patrol on foot. The people from the bar turned quickly as soon as they saw the patrol and moved back to the bar shouting and jeering.

Once she hit the fresh air, Stele had no control over her body at all. She slipped from the grasp of her friends and fell over, laughing as she hit the ground. Domino and Questa bent over to pick her up, but Stele began to sing Ariane's songs at the top of her voice, happy to remain on the floor.

"Officer cadets! Attention! What is the noisy cadet's name?" a voice from the back of the patrol said.

Stele squeezed her eyelids closed and opened them again in an attempt to focus on the person behind the voice. She managed to make out the duty sergeant Staff Sergeant Ring. This could be trouble. She concentrated on making sure her words were clear and not slurred. Perhaps they'd consider it was high jinks and let them go. "I'm Stele Hosun, and this is Epsilon pod."

"You'll report to me at first light with the rest of your pod, in ceremonial kit and I'll decide on your punishment. You two, please take officer cadet Hosun back to her bed," Ring said.

At first light, they stood outside Ring's office in their ceremonial kit, with their boots shining like glass. None of them had slept after taking what was left of the dark to prepare their clothing and boots. The ceremonial uniform consisted of a bright red jacket with blue upright collar and cadet rank markings on the shoulders. The cadet rank markings were made of a dull flexible metal that required several crons' work to ensure they shined. The blue trousers had stripes at the sides made of the same material as the rank markings, and they also required shining. Stele knew that it was all part of training but knowing that the metallic elements of the uniform would be replaced with a perma-shine material when they were commissioned made their work seem such a waste.

Stele's body raged hot and cold, and Naveh, her head hurt. She never wanted to drink again. She didn't have the control. She finally had to admit to herself that she never had and probably never would have.

Staff Sergeant Ring opened his door and gestured them inside.

"Epsilon pod, ATTENTION," said Questa.

Domino and Stele followed Questa into the office. Stele saw Kian standing behind the desk and kept her head high despite wanting to hang it in shame. This was exactly what Stele had told Kian would happen. She would let her down. But it hadn't happened until now. Stele had surprised herself. Was her return to form inevitable? Was she kidding herself that she could forge a better life for herself?

"Ma'am, as you heard, this pod was fighting in a bar outside the academy and making a lot of noise across the base last dark. I made them report here at first light."

"Thank you, Staff Sergeant. Thank you for getting them here this morn. I will take over."

Staff Sergeant Ring left the room.

"Epsilon pod, last dark was inexcusable." Kian looked at each of them in turn. She stood ramrod straight, her face was stern, her jaw stiff. "Fighting in bars is not conduct the ADF expects from its officers. Do you wish to say anything that might mitigate your punishment?"

"It was my fault, Colonel. I was drunk, and Domino and Questa were trying to get me home. The fighting was also down to me. I took exception to someone's actions and used my fists. Questa hadn't even had a drink. It's me that you should punish, not them."

"That's exactly the way the duty patrol saw it last dark. Quess and Gratis, remember who you are and the uniform you wear. Do not let that uniform down again. You are dismissed. Hosun, remain where you are."

Stele wanted to hang her head in shame again, but kept her eyes focused straight ahead. She was in so much trouble and wondered if the ADF would throw her out. Once Questa and Domino had left, Stele breathed a sigh of relief that they wouldn't be punished for her mistakes. Now it was all on her, as it should be. She stole a glance at Kian who was staring at her, still standing at attention, and her face revealed nothing.

"Hosun, stand down. We need to talk."

Naveh! Kian never called her Hosun. It was said with such a controlled and even tone. Stele knew at once what it felt like to lose the trust she'd worked so hard to earn. She'd thrown it away like the wrapper from a sweet arden. And creff, she liked Kian and had come to care about what she thought about things. She had supported Stele through thick and thin with the drink and given her a reason to make something of herself. Stele had thrown it back in her face.

"Sit," said Kian as she slumped into a chair, her face still emotionless as she took in a slow breath.

"I'm so sorry. I've let you down. I told you I was bad news." Stele stood to attention and stared at a point above Kian's head. She couldn't lose control here, not now. This was what she did on Nero when things got tough. She lashed out. She was trying to earn Kian's respect, and this episode had destroyed all that. She balled her hands into fists. She wanted to use them, but she had no one to use them on except herself. She was the only one at fault here.

"Yes, Stele, I expected more from you, I have to say. Tell me what happened. I need to understand."

"I've found life difficult in the last few weeks. We all went out to let off a little steam, and I decided I was in control enough to have a few drinks. I thought they'd make me feel better." The confession relaxed Stele a little, and she gained enough confidence to steal a glance at Kian.

"Why haven't you talked to me about what has been difficult for you? Am I so frightening?" asked Kian, still looking grim.

Stele looked up. "Of course not. I'm going to be an officer and whining to you isn't the way I should be doing things. I need to solve my own problems."

"I agree, Stele, but you're not an officer yet. You have some unique problems to overcome and difficult issues that you're likely to encounter. I'm here as your mentor to help you through them." Kian leant forward, pulled up another chair, and patted the seat. "Come and tell me about what's been so difficult. I'm sure we can work through it."

Stele sat in the chair but still at attention. How could she talk about Drax to her boss? Were Kian and Drax friends? She looked at the wall above Kian's head again. She wasn't sure she wanted to go down this road, but if she wanted to stay with the ADF, she had no choice but to be honest. "I'm worried that you'll think less of me if I discuss my fears. I should be strong and able to cope."

"You're strong, Stele, particularly when you don't doubt yourself or drown your fears in alcohol."

"I'm frightened of failing. Frightened of my anger. Frightened of making a mess of my new start and your faith in me. And the more I think about my fears, the more they seem likely to happen. I can't fail because I need to succeed so that I can see Ariane. But it's as if it's my destiny to fail, and I can't rid myself of the fear."

Stele thought back to midway through training when things had been going all right and before Sergeant Drax arrived. She'd been confident and clear with her goals. She was sure Drax was setting her up to fail by making her responsible for Epsilon pod and finding fault with everything she, and they, did. Each failure for an individual was also considered a failure for Stele, and Drax kept Stele in her sights.

Kian's voice brought her back to the present.

"So, tell me, Stele, what or who is making you feel you are failing?"

"I've lost confidence in myself. I feel as if I'm going to let you down, and I'm like a tree in the breeze wavering between fear and anger. The anger is getting worse, and I can't control it. I feel I need a drink. It all started two moon cycles ago." Maybe she could get around the Drax problem by not mentioning her by name.

Stele could hear people outside and footsteps in the corridor. Kian made no move to speak for some cron.

"Ah, I think I understand. Did someone arrive those two moon cycles ago?" Kian asked.

Stele looked at the floor. She couldn't reply, so she just slowly nodded her head. Kian was more perceptive than she had expected. Now what should she do? She would *not* resort to tears and blinked desperately to keep her eyes clear.

"I'll take that as a yes. I'll see what I can do. Look at me, Stele." Stele looked up and into Kian's starburst eyes. "You'll not see anything different, and do not expect to. I'm now aware there's a problem, and you must let me deal with it. Your test will be to carry on and not let it affect you. Your training is going well, and you can have a good future here. Don't let anger and alcohol rule your life. Do you understand?"

"Yes, I understand. I let everything get on top of me. I wanted to cope

with my issues but instead I let them get worse. I let you down. I'm sorry."
Stele's headache pounded in time with her heartbeat and her dry, stale
mouth caused her words to misshape and sound more Pargent than Nero.

"We should meet more often, and we can discuss how things are going.
Perhaps after dark-meal every other sun cycle? Will that work with your
timetable?"

Although the problem wasn't solved as such, at least Kian would be
there to talk to and discuss the things making her angry. "Yes, and thank
you. I should've spoken to you earlier. I was so intent on trying to cope
alone and deal with things as I thought an officer should. I hope you'll
forgive me." Stele expected a long journey to regain Kian's trust, but she
could do it. Kian said she wanted to understand. No-one had ever said that
to her before. This was a second chance to prove herself, and she'd take it
with both hands.

"Now, we have to do the formal part. Let's both stand," Kian said.
"Hosun, getting drunk and fighting with civilians is not the behavior we
expect from our officers. I spoke to Staff Sergeant Ring on your behalf and
explained that you have a bad relationship with alcohol. This is your first
transgression. Let it be your last. You will get a written admonishment in
your docket and a punishment."

"Yes, ma'am."

"Your punishment will be to provide double duty in the simulation
exercises for the last five sun cycles of training."

"Yes, ma'am."

"Dismissed."

Stele saluted and turned. Before leaving she stopped to look at Kian,
mesmerized. Her mentor had cleverly made her punishment into something
that would help her. Kian nodded. It was a sublime move. "I get punished
by getting extra simulation practice? Getting the extra time on the training
bridge will help my confidence. Thank you."

"Don't thank me," Kian said, looking serious. "You're going to have
to work hard, and you'll need to keep on your toes even when you're
exhausted. There will be little time for relaxation."

"It's going to make sure I do well in my final test. It's good."

"But, Stele," Kian said, "you cannot get drunk again. You've been
found guilty, and it will be on your record. You aren't the first officer cadet
that has trouble with alcohol, but you need to keep a clean sheet from now.
Dismissed."

CHAPTER FIVE

THE VISION OF Ariane came alive in front of Stele, and she drew a deep breath. The intricate detail, luminescence, and shading were so real yet virtual at the same time. She lifted her hand to touch Ariane's face, desperate for Ariane's warmth beneath her fingertips. Instead there was just the cold emptiness of the hologram in its place. They'd been sharing messages for a few moon cycles now, and the frequent contact was a real boost for Stele. As Ariane listened intently to Stele's worries, the projection showed every nuance of her facial expressions, right down to those slightly parted beautiful pink lips that tortured Stele in her memories.

She longed to be with Ariane so that she could feel her smooth warm skin under her fingertips, to be able to run her fingers through Ariane's silky hair and to inhale the intoxicating smell of flarnic that was all Ariane. A shiver ran down her spine and pooled deep inside her. When she lay in bed at night and closed her eyes, she could see Ariane's body curled up next to her. The soft curve of her breasts dipped into a valley that hinted of journeys yet to come and was tantalizing. As was the arch of Ariane's spine trailing down to another valley that was full of mouthwatering promise. Ariane was never far from her thoughts. They spoke together regularly, and Stele reveled in the contact. It brought her close to Ariane despite there being a galaxy between them.

"So that was what happened, hangover and all." Hot tears ran down her face. "I made a real fool of myself." The bitter taste of the shame of standing in front of Kian returned. The vulnerability of sharing this side of herself was a new feeling. She'd admitted to Ariane that she didn't handle any of this well. Somehow it gave her a sense of freedom and security and at the same time Ariane was there for her.

"I'm sorry that you've had such a difficult time, but at least it's out in the open now." Ariane smiled at her, her purple eyes sparkling. "I want to hug and kiss you, help you forget that your life has been so trying."

Stele was mesmerized by her and tried to put all her thanks and love into her gaze, tried to send all her emotions across space. She loved Ariane. Her heart stuttered, almost faltered and beat faster and stronger than ever. She didn't have words for her feelings before, and perhaps it would be a while before she could voice them out loud. But in that moment, everything came together, and Stele was sure.

She'd been wet with tears and vulnerable, and the truth had hit her between the eyes. Now she wanted to take the galaxy in her arms and hug it. She drew in an unsteady breath. "In all those years together, we never did more than hold each other and now we can't even do that." She bit her lower lip. "Ariane, I want more. I want to show you how I'm feeling." She opened her arms to Ariane, taking a half a step even though it was impossible to fill the gap across the universe between them. Ariane mirrored her movement, and they were now so close that their bodies virtually touched. They closed their arms, but instead of embracing the other, the holographic images gave no resistance and they ended with their arms wrapped around their own bodies.

"We're sharing a hug."

Ariane's smooth, silky voice wrapped around her in a tender blanket, intensifying the feeling of a shared embrace. Stele kept her eyes firmly on Ariane's, and it seemed the vast darkness of endless space between them shrank just a little. Ariane's face and her striking eyes reached out and soothed her soul. Stele had imagined this for so long. She wanted it to be real; it almost seemed to be. They were so close but the heat from Ariane's body was missing. Nevertheless, the longer she lost herself in Ariane's presence, the more it felt like Ariane had her arms around her, wrapping her in her warmth.

In the past, Ariane had provided her with a cocoon of care and shelter whenever she needed it and made her feel like she was worth something when no-one else believed in her. Together, they'd created a safe space and over time it had nurtured her. And now it was awakening feelings that were taking her forward. It was bringing out a new and fierce protective side that needed her to be there for Ariane and to take care of her.

The need to share this moment with the woman of her dreams threatened to overwhelm her. "Keep looking into my eyes and listen to my voice." Her voice was deeper and cracking with the promise of what was to come. "Imagine my arms around you, holding you close."

Ariane nodded, her eyes fixated on Stele and appearing to grow larger as if she knew where Stele wanted to take them. It was so easy for Stele to disappear into the swirling purple depths of Ariane's eyes, so full of dancing light, reminding her of her favorite cavern on Nero. She lost herself in those rememberings until there was only the two of them in the universe.

"You are so beautiful, Ariane."

Ariane's smile spread to her eyes, and they filled with anticipation of what was to come: learning each other's bodies and the expectation of exhilarating emotions bursting alive. The promise in those eyes combined with the memories of all the nights Stele had to make do with her own body made something low in her abdomen tighten. Heat started to pool even lower.

"I need to touch you, Ariane." Stele slowly lowered the zip on her jumpsuit, creating excitement as much as giving Ariane a chance to stop her if this wasn't what she wanted. Her heart skipped a beat when Ariane mirrored her movement, undoing the fastening on her own jumpsuit. Stele's fingers slipped under the fabric above her chest.

"Can you feel me undressing you?"

Ariane's quiet question intensified the feeling of not her own, but Ariane's hand, touching her shoulder, pushing the fabric of the jumpsuit out of the way and revealing her body to her lover.

"Oh, Ariane. You are exquisite." Her zip had fallen open to reveal her smooth dark skin underneath. "Can you feel me trace your collarbone?"

Ariane nodded. They moved together, touching themselves as they explored each other.

"I need more." Stele's entire body was alive. Cold sweat formed on the back of her neck and made her shiver.

Ariane's chest heaved, and Stele was mesmerized as her dark nipples became erect. A small shot of pleasure erupted and settled deep in her core when Ariane's fingers fluttered over her own chest.

Stele struggled to concentrate as she was sharing herself with Ariane. This was nothing like thinking about Ariane as she took care of her own needs. This was so much more. She could share her feelings, her passion even though they couldn't physically be together. "Keep looking into my eyes and listen to my words," she whispered. "You've always been there for me, and I worship you with my heart and soul."

She moved her hand farther down and watched as Ariane nervously faltered but followed her move. Ariane's breathing became thready and her lips, oh those luscious lips waiting to be kissed full of the promise she'd been anticipating…

Ariane opened her mouth, but no words came out that Stele could hear. "Keep that hand moving," Stele said.

The way Ariane was looking at her and sharing herself with her made Stele's heart swell. It was such a delicious feeling and she needed to share her most innermost and secret self with *her Ariane*. Her chest tingled and her body had a life of its own, moving to the music of Ariane's movements. She cupped her breast and gently squeezed her nipple. She let her hands sing their tune. Creff, this was exquisite torture. Her entire body was on fire and the wet heat between her legs became unbearable as her core ached with intense pressure. "I want to show you how much I care. Can you feel me?"

Ariane nodded, and her lips parted. Her heavy breathing was the only sound coming across the galaxy. "Yes," she said, whispering the word as if the breath had been borrowed from another.

Stele struggled to stay in control. Her deep inner emotions of nurture, and protection, and shelter were beginning to overwhelm her. She took a deep breath. "If we touch each other here, it would be a beautiful moment for us both." Stele glanced down toward the dark triangle of hair between Ariane's legs. Their bodies were in a duet that was playing out to a pre-ordained tune.

"We're touching each other. I can feel you, as you can feel me. Be gentle with yourself at first and get harder as you need."

Ariane licked her lips. "Oh, Stele, Naveh…"

All those nights Stele had spent thinking about this exact moment nearly undid her. She was within an ace of exploding. Her heart thumped against her chest. Her mind blanked, and she was overtaken with the enveloping passion that was Ariane, the heat and the exhilaration pushed her over the edge. She reached out with her free hand for the safety and warmth of *her Ariane*. She couldn't see any longer through eyes that were full of tears. "My darling…"

They fell into a safe and comforting silence, and small shudders ripped through Stele's body as her breathing slowly returned to normal.

"It's no good wishing, I know. But I so wish we'd done this together before you left," said Ariane.

"Let's keep wishing." Stele would fix this and find some way for them to be together.

***

"Epsilon pod. Attention on deck," shouted Stele in her best command voice. This had to be perfect for Drax, otherwise the whole pod would be in trouble. A bad performance in this final inspection could result in comments on their dockets and affect their postings and careers. Drax started her inspection, but Stele was confident that there was nothing wrong. The pod had even bribed a corporal to do a practice inspection and asked him to be extra picky. He'd said that the pod was the best he'd seen.

Drax ran her finger across a countertop. "Hosun and Quess, on the floor. Give me ten."

Stele reacted instantly and was pleased to see Questa in time with her, not allowing Drax to accuse them of being slow. Stele fought for breath and realized there must be something wrong. Her stomach churned, and she held fast to her anger. *I will not react.* They were going to fail. Like everything in her life, it was going wrong. *They were going to fail.*

The pod door opened, and Sergeant Drax saluted. "Ah! Colonel Ray. Pod ready for inspection, ma'am." Drax pointed at Questa and Stele, still on the floor. "Everything is in order. I was just testing their reaction time, ma'am. It was good."

"Excellent, sergeant. Carry on."

Stele stood and quickly snapped to attention. Questa mirrored her actions. They'd be fine now that Kian was there. Her thoughts of failure and her anger dissipated.

Kian inspected everything carefully and turned as she reached the door. "Well done, pod. Excellent work. I've given you top marks. Keep up the high standards." With that, she was gone.

Sergeant Drax didn't follow the colonel and didn't give Stele a chance to cheer for their good performance.

"Outside in the corridor, now," she said.

Stele held her breath as she followed Drax, wide-eyed and anxious. What scheme had Drax engineered now that would cause Stele trouble?

Drax pointed her finger at Stele and backed her up against the wall in the corridor. "You think you've got away from me, but I'm going to keep my eye on you."

Drax looked as if she might explode. Stele stared at Drax's tongue as she spoke. It looked like a long, thin, slimy epo in its dark lair as it bobbed back and forth. This was likely to be the last time she had to deal with Drax and for the first time, Stele didn't think about punching her. She was ranting because she'd lost the battle between them. Stele had finally won out, and nothing Drax could say or do could affect her anymore.

"You think that because you've become the colonel's favorite, you'll get special treatment from everyone. Just remember you'll be usurped when the next young gun appears from Nero or wherever. Her latest little fancy. You'll be nothing. Remember who told you this and—"

"Hosun, to me," said Kian, stepping into the corridor.

Drax marched off, and Stele relaxed. She'd been holding her breath as Drax ranted at her. Kian's rescue was timely.

"I need to speak to you privately as part of your mentoring. Come walk with me, we can go to the park. Switch your Mesh to discreet," said Kian.

Stele stopped dead. Creff, what had she done now? Her stomach lurched. "I didn't react to Drax...I mean, Sergeant Drax. I didn't even speak. She was the one ranting..." Stele sounded like Domino with words tripping off her tongue.

"You've done nothing to worry about. We'll discuss it once we're in the park."

As they reached the grass, Kian looked around as if searching for someone or something. "I'm not sure where we can go so we can be out of sight."

"I can help. The two memorial rocks to the Founders are a good spot; it's where I speak to Ariane." Stele wondered why Kian appeared nervous but decided to wait and see.

They reached the rocks, and Kian was quiet for a moment. "I'm sorry for the subterfuge," she said. "I've made some enquiries and well, it should be possible. You'll probably need more credit than you have, but I'll lend you the difference. You've enough leave so there's no problem, and all your friends will be gone too. It's risky, but you'll need to make the arrangements yourself. I just can't be seen to be involved. Okay?"

Stele had no idea where Kian had gone with the conversation. "I'm sorry, Kian, but what are you saying?"

"You. Seeing Ariane. On the Vanguard. Going to Nero."

"What?" Stele had misheard. Kian was helping her to go see Ariane. This was epic. She'd dreamed about being with Ariane and loving her. Adrenaline zipped through her body and made her feel ready to take on the world.

Kian looked at her and said nothing. Stele was used to Kian thinking before she spoke, but this silence was killing her. "You're going to help me to see Ariane?"

"Yes. I'll give you the name of my contact, and you'll have to arrange a meet to discuss smuggling you to Nero. The ship will take two sun cycles to get there and a similar amount of time to get back. You'll only have a couple of sun cycles between journeys, and you won't be able to get off the ship. It'll be an uncomfortable journey."

"But I'll get to see Ariane. It's been so long. Wait, I'll need six or seven sun cycles off planet. How can I do that?" And there was the problem that tore away the tantalizing possibility of being with Ariane.

"Well, when you graduate from the Academy, you'll get nearly a moon cycle leave before your first posting."

"Oh, I'd forgotten that." Stele wanted to jump around, barely able to contain her excitement, but she managed to keep herself still. "Domino is going to Weston and Questa's parents are taking them on a tour around the Federation whilst they're here to see them confirmed as a Sub Lieutenant. I hadn't decided what to do. I could say I'm going to spend some time in the mountains on my own to relax. I can add in the trip as part of my mountain exploration." Stele wanted to do this, but it was chancy. If she was caught, she would have to give up what she had now for those few moments with Ariane. Glorious moments close to her, fitting together and being as one. There was no contest; it was worth it.

"You'll need to decide about the risk and whether it's worth the reward. For me, there will be none. For you, there could be problems," said Kian.

"Well, if I'm caught by Nero, what can they do? Banish me? The risk is all Ariane's, and we both need to think about it. We can chat about it when we next speak."

"You need to think about yourself and your career. You have a bright future and if you get caught, the ADF will probably throw you out."

A bright but lonely future. "Yes, but without Ariane, it'll be like living in a gray world with heavy skies and no love." Stele thought about Kian's solitude. Is that why she wanted to do this for her?

"Once you've decided, let me know, and I'll give you the details you'll need. The Vanguard is on its way back from Nero, so we have a bit of time."

Stele was still wired as she left Kian and headed for her pod and her friends. Her one thought was about whether she should tell them about it. She didn't want them to worry about what she might do and what may happen to her. She'd discuss it when they got to their postings after the event if she was still free.

***

"My love, we need to talk seriously for a moment," said Stele. She and Ariane had been flirting with each other and laughing about some of their younger days. "I may be able to get to Nero to spend a sun cycle with you. There's a lot of risk to everyone involved but more so for you than me."

"Yes," said Ariane. "Yes."

"If we get caught, I suspect that we'll be—"

"Still yes."

"We'd be imprisoned, along with our families." Stele had almost held her breath for this conversation. Maybe one of them should be serious and responsible, but Stele found it difficult.

Ariane smiled and waved her hands in the air. "I know, but we need this. You can feel me for real: we can touch each other. We can kiss."

"I want this as much as you. But I want to be sure you understand the chance we'd be taking."

"How will you do it?" Ariane asked.

"I'm paying to be smuggled on the Vanguard along with tak and gemstones. I'll know the finer points nearer the time."

"Do you have the credit? I'd like to share the cost. It's not fair for you to have all the responsibility."

"It's fine. It's no problem for me at all. I'm not telling anyone until we've met up and all is well. I don't want to jinx things. There'll be less chance of it going wrong. In the meantime, sing something for me. Have you written anything new?"

After the mesmerizing time with Ariane, Stele switched off her Mesh and wandered down the Strip. She was dressed like many of the young people on Alton in a jumpsuit, although hers was a pale gray and not the bright colors and patterns many people were wearing so that they stood out in life's dance for partners. Stele wanted to be unremarkable and not memorable. She went into one of the tak shops and got herself a tak from the counter. She sat in a booth at the far end and faced the front door. At this point she'd done nothing wrong, but she wondered if guilt had a look. Her intentions were illegal, and she was guilty before the fact. She tried to sit straight and look around her as if she were enjoying an afternoon off. She dried her hands off on the legs of her jumpsuit. She didn't want anyone to notice her nerves. She heard a door open behind her and a draft of cool air that smelled of Gandon wine fell across her skin.

A man slid in the booth in front of her. "I remember you, black eyes."

Stele winced. Black eyes. She'd never lose that name. "I remember you too. Zentos, is it? I didn't expect to meet you again. A one-way trip and all."

He'd provided her meals in silence when she was in the banishment suite.

"Well, seems I can provide a service to you. I'll be quick. Let's discuss credit. Once all is good, I'll give you instructions."

Stele took a sip of tak. "I've been told it'll cost me two thousand credits." Stele had to work out the trade with Zentos, but Kian had said to stick at two thousand for as long as she could so that when she gave way, Zentos would think that she was pushing her limit. Her mouth tasted like Seloton sand. She took another drink.

"I'm expecting five thousand."

Stele took a quick breath. That was beyond her means. She could borrow against her future but five thousand would cripple her. "Five thousand? That's a big leap from two."

"Did she tell you that? Well you're replacing tak and gems. Five thousand is what I'll lose."

"Lose?"

"The Treemons don't know what's going on, and the ship has to weigh right. I have to make sure that I always have the same extra weight, Alton to Nero and on the return journey. I take tak from Alton to Nero and have clear gems from Nero to Alton. I need your money to replace my profits from tak and clear gems. I have to lose your weight in tak. See?"

"But two thousand is all I have."

"I'm not running a charity. I need the five."

"I still only have the two. I'm sorry to have wasted your time." Stele stood up to leave. She had never bartered before, but it seemed the right thing to do.

"Okay, black eyes, don't get in a tangle. Sit. Can you borrow some and make it three?"

He put his hand out to her and his eyes bored into her. Was he trying to intimidate her? It didn't work. Stele had three thousand for this, but if she could save a bit more, she would.

"I think I can borrow five hundred. Would you take two thousand five hundred?"

Zentos was silent for a time. He stared at her all the while and Stele didn't back down.

"You strike a hard bargain, black eyes. We have a deal. Put the two thousand here," he said, holding out his wrist and indicating the credit strip on it. "You'll receive details nearer the time about getting on and off and what to do while you're on board, and you can send me the five hundred. I can feed you, but it won't be tasty or hot. We shall see. As far as I know, there are no banished due to come through in the next few moon cycles, so you should be all clear."

Zentos stood, nodded, and left through the back door. Stele nursed her tak and contemplated what she'd just done. She was two thousand credits down, but she was finally on her way to see Ariane.

CHAPTER SIX

IT WAS THE last sun cycle of Stele's Officer Training. Once complete, the graduation ceremony would follow, and she'd be on leave. But before that could happen, Stele had her final testing. She'd prepped herself for the simulation test in the Command Warfare role. The training team would be assessing and evaluating her results and performance, including the speed and accuracy of her decisions and how she treated the rest of the bridge team and the rest of the fleet. The results would affect her first posting and her early career as she and her cohort vied for places in the ADF.

The Academy had a variety of fleet mockups that they used as training rooms, and the one that had become Stele's second home since her punishment was the bridge of a destroyer. Destroyers were one of the largest star ships in the ADF, and they held over thirty people on the bridge. For exercise purposes all junior roles were missing, but the ten senior roles were filled by training staff and other cadets to give the cadet being tested a real taste of life fleetside.

The bridge looked like most bridges in the fleet with most of the electronic equipment. A view of space was available right around the ship when switched on. Many would-be bridge officers suffered with illness, unable to cope with an all-around view and nothing solid on any horizon. For Stele, the emptiness of space was exhilarating. The insignificance of the ship against a backdrop of distant stars and planets gave her skin an electrical charge as she contemplated having the expanse at her fingertips. Personnel that were within the vastness of the fleet ships were impossible to see and the contrast between such a small thing as an individual, and the endless dark was something Stele held in wonder.

She found herself in her element. Adrenaline surged through her veins at the view and the feeling of being alone in space. Developing strategies to deal with incidents and incoming targets was just an added bonus, a welcome puzzle to solve in the enormity of coping with life in the galaxy. The rest of the bridge had consoles for navigation, communications, operations and warfare, steering and propulsion, engineering and the control platform used by the captain or bridge commander.

Stele was approaching the third sixty cron of action in her test as the bridge commander, her brain strung out thinner than the seals around her atmospheric suit. She swallowed down the thought that she might not have what it would take to pass this final practical test.

The bridge was located in the Academy at Alton but built as if it were part of a destroyer, ADF Burton. She'd have to deal with a number of issues designed to test her knowledge, her ability to deal both with a stream of stressful situations and ultimately, with the unknown. Stele had already dealt with fire and smuggling space pirates. Now she was dealing with a full invasion fleet and was up against their command cruiser. She would be outgunned and outclassed, and the situation would be used to see what she would do. Stele considered her approach. She looked at the display and followed it by switching on the full spatial view. She looked around her and noticed a number of the training officers holding on to their consoles. They weren't used to life on the bridge and were feeling the effect of the all-around vision. She smiled. It felt good to get one over on the trainers occasionally. She focused and visualized her plan. First, she had to deal with the other ships in her Task Force and let them know her strategy. "Comms, get me the Klipton and Mando."

"Ready, commander," said the comms officer.

"Frigates Klipton and Mando, see if you can get closer to the enemy fleet. Full shields and follow as close as possible. Fire full spray shots to their rear once they spot you. I'm using you as a diversion. Don't allow them to slow, and keep pushing them towards Alton. They won't have seen the Burton as we'll be out of range, and they'll think getting away from you is the right option."

"Aye, ma'am," came the reply from both ships.

"Comms: tell Alton artillery defense grid Alpha and Gamma, we're pushing an enemy force in their direction. It will be at the limit of their artillery range, but try and take them out before they realize how close they are to the Alton defense grid."

"Yes, ma'am," said the comms officer.

Now Stele needed to get her own ship's defenses ready. She ran through lists on her Mesh, lists in her mind, and holoplans of her personal strategic plan. She took a step forward and looked at the display in front of her to see the placement of her task force. She needed to talk to the gunnery teams to ensure they understood she was planning to turn the ship in an overhead loop and cruise upside down, with the guns having to fire whilst their teams were in a different position. It was a risky strategy, and even more so to use it when un-rehearsed. But she had researched and planned it, and to her knowledge no-one had attempted it—certainly not with one of the biggest ships in the fleet. She didn't have time to second guess herself. She just had to get it done. It was the only strategy that made sense to her in this situation. If she did anything else, the invasion force would win, and the Burton would be blown out of the sky.

"Starboard Magnetron Gun team and Starboard Torpedo Team. Ready for action on my mark. Fire for effect against the enemy cruiser when it comes into view. I will be swinging around and flipping using Plan Hosun Two so keep your wits about you," said Stele. "Helm, make sure the ship is ready."

"Yes, ma'am. Helm ready."

"Port Magnetron Gun team and Port Torpedo Team, standby. I repeat, I'll be swinging around and flipping using Plan Hosun Two, so be ready. Helm, are you following that?"

"Yes, ma'am."

Stele knew that she now had to maneuver the destroyer with care and could hear her voice shake as she gave her orders. A thousand plus crew and a marine contingent of five hundred would depend on her not making a mistake if she were in the real world.

"Helm: increase speed to Mach 8. Head for Point Zulu." She quickly thought through her plan and could see all the bridge officers following her instructions using their Meshes as memory aids. She shoved both hands in her pockets so that no-one would see them shaking. The navigation training officer turned and smiled. Was that a good thing? Or maybe this would be a costly mistake? She'd created the plan as a fun research exercise and never expected to use it. Plenty could go wrong with it. But it was too late to worry. The ship was ready. The final elements were in place.

"Helm: slow." Stele steadied herself. "Starboard armory teams, standby… Starboard armory teams: Fire! Armaments, results as soon as you have them, please." Stele headed the ship straight into the next maneuver. "Helm. Stage three of Plan Hosun. Full speed across the bows of the attack fleet and then slow." She was about to take the ship into its defensive roll and flip. But how successful had the initial attack on the enemy been? And the Burton, her ship…did they still have shields? She needed at least eighty-five percent for this maneuver. She asked for any results. *Keep your face straight, look ahead. Appear confident.* She could do this. "Operations: what is the state of our defenses?"

"Shields still holding. Slight damage to decks twenty-five and twenty-nine, starboard side."

Stele clenched her jaw. *So far, so good.* "Armaments, any results yet?"

"Yes. The enemy cruiser has lost sixty percent of its shields. Its defense grid and forward guns are down, and it's heading at speed along with the rest of its fleet straight for Alton Gamma Artillery. Wait. The cruiser has started slowing and is turning to face us."

Everything was proceeding exactly as planned. "Helm. The flip maneuver. Go!" Stele could almost taste the excitement and adrenaline across the training team and the test bridge crew. "Port armory teams, standby, standby."

This was the point that she killed her own ship and crew if her plan failed. Stele felt her stomach twist, fear manifesting itself. She wasn't physically upended, but it felt as if she were. She could see from the all-around view that the destroyer was now upside down and turning in a circle. She counted as they came around and finally said, "Port armory teams…fire."

"Enemy cruiser engines and guns out of action. Invasion force damaged and turning away," a voice reported over the comms.

Yes! The flip had worked. Stele bounced on her toes and wanted to shout out loudly. Warmth spread through her body as she tasted real success for the first time. The sun cycles of worry and stress had all been worth it for *this* moment. It wasn't the real world, but the figures she used for the maneuver were real, and the exercise bridge had computed her instructions and given a win against an attack by an enemy fleet. She hoped it would give her a good final score for the academy.

"Exercise over. Stand down, all teams," the disembodied trainer's voice continued over the speakers. "Go get cleaned up."

Stele left the exercise bridge and ran to tell Questa and Domino of her success.

***

Stele straightened her dress blues and gave Kian a smart salute. They were standing outside the front of the Academy. They turned to one of the official robot recorders filming the proceedings of the cadets finishing their training. They stood next to each other and smiled, and Stele could see the results on her Mesh. Her smile was radiant. She couldn't stop her eyes filling with tears. She wanted to savor this moment, hold it close, and squeeze every last feeling from it. She wanted to remember this sun cycle forever.

Was it only twelve moon cycles ago that Kian had rescued her from the drunk holding cells she'd thought she was in? Stele had been so broken, unable and unwilling to see beyond the next glass of Gandon wine. Always angry, no home, no friends, no future, and no Ariane. Everything had changed, and despite some missteps along the way, she'd forged a new life. She had a home where she was accepted, friends who loved her, and a future. She owed Kian.

If only Ariane was here. Stele wanted to show her that she could be more than she was expected to be by everyone on Nero. Stele would have the robot recording of the event to give to her, something to make Ariane proud of her.

Kian was so special, and Stele had come to think of her as family. For the first time in her life, Stele had someone who believed in and supported her. Whilst Kian tended to be present for all graduating Neroians, as none had family, she'd made Stele feel special from the beginning.

"Graduation is here, and you're ready to ship out. How does it feel?" Kian asked.

She'd given Stele her trust, encouragement, and care, even if Stele wasn't ready to accept any of it at the time. She'd made Stele feel she could be more than she'd been, that she could *be* someone. Kian had also encouraged other Neroians to attend the ceremony, so Stele had an extended family of serving officers and other ranks here for her.

"Nervous. I've got this far, but I can't get away from the feeling that my future could be plucked out of my hands any cron." Stele sighed, taking a moment to find the right words to answer Kian's question. No one had ever cared how she *felt* before. No one other than Ariane. "It's like when I had to leave Nero. There's this sinking feeling in my stomach." Stele straightened. She didn't want to dwell in the past. She was an officer cadet now. No longer floating, waiting for the next disaster, the next knockdown, Stele was part of something bigger than herself. "Things can only get better though, right? I'm looking forward to starting my new job. I've got a whole heap of leave to use as well."

Kian smiled and slapped Stele on the back. "Your results were excellent, particularly the last simulation. What made you think of doing a flip with a destroyer? No-one's ever done anything like that before."

In truth, Stele wasn't sure where it had come from. "It was just how I saw the attack going. It took the technology to its limits, but...I just... *knew*." She shrugged, aware how weird she sounded. "It means I got the posting to the Dartington. When I started, I didn't expect to get such a good posting. I'm surprised...and excited!"

"The bridge of a Capital class Destroyer is a top posting, Stele. You deserved it. You earned it."

Kian had given her back the self-belief her parents and Nero had taken away, and Stele wanted to put her arms around Kian to thank her. But she couldn't hug a colonel here...or could she? She hopped from foot to foot and tried to vocalize some of her thoughts. Nothing came out. She put out both her arms and managed to get Kian into a hug. Kian looked startled but smiled and hugged her back.

"Thank you," whispered Stele, enjoying the familiar smell of pilton fruit and the sanctuary the moment afforded her.

Stele turned from Kian to find not only the Neroians but also the rest of her Pod and their families awaiting the ceremony. Stele thought back to Nero and all those sun cycles when she was alone, even beyond Ariane's help. She had led such a solitary life and spent so much time in her head, dreaming of a life where she had friends and people to talk to, where she was a part of a network, where she had a sense of belonging. The ADF had given her that. Now she had close, special friends from her pod and their families. The surprise was that they were all so different, as Domino had remarked all those moon cycles ago, a Neroian, a Pargent, and a human male. Yet they were now all connected.

She belonged.

Questa's family were easy to spot, their red faces and blue skellen stood out amongst the sea of mostly humanoid people and Stele smiled as she returned a wave from Questa.

Domino came over with a group of people. "Stele, let me introduce you to my family. I know you know all about each other from my constant chit chat, but this is my father, Hugo; my mother, Thenty; and this," Domino pointed to a young woman, "is Weller, who has my share of the family brainpower, as well as her own."

The whole family looked at Stele, their eyes clearly drawn to her own unusual ones.

"It's a pleasure to meet you, Stele," said Hugo. "And I apologize for staring. I've heard so much about you, yet your eyes are a shock on first meeting. Domino has shared with us how you came to be in the ADF, and I was so pleased that he had a Neroian in his pod. You'll find that we are all curious about Nero."

"I told you, Stele. They're as full of questions and chat as I am," said Domino. "Well, apart from Mama, who is full of smiles and love."

Thenty smiled, looking at her son with obvious fondness. She nodded to Stele.

Weller came close and put her hand on Stele's arm, still staring into her eyes. "You will class me as curious too, I expect. But for me it's in a good cause. I'm a research scientist studying the creation of energy from Neroian gems. There's little material available, and as this is the first time I've left Weston, you're the first Neroian I've met. Tell me about gem nests and how the gems are found?"

Weller was as garrulous as Domino, and like him, barely drew breath between sentences. Stele had to smile at both the warmth in her questions and her similarity to Domino. She took a deep breath and was about to speak when her thoughts drifted. Stele hadn't thought about the landscape on Nero for some time and was discomforted to realize that she missed the blackness, the caverns, and the gems. It was a beautiful landscape full of hidden surprises. They were a big part of her past, and she realized how much she missed them.

"Nero has gem nests everywhere. Those above the surface have long since been mined and the gems turned into sculptures, household items, and anything else you could think of. Now the nests are all below ground, in networks of caverns and tunnels that run through the planet. You can be walking through a vast cavern with openings to the sky and find light from a nest creating an aura and transforming the whole cavern into a place of inspiration." Stele waved her hands as she spoke, trying to show the vastness of the caverns. She thought of Ariane and the way her music reflected the light in those caverns. But she wasn't here to share this moment with Stele. She rolled her neck. This morn was not the time for negativity. This sun cycle was for celebration.

"So, how are the gems mined?" Weller asked.

She was watching Stele closely, and Stele was aware that her face had probably shown a number of emotions in a matter of moments. Weller was resolute in her task though, and her hand still gripped Stele's arm.

"They're selected and removed mostly by hand by a group of mineworkers who pick gems based on what they believe will be used by the artists," Stele said.

"So is it mapped? Is it possible to find different nests?"

Stele thought about her ten sun cycles with the mineworkers as the Ruling Council tried to find her work after her education was finished. "The mineworkers have favorite places that they visit, and some explore further afield if looking for special gems. They know where they find things, but it's secretive and there are no maps." She shook her head and smiled. "It's amazing that there's a whole world underground that's both majestic and beautiful." Most Neroians didn't value what they had. "No one visits the tunnels and caves. They have no wish to see what's under their feet." Instead of appreciating their beauty and value, they trod on, stepped over, or ignored the gems and where they came from. Just as they had done with Stele.

"Do you think there are any black gems?" Weller moved closer to Stele and indicated to Hugo and Domino to move in close with her free hand.

"The whole planet is black, so they would be difficult to find, and no-one has ever looked for them as far as I know. That's because there's no black shard for rite of passage for black eyes and therefore no black gems, as I'm sure you know."

"What does a shard look like?" Domino put his hand over Weller's on Stele's arm.

He was being his usual crass self, totally unaware of the effect he was having on her, and she was feeling exposed. The rite of passage ceremony when there was no black shard had been difficult, and she was struggling to maintain her composure. Domino and his family were making her think about Nero, the planet that had discarded her like trash. A childhood memory assailed her, and she recalled looking at the five shards and praying to simply have the same eyes as everyone else.

Stele blinked away her tears. "They're all about my height. Each one is slightly different, but they're bigger at the bottom than the top. Each shard looks as if the top were sheared off. They're solid and made from each of the colored gems that match Neroians' eyes. They're also indestructible, or so I was taught as a child." Stele thought about kneeling in front of the purple shard as a child. Both her parents had purple eyes, and if she'd had them too, she wouldn't be different. She wouldn't be worthless, she wouldn't be trouble, or difficult, or dangerous. She had stood and kicked and punched that purple shard for not allowing her to be the same as her parents. What followed was her first meeting with the pacifiers who calmed her, that first time by speech alone. She had done no damage; the shards were indestructible.

Weller nodded. "I've examined and experimented on every piece of black rock that I've been able to find from Nero and haven't found anything special about any of them. I'm still searching for more pieces. As Domino will have told you, Weston's Science Academy, where I work, has been exploring Neroian gems since the first settlers arrived. We were sent bits and pieces in the past and had numerous bits of black rock in storage for a long time, but none of them are gems. I did find a handful of jewelry made from black gems in a place that I shouldn't have had access to. They were much more interesting."

Stele thought of her tear-shaped rocks that she'd found by a nest and that she'd shared with Ariane. "In what way?"

"Well, I've been researching energy sources that could provide high grade fuel for the Federation with mixed success. We've made some energy but not the sort to fuel ships or cities. Using the fragments I found, when mixed with Amandite and heated, the power was extraordinary, even just from a few pieces off a bracelet. Those gems could create a new way of providing energy that the Federation hasn't seen before. It could be used throughout the Federation if, and that's a big if, there are more black gems on Nero and they're willing to make them available."

Stele laughed and shook her head. "It took several lifetimes before they agreed to release clear gems to provide lighting for other worlds. Prepare yourself for a long wait. They don't even believe black gems exist."

She looked around, aware of a number of the Neroian ADF members standing close to her. This shouldn't be made public. She drew Weller and her family away. "What do the black gems look like? The ones you found in the bracelet?" Stele asked, expecting them to be similar to the other gems on Nero, in a variety of sizes and shapes.

"They're small tear shaped gems, which are beautiful and make exquisite jewelry," Weller said.

"So you think the tear drops are going to be valuable eventually?" Stele asked.

Weller nodded. "Of course. Energy, and who controls it, means money...and power. Why?"

Stele withdrew the tear drop from her pocket. Her Ariane touchstone. "I have one here."

"It looks ordinary and unremarkable," said Hugo.

"I didn't expect it to be anything else other than a talisman for me and my girl." *My girl*. There it was again. "I find that it settles me when I hold it and think of her," Stele said, putting the tear back in her pocket.

"Cadets, fall in for parade," a loud deep voice called from the raised platform in front of the Academy.

Music started playing, and Stele walked along with Domino and Questa to her place among the other cadets. Their families took their seats in the raised seating to watch the proceedings.

Admiral Heddin, the Fleet Admiral in charge of the ADF, looked almost regal in his dress uniform that was more gold than blue. He made a speech about the ADF, its acceptance of each according to their skills, and the future being in the hands of these cadets. Each cadet was called by name and pod order, and they moved to the platform to get their commission. Stele stood and rocked on the balls of her feet.

"Epsilon pod," Admiral Heddin called. "Domino Gratis from Weston."

Stele cheered and clapped as he crossed the platform. The warmth that flooded through her beat the nerves she was suffering from.

"Stele Hosun from Nero."

She walked to the admiral on the platform, the cheers and clapping a little more muted.

Admiral Heddin handed Stele her commission. "Well done. I look forward to watching your future journey in the Force," he said and shook her hand.

She stood to the side and clapped and cheered as Questa received their commission, watching their blue skellen moving like pilton trees in a gale. They'd each received their commissions as sub-lieutenants in the ADF, and Stele knew for the first time in her life that she was on the brink of a new adventure.

CHAPTER SEVEN

THE VANGUARD WAS the only ship that ever landed on Nero. Its inhabitants had never wanted anything to do with other worlds, so an ancient agreement was made between the Federation and Nero. The Treemon family were given the job as liaison between the Federation and Nero with a right to trade. Each generation of the Treemon family entered into an agreement to provide transport for Nero and to protect the trade of the planet and its population. None of them were Nero born, nor lived on Nero, but they'd been given the right to land a ship at the terminal and had free movement within the docking terminal on Nero.

Stele moved through the shadows in the space docks. She moved smoothly and stepped gently so that the only sounds she could hear were her heart beating and the distant sounds of the Vanguard in space dock. She was on her way to see Ariane. This was the first step. Each step was risky, and each step would be difficult, but it would all be worth it for a few hours with Ariane. A few moon cycles ago she didn't think any of this would be possible. They would soon be together, to talk about their lives and their future and to love each other with their bodies and words. Stele hurt deep inside thinking about it. She ached in her heart, and she ached in her soul. To be able to feel Ariane's skin and her warmth was all she could think about. Her hologram was no longer enough. This would be the first time they'd managed to meet since Stele's banishment, but she hoped they'd able to do it again. Ariane was a drug she craved.

Kian had given her a helpful tip: *stand completely still next to a bright light, and in its shadow, you'll be unseen. Even if people are looking for you.* There was no-one around to see her, but she hoped Kian was right. She was dressed as a crew member of the Vanguard in their gray kit and once the cargo was loading and unloading, she'd sneak on board. She knew her way, after all, since she'd been there before. Stele had arrived on Alton in this ship after she had been banished with nothing and no-one.

She thought back to her feelings of inadequacy and fear on that trip.

Valden Bush

There was no comparison with the woman she was today: stronger both mentally and physically and going after what she wanted. *My Ariane.* Tonight, it was vital to get things right. There was no room for being cocky; if this went wrong, both she and Ariane would be in serious trouble, as would Zentos, though he was being paid so her concern for him was small. For the first time in her life, she *was* someone, and she *had* someone. Yes, she was risking everything, but Ariane was worth it.

From her dark and shadowy viewpoint Stele could see movement and the hold was being emptied of containers. Now was her chance. She edged across the empty adjacent bay to the side of the cargo gate. Her heartbeat was accompanied by a sound in her head like a large drum softly sounding. The containers were being unloaded using some kind of self-propelled hover mechanism. Stele needed to get close enough to get on board without drawing attention. This was the most dangerous moment of all. She stood almost to attention before confidently walking forward across the open space, looking as if she should be there as she marched into the cargo gate and over the gangway into the port hold. The stale smell of food and engine oil hit her as she silently moved forward, and she shook off memories of her previous trip.

She crossed the port hold, a dark and cavernous area with small emergency lights. From there, she navigated narrow, brightly lit corridors and finally went into the back of the starboard hold. The door to the banishment suite was open. She entered slowly and checked for any other occupants. All clear.

She followed Zentos's instructions and lay on the floor between the beds so that she was out of sight of casual inspection from the doorway. The only sounds were the distant movements of the cargo being unloaded and the thumps of her heart beating as she waited for Zentos to come and seal her in. She heard footsteps and stayed totally motionless though her heart sounded like a charging decko, and her breathing echoed like firing torpedoes in her ears.

"This door is open, Zentos. Have you been stealing the tak?" asked a woman, then she laughed loudly.

"Ma'am, you know all my secrets. You know I like a little quiet time when I can steal away and why not have it in luxury in this suite? I just cleaned it ready for the next trip," said Zentos.

"You know I don't mind, but you must try and keep the door closed.

If my father finds out, we'll both be done for. He'll bust me to Ensign and you off the ship."

The door slid shut and the voices became distant.

Stele slowly peered over the bed toward the door to check that it was closed. She let out the breath she'd been holding. She looked around at her home for the next few sun cycles. It had gray walls, two strap-in seats, and two beds with a door on the far wall to the head. An entertainment rig sat on a metal shelf. The suite was small and basic, but clean.

It was also daunting. She'd talked of risk and what could happen to them if they got caught. But she was here now, and this was all real. She could be captured. Fear was something that rarely came to the fore in her life, usually replaced by anger. Just occasionally though, it took her by surprise. But her hope outweighed her fear. Hope that could easily be quashed and there it was. Her fear of losing something she didn't have yet. But how she wanted time with Ariane. They had been together so little and now they both knew what they wanted.

The cycles would pass slowly locked away in here with little to do and no one to talk to. Luckily, she could use the entertainment rig because it wasn't attached to any ship-wide network. She had brought a few things with her and had her Mesh that would allow her access to everything in the rig.

Lying on the deck, she saw the boxes containing tak that Zentos was smuggling onto Nero. Stele laughed quietly to herself. She was worth several of those boxes of tak. Not many people had their worth calculated in such a way.

She froze as the door slid open again.

"It's Zentos."

Stele emerged from her hiding place.

"I've bought food for the next two sun cycles. The hot should stay hot and the cold, cold. I won't be back again until I need a break from the rest of the crew. I need to keep to my routine, so ration yourself," he said.

Stele looked at the box that allowed hot food to retain its heat and taste and not affect the cold food and drink. They were rare outside the ADF. "Marine issue container?"

"It works." He handed her a pass. "This will lock the door on the inside. I have one and so do the bridge crew. You won't be disturbed."

She didn't want to see anyone. If she did, it would be the end of her dreams.

"Strap in. We leave shortly," said Zentos, before he smiled and left, closing the door behind him.

Stele got up from the floor, locked the door with the pass, and strapped herself into a nearby seat. Even though she'd been in space for the journey to Alton, the thrill of exploration and adventure ignited within her. The excitement of seeing Ariane soon and the passion of her dreams was almost overpowering.

***

The journey to Nero was safe but tedious. Although only two sun cycles, it was a long while to be enclosed in a small room. She had seen Zentos a couple of times when he visited to get away from the crew, but it was only to give her food rather than companionship or conversation.

Zentos opened the door and entered. "We're coming up to Nero."

Stele's eyes prickled with tears. She was breathing the same air as Ariane, and they would soon be together, as they should be, as they'd always been destined to be.

"Belt yourself in. I'll be back shortly with food."

A knock disturbed her, and Zentos re-entered with a container which he handed to her.

"It's not the best food, but it's edible. I'll get your woman and bring her here. I'll inform you when she'll need to leave. You'll have one sun cycle." He pointed to the boxes beneath the beds. "I need to unload those now."

"Thank you," she said, though the words didn't seem adequate.

He nodded and left, but quickly re-appeared with a gray box, which he loaded with tak and left again. She cleaned and tidied the room in case the female officer appeared and lay down between the beds to wait for the ship to dock.

She opened her eyes. She must have fallen asleep. And there, on the other side of the little gray room, leaning against the back of one of the chairs was the person she'd just been dreaming about. Ariane looked just as beautiful as Stele had remembered. Her dark hair curled around her shoulders and her eyes, that always seemed to see right through her, were looking straight at her. The world stopped. Stele could see everything and nothing. She was drawn into Ariane's purple eyes and the dark abyss at their center, as if a black hole was sucking her through its ring of fire into oblivion. At this single moment it was as if there were no one else in the galaxy except the two of them.

Ariane opened her arms and smiled. There was nothing transparent about her: she was definitely not a hologram. Stele wanted to touch her to get the warmth and softness from her body. She got up and drew her into her arms, just as she'd done a hundred times in her life in the past whenever the world seemed against her. She breathed in Ariane's hair, and she smelled of flarnic, of safety, of home. She'd never needed Nero, or even a home planet. All she'd ever needed was Ariane.

She relaxed into the feeling of their bodies molded together. Ariane's curves touched her body, creating hot spots of longing. Stele took hold of Ariane's shoulders and gently held her away from her so that she could see her face.

Now she was only a breath away from her. "Hello for real," she said. She held Ariane's face gently and slowly, so slowly she pressed her lips against Ariane's. They were soft and cool. She was just as Stele had imagined she would taste. Stele wanted them both to remember their first kiss. That kiss that she'd dreamed of. Ariane's lips that were both tender and gentle, perfection indeed. Ariane pulled Stele closer and added more pressure to her lips. Stele's body ached, but her soul was on fire. All this need and waiting had ignited her passion with only a small spark.

She'd pictured this moment for so long, the safe harbor of Ariane's arms and the joining of their bodies. But now, she didn't want to push. Conscious that this may be their only time together, Stele wanted it to be perfect. She wanted to take everything slowly and allow them both to enjoy the peacefulness they had found in each other's arms. This time together was special, and it would be Ariane's first time. She wanted to share her feelings of wonder and joy at the act that would give them a joining that would be irreplaceable, made with love and hope.

Stele moved away from Ariane's magnetic lips. She saw her own smile mirrored by Ariane, who drew a deep breath.

"That was a real hello." Her eyes twinkled. "Can we do it again?"

Ariane pulled Stele to meet her lips, and she was lost all over again. All thoughts of before and now became one as adrenaline coursed through her body.

They had explored each other's bodies as holograms but never in real life. Ariane was so much more than the hollow three-dimensional projection she'd been messaging, so much more than the young woman who had been her best friend and hugged her when she was in trouble. Ariane would be guided by Stele, and she needed to make sure that this was special, but also, if it was their only time, it had to be something that they would both remember. When they'd talked about this trip, they hoped it would be repeated or that their circumstances might change. There had to be some chance of that. What happened this sun cycle would matter.

Ariane took a step back. Stele was instantly aware of the space she left and the almost cool air in front of her.

"Mm." Ariane licked her lips. "My legs are shaking, and you're going to have to let me sit before you kiss me again."

Ariane took Stele's hand and pulled her over to one of the small beds. Stele flopped onto the bed and lay on her back, lying on the bed with Ariane half on her and half on the bed. Ariane's giggle, that wonderful sound like gems tinkling in the breeze, lit her longing. She'd missed it in her absence from Nero.

She turned slightly onto her side and pulled Ariane up close so that they lay side by side. Stele whispered to Ariane about the wonder of her warm skin, her softness, and the light in her eyes. She stroked her face as she leaned in for another gentle kiss. She nibbled along Ariane's lower lip before using her tongue to follow the same path. Ariane copied the action and moved slightly away, running her fingers along Stele's lips.

"I love this. I love kissing you."

All the thoughts about what a kiss from Ariane would be like hadn't come close to the real thing. Whatever she'd expected was somehow so much less than the reality. "I love your lips, my Ariane." Stele ran her hand through Ariane's hair as they exchanged more kisses.

Her thoughts were taking control, her heart was beating loud enough to mirror a decko mating dance. She needed to feel Ariane's skin under her hand, needed to find all those secret and exciting places that Ariane didn't know she had yet.

Using both hands she undid the fasteners on Ariane's jumpsuit and slid it from her shoulders. Ariane didn't look away from Stele as she raised her body to allow them both to pull it down to her waist. She was no longer a disembodied voice or a hologram with no center, she was lying in the here and now, waiting. Stele ran a hand down Ariane's back and she shivered. Her whole face came alive with her smile, and Stele implicitly understood their togetherness.

She looked down Ariane's magical body. Her taut stomach disappeared into the folds of material. She'd been quietly waiting for this. Waiting for the things that she'd dreamed of for so long, imagined feeling those soft places. Stele would worship her, as both her lover and protector.

She trailed her hand over Ariane's stomach and up to her breasts. Ariane's nipple hardened beneath her fingertips, and she took a sharp intake of breath.

"Are you okay?" Stele didn't want to hurry Ariane or push her somewhere she wasn't yet comfortable with. It was one thing to play virtually as they had a few moon cycles ago, but she didn't want to go too quickly for Ariane now that they had time.

"Yes," she whispered. "This is more than okay. This is what I've been waiting for, to have you in my arms and your body close to me…and these kisses." Ariane pressed her lips to Stele's again and sighed. "I want you to feel the music in my fingers as you give me the poetry in yours. Please don't stop."

The soft sheen across Ariane's bronze skin took Stele's breath away as she explored the valley between her breasts and ran her hands down her bare skin. She luxuriated in the exploration, finding the tender spot on one side of her neck and the ones around the front of each hip. She took each spot in her mouth before running her tongue down the center of Ariane's abdomen, pushing back the material until she came to the softness of hair. Ariane ran her hands through her hair, and joy filled Stele's heart.

She helped Ariane remove the rest of her clothes and boots, and she removed her own with Ariane's help.

"Let me see you." Ariane gently pushed Stele back to the bed and looked her up and down. She reached out and traced the lines of Stele's stomach muscles.

Stele needed to feel Ariane's skin against her own. She pulled Ariane in close as she sought her lips once again. She ran her hands up and down Ariane's back seeking the hollows and coming to rest on her backside. She gently pushed one of her legs in between Ariane's.

One of her dream images of Ariane was just this pose, her hands holding Ariane so close that they would appear completely molded together, forever joined. She took a deep breath and moved slightly away, Ariane looked at her and smiled. She moved her hand down Ariane's body until it reached soft hair. She was where she should be, wanted to be and she was going to show Ariane how much she loved her even if she couldn't yet voice it. She looked at Ariane as she moved her hand lower asking for permission.

Ariane answered by pushing her body up into her hand as Stele moved into the warmth of that special place. Home was being with Ariane, but giving her love, this was home. She ran her hand tenderly along the folds, finding the gem that was hidden between them.

Ariane moved her body in a rhythm with Stele's hand. Her heartbeat pounded against Stele's chest, playing a duet with her own. The symphony was getting louder and faster. Stele could feel changes in Ariane's body responses and so softly and carefully, she entered her. There was almost a crash of cymbals in Stele's head as Ariane stopped moving completely before shaking and shuddering as she held onto Stele's arms.

She had only ever been alone in her soul. She'd always been alone, even with family and friends, both on Nero and Alton. She was different and would always be so, but now she was no longer alone. Ariane had found a way to meld their beings together.

Ariane's breathing slowed, and she opened her eyes. She wrapped one of her legs over Stele. "We've been missing a lot, haven't we?" She nestled her head on Stele's chest.

Stele wasn't sure she could put anything into words, so she nodded. She needed release, but she didn't want this feeling to end.

"I'm not sure I know how to do this." Ariane tentatively put a hand on one of her breasts and stroked it.

"Just follow your instincts," Stele whispered. "You're doing fine so far. I'm so ready for you." Ready enough to explode.

Ariane put one of her legs between Stele's and kissed her. The pressure of Ariane's breasts against hers and her warm lips on her mouth made the heat inside her almost unbearable. She was so close. She pushed her hips up into Ariane's body. Ariane stopped kissing her and moved her hand down between their bodies. Her caress was like a whisper, and Stele needed nothing more. Everything in her body raged on fire and the galaxy was full of shooting stars.

Stele had enough energy to pull Ariane up her body and the two of them lay together molded body to body as if they were wrapped in the other. Stele vowed she would move the universe to make it happen so that they were together always. They may have different places in the world, the banished black-eyed outcast and the rising star. Stele may not fit in the world on Nero, but she did fit with Ariane.

The sun cycle moved at light speed, and before they knew it, their time together had ended. Ariane cried as she left the Vanguard, and Stele had to hold onto the wall to keep from falling to her knees. When the door shut, closing Ariane and Nero out, she struggled to her feet.

Stele strapped herself into the seat into the banishment suite on the Vanguard and cried. Saying good-bye to Ariane had been as difficult as she'd expected. They'd clutched each other tightly with the desperate knowledge that it would likely be some time before they could meet up again. Trying to be strong for both of them, Stele had clamped her mouth shut and still had the pain in her jaw now. She wrapped her arms around her knees and told herself repeatedly that anything was possible. But all the while, she was hurtling through space, away from her love.

Having spent a sun cycle in Ariane's arms, being close and showing her everything she was feeling, her future was with Ariane. But it was hard when she had just found herself on Alton and got the beginnings of a successful career in the ADF. How could they make that future happen? She was going to be travelling through the stars for the foreseeable future. If Ariane left Nero, she'd leave everything she'd ever known and leave her parents to face the reprisals. They'd talked about it as something to work toward, but Stele had no idea how to make it happen. She couldn't go to Nero. It was for Ariane to make all the sacrifices.

She closed her eyes, raw and burning from tears of loss, and willed herself to remember every moment of the short time they had spent together and to believe in the wonder that was Ariane.

CHAPTER EIGHT

WOW, IT'S REAL. This was Stele's new life, and the thrill of anticipation tingled through her body. She rested her hand on the warfare screen in front of her to still herself. Standing on the bridge of the Dartington felt... right. The pain of leaving Ariane was still fresh and raw, but she had to keep moving forward.

Stele had been on the bridge for ten crons and had already taken in her surroundings carefully. It differed little from the training set-up she'd been used to in the Academy. The biggest contrast was that the people at the different stations were no longer her fellow officer cadets and staff. Instead, she was surrounded by strangers, most of them a lot older than her. She looked to the communication station and could see that a commander was on point accompanied by the familiar face and blue hair of her Pargent friend, Questa. She gave them a quick smile.

"Good luck," she mouthed silently. Questa smiled, and their blue skellen waved.

The other big contrast was the number of command posts. Stele could see an admiral in one command post and a captain in another. Normally there was only the one command post. There was no one at the Warfare Officer point except herself, which left her feeling exposed. Where was the officer she would be shadowing? It appeared she was going to have two senior officers giving her instructions and orders. Stele relished the challenge and the chance to excel, even if the thought was giving her slightly shaky legs. She was glad of her hand on the display in front of her.

Admiral Simpkin turned and looked at her from one of the command posts before gesturing her to come closer. "Hosun, welcome to your first duty as warfare officer on my bridge," he said.

"Yes, sir."

The admiral gestured over to Captain Harmer to come and join them.

"Be clear, you are not an assistant. You are the warfare officer in training. I run the operations for the whole of the ADF from the Dartington, and although Captain Harmer is the commanding officer of the ship, I'm the fleet admiral, and he follows my fleet instructions. That means we'll both be giving you instructions. Do you understand?"

"Yes, sir. Obey all instructions, sir." The thought of getting it wrong surged adrenaline through her veins and she closed her eyes against the dizziness.

"This post is a skilled one. Few people are capable of understanding the different spacial and strategic views along with the difficulty of being commanded by two superiors. It can be confusing and frustrating. Captain Harmer started his career as a warfare officer and has been acting as my warfare officer in addition to running his own ship. Your instructors at the Academy believe you have the skills necessary for this role. We've decided to train you ourselves and see how you get on. How do you expect to deal with two sets of commands? Captain Harmer and I are interested in your approach."

How Stele answered this question would reflect on how they would treat her in the future. "I understand from talking to my instructors at the Academy that you have a louder voice than Captain Harmer, sir, so I expect to start by obeying the loudest voice first."

"Ha! I can see you've the right idea. We'll try not to give differing commands but there may be times in the heat of battle when you'll have to make difficult decisions. We've not had any serious battles to fight, but we practice constantly to keep the fleet on its toes. I'll be pushing you and testing you at all times, so never think that any sun cycle on my bridge will be an easy one. There is no such thing."

"Yes, sir."

Captain Harmer nodded. "The biggest problem we're likely to have is the odd skirmish with pirates who like looting our trading vessels. We need to be both vigilant and strong. We must ensure that pirates don't think the Federation is an easy touch. We have many trade routes through our air space that would be rich pickings if pirates decide they can beat us."

"The first thing we need to know is how you managed to flip a destroyer like Dartington without breaking it," said the Admiral.

"I can show you my research, sir." Now she was on familiar territory. Stele's stomach settled. *I'm going to be all right.*

***

When she'd first arrived on board, Stele had gone to her new pod on the Dartington with her kit bag over her shoulder and found a woman lying on one of the beds staring into nowhere. Her legs were moving and her arms waving as if she were dancing in time to music. Stele realized the woman was looking at something on her Mesh. An adjacent bed was empty, and the only one that looked neat and tidy, so Stele moved toward it. It seemed as good a bed as any of the others to claim.

The woman looked up and smiled. It was the kind of smile that could break hearts. Not hers, of course. Now that Ariane was hers, other women held little interest beyond friendship.

"So, the only neat spot in this room will soon be mussed up like the rest. Who are you, and where've you come from?"

"I'm Stele Hosun, ma'am, trainee warfare officer from Nero and fresh out of the box."

"Naveh! I've never been a ma'am, and I'm not starting now. I'm Dash, lead pilot of the Sprint squadron. Help yourself to that pit. It's been empty a while." She jumped up from her bed and moved toward Stele. "Dash is my nickname because I rarely stay still. You caught me dancing."

Dash had got up quickly as if it were part of the dance. Although she was the same height as Stele, Dash was a complete contrast to Stele with her light skin and white hair.

She stared at Stele. "You have unusual eyes. The only people I've seen from Nero have black lines in their eyes like the colonel of the Marines on board."

Stele sighed at Dash's inevitable line of questioning. "I'm one of a kind. I'm the only black-eyed Neroian, and I was banished several seasons ago, just like the starburst people." She sat on the end of the bed. "I seem to be doing all right as part of the ADF though, and it's been good making friends. It wasn't so easy on Nero."

"I'm sure the pilots will enjoy getting to know you," Dash said and winked. "Did you come alone or are there any more of you?"

"Yes, there's a Pargent called Questa in a pod close by... They're a good friend. And there are more new officers from training; half of our graduates were posted here, but I'm not sure where they are."

"Ooh, a Pargent. They must be accomplished. Only a few of them are allowed into the ADF and this sector of space, away from the Allied Nations. A friend, you say?" Dash raised her eyebrows.

"Yes. We were in Epsilon pod in training together and we've got on well. They are far from where they grew up. As I am, and it means we understand some of each other's problems. A Pargent only gets together with another Pargent."

"Did any more humanoid females come on board with you?" Dash looked at the bulkhead as if she were feigning disinterest.

Stele put her kit bag on her bed and glanced toward Dash, who kept her gaze away. She was still pretending she didn't care, but she was obviously more interested than she was admitting. "Yes, there were one or two but I'm not sure where they've been posted. Are you looking for someone in particular? I'm sure Questa might be able to—"

"No, no one in particular. I like to keep my eye on the ladies." Dash turned and looked at Stele, a flirty smile playing on her lips.

Stele felt her face flush. "Sorry. I'm a little slow about these things. Nero didn't allow same-sex pairings, and I'm still getting used to the openness on Alton. I have a girl myself, but she's on Nero." Stele grinned at her own words. She *did* have a girl. "I'll work on trying to keep up."

Dash laughed as she jumped up. "Please don't worry; it's charming. Get yourself unpacked, and I'll catch you up on the essential things you'll need like showers, clothing, and food. Once we've done the boring, we'll hit the fun stuff like the bar and social spaces."

"I won't need the bar." The stories about pilots and their partying were legendary. But Stele had been doing well avoiding alcohol and wouldn't be pressured into drinking. She couldn't afford any more formal warnings that would ruin her career before it had started. "I don't drink."

"Don't worry. A lot of the time we aren't drinking either. We have to be clean for twenty-four hours before we can fly…and we're tested frequently. So, there's always a group of us that can't drink, and we don't push. Well, mostly. You have problems? I haven't heard that Neroians don't drink."

Stele couldn't hold the direct stare from Dash's striking blue eyes. "Um…er…"

"Sorry, I shouldn't be so inquisitive. Like, do you want to tell me your life history in the next twenty cron? Probably not. Just tell me to shut up."

Stele held up her both her hands. "No way. I won't tell you my life story until you've told me yours." Dash laughed. "But yes, I've had a few problems with Gandon wine. I don't drink at all now. It's much safer."

"Safer for you?" Dash asked.

"For us all. I'm likely to start a fight I can't win. It's also quieter. I've been known to attempt singing, but my tone is far from melodic."

"I'm looking forward to finding out more about your story. I think we'll get on well. The pilots and shooters on my squadron are a good bunch and enjoy new company, especially if they can win a few hands of Zot and get credits from you. Come on, let's hit the high spots of the Dartington and we can meet them. While we're out we can get some food and tak."

Domino was now a light weapons specialist on the Dartington and was on one of the squadrons as a gunner. She didn't see him as much as she had hoped. Stele missed his everyday chatty dialogue. She, Questa, and Domino had several chats via their Meshes, but they didn't get to meet up. The rest of that first moon cycle, Stele spent most of her off time with Questa and her new pod members who were all pilots, and Stele appreciated their carefree approach to life. They protected the Federation's cargo ships and attacked the pirates. They never knew whether their flight would be their last as they headed out into the vastness alone, where it could also mean instant death as they provided much of the forward strength and information gathering of the fleet. Stele was sure that putting her in a pilot pod had been a conscious decision by the brass to ensure she understood the ramifications of any of the decisions she made or commands that she gave on the people whose lives she held in her hands.

***

"Alert! Alert! Code one. Repeat, code one."

Stele woke from a deep sleep hearing the disembodied voice over her Mesh and the klaxon sounding in the room. As she opened her eyes, the room flashed with alternating white light and a bright red glow. If the noise hadn't alerted her, the light show would certainly have made her aware that something was happening. Code one was the top alert and meant that the ship was either under, or about to be under, attack. Stele felt her adrenalin spike. This was what her job was all about and reacting to the unknown gave her a better rush than a glass of Weston Green. She jumped out of bed and threw on clothes. No one spoke as Stele made her way to the bridge while Dash and the other pilots headed off for the flight deck. The corridors were packed with people moving toward their stations. Everyone moved with silent purpose, but there was no hurry nor panic. It was a much-rehearsed reaction.

Stele quickly arrived on the bridge wondering how she had ever managed without her automated direction. She and Questa had spent the first couple of sun cycles getting lost and causing much hilarity amongst the pilots until Dash told them they could download an update to their Meshes with direction finding.

Admiral Simpkin's normally smooth hair firmly stuck up on one side looking like the silhouette of a forest on the horizon. He looked around the bridge. "Code one. We're under attack. Defense plan three-alpha-delta. The captain is busy defending the Dartington. Hosun, look at what we have on the sector maps. Three space pirates, if I'm not mistaken. I'm not sure where they have come from. What are they doing? Be quick."

Stele looked at her screens and saw three sleek-looking pirate fighter craft, smaller than most of the six fleet ships they'd just ambushed but bristling with armaments. She suspected the pirates could give the ADF fleet a real problem, but they seemed to be moving off out of range and toward the Alfed jump gate. The jump gate gave access between the Federation and the Allied Nations and was the entry point for a major cargo route across the sector. It was possible to take other routes between the two sectors of the galaxy, but this jump gate provided much faster access.

"Admiral, they've moved out of range and are closing in on the jump gate. Looking at their movements, they've come from Seloton and before that, Bacton. They appeared here from nowhere though."

"How did they get here unnoticed?" the admiral asked.

"They can't be using mobile jump gates, can they? Stele said. "They're illegal here in the Federation. But they look as if they're watching us." She tapped the screen in front of her. "I suggest that the squadrons are recalled to avoid potshots from the pirates. They could launch their fighters, but this is the third time they've played with us like this since I've been on board. I think they're testing us to see if we've noticed what they're doing and what we do about it," said Stele.

"Let's see. Quess, try and can get one of the pirates on the comms," said the admiral.

The screen filled with the picture of a bridge much the same as the Dartington, but it was more compact and housed casually dressed staff.

Standing at the center was a towering humanoid male, much bigger than his crew, with a bald and glistening head that had a green shadow to it, reminding Stele of the domed roof of an Alton temple. Stele recognized him as a Komodon, a combination of human and Varanids, lizard-like creatures who held humans captive on their small Zuton worlds at the far edge of Allied Nations space and at the beginning of the Wilds. He nodded at the screen. It was unusual to see many Komodon travelling in space since few managed to escape their slavery. Stele had only ever seen pictures of them in books at the academy.

"Nice to see you again, Admiral. Hello, bridge crew." He grinned, showing gold-colored, sharpened teeth. "Never let it be said that I'm not polite."

"Hello, Rudd. I had a feeling this might be you. Testing us out, are you? You were in the ADF. You should know that we'll spot you whenever you appear here."

"Yes, but you can't be everywhere, can you?" Rudd put his hands on his hips and thrust his bulging stomach toward the screen. "I'm just biding my time until you get sloppy. Oh, and look, you've got a warfare officer now. A woman too! She won't last long. That's a difficult job, little lady."

Stele bristled at the comment but said nothing. This conversation was between the pirate and her admiral.

"I've heard tales of a Neroian woman with black eyes. Could that be her? How interesting, Admiral. If you get tired of her, please feel free to pass her on to me. I know how to *treat* my women…especially if they're the stuff of the ancients."

Stele shuddered. Any man would be bad enough, but Rudd had no hair, fat lips, large red eyes, and a mangy, long beard. The thought of him putting his hands on her was repulsive. Stele refused to look away. She wouldn't give him the satisfaction of seeing her react.

"Not likely, Rudd. She can certainly do the job you were so spectacularly incapable of. She outclasses you."

"I suppose I'll find out if I decide to capture her…" He ran his sharp, thin tongue over his lips. "Life has become much more interesting in the last 20 cron."

The screen darkened, and Stele saw the three pirate ships move to the jump gate. And they were gone. Stele could still feel Rudd's red eyes on her despite the screen having gone dark. She shuddered involuntarily, strangely aware that he would be back to cause far more serious problems.

"Hosun, I want a meeting of all ship captains and their warfare officers in my meeting room in ten crons," Simpkin ordered. "We need to work out what they're doing and why. We also need to develop a new defense plan."

It wasn't Stele's first strategic meeting since she had been on board, but it was the first she had attended that had all the captains and warfare officers from the six ships in their Fleet. She knew them all by name because she dealt with them, issuing instructions, on a daily basis, but she'd met none of them. Her stomach churned, and she took hold of Ariane's stone to keep her calm and grounded.

She sat next to Captain Harmer, hoping that being close to him would somehow protect her. She looked around the table and wondered who was checking her out as the newcomer with the black eyes. She continued staring at each of them, brazen in her approach. She didn't know what they expected from her, but she wasn't going to back down. She just didn't want to make a fool of herself.

"This is Sub Lieutenant Stele Hosun. She's recently taken the role of trainee warfare officer for both the Dartington and the fleet, though she's soon likely to graduate to the full position, having proved herself well."

Stele looked at Simpkin in surprise and allowed a small smile to play on her lips. His feedback so far hadn't mentioned ending her trainee period.

He nodded at her. "We believe that Rudd has been openly travelling around the Federation visiting many of the planets, flexing his muscles. The intelligence we have suggests that he has managed to either buy or accost a number of other small pirate fleets; both Chin Lee and Joost Hammamet have been murdered, and Rudd is now running their fleets. The intelligence has also suggested he is looking for something, although no one has been able to confirm that. I believe there are a number of trade routes that he could have his eye on. Other suggestions?" Simpkin scanned the room.

"Captain Tryss, frigate Sutton. Might this be something personal between you and Rudd? Does he want to destroy *you* rather than the fleets? We all know how he believes failing as the fleet warfare officer under your command was down to you and not him."

Simpkin nodded at Tryss. "You may be right, and he will confirm your suspicions but, in the meantime, I think we should consider escorts for all trade vessels, particularly those with passenger vessels and valuable cargo between the major routes. Does anyone else have any better suggestion?" Simpkin waited but everyone simply shrugged or nodded their agreement. "Hosun, prepare some first cut details of what that will look like for fleet movements and how it will be best to control it."

"Yes, sir." Stele automatically replied before she considered the compliment that the admiral had given her by asking for first cut details. She was both proud and elated. It was an enormous task and one which Simpkin had asked her to advise him on. She could do this. She relished the challenge. She would *not* think about failure.

"I think we need to go back to Alton and deal with it from there," Simpkin said.

Stele's breath hitched at Simpkin's announcement, and she thought about seeing Kian. She was her new family and being close to her again gave her a lightness in the chest she hadn't had for some time.

***

Stele liaised with officers in Command Central as the best minds in the ADF tried to work out what Rudd was doing. Admiral Simpkin encouraged her to be honest and to say what was on her mind, a happy contradiction to how she was expected to behave on Nero. She produced a number of options for the admiral with the help of Command. Stele had some down time while Admiral Simpkin perused the options she and Command had created, so she contacted Kian, hoping to connect with her mentor. She had missed her as a child might miss a parent and wanted the physicality of that tight bond.

Kian's message came in. *"I know just the place. I'll pick you up from the Dartington amidships gangway at sunset."*

"See you there." Stele couldn't relax once the message had arrived. Her body seemed to have a mind of its own, and she couldn't sit quietly. She paced around the ship waiting for sunset to arrive. It hadn't been that long since she'd seen Kian, and they had messaged often, but Stele missed the strength of their bond and their face-to-face talks.

Kian jogged up the steps and pulled Stele into a tight hug. They'd only hugged a couple of times before, once at her graduation from the academy and once when she left for the Dartington. There was a time when the only physical contact Stele had was with Ariane and she needed no more.

But she had come to know that the feel of Kian's arms around her was something vital to her emotional well-being. It wasn't long enough for Stele, who loved the security of Kian's arms. But it wouldn't be proper if they hugged for anything longer. They walked out toward the space gates at the end of the dock before Kian turned them down an alleyway.

"This is the best kept secret on Alton. The food here is excellent. Plain but cheap. There are a number of stateless people who run the restaurant, with the full knowledge of spaceport security. They arrived on trade ships and were abandoned, awaiting clearance to enter Alton. While they waited, they started to serve snacks and their enterprise grew into a restaurant. They've not yet entered Alton and thus are stateless, but the security officers have allowed them to remain because they run an excellent service."

Stele followed Kian down the alley, and they entered a nondescript small, gray warehouse. The enticing smell of spicy, exotic food filled her nostrils, and after time on board ship eating bland ADF rations, she already wanted to eat everything on the menu. The restaurant was small, with a few mismatched tables and chairs.

"Hello, friend," one of the staff greeted Kian, obviously knowing her well, before she seated them at a table.

Kian shook the woman's hand. "Hello, Xim. How have you been?

"Same old, same new," Xim said. "What can I get you?"

Kian looked at Stele, but she shrugged. "You know the place. I'm happy to eat whatever you put in front of me. Everything smells amazing."

"Okay." Kian ordered a series of plates and drinks, and Xim left them.

"I'm so pleased you contacted me, Stele. I've heard good things from the Admiral and Captain Harmer about you. Are you having fun?"

"It's amazing. I'm actually good at something for the first time in my life, and people have congratulated me when I've moved the Fleet across space; they applaud me for enjoying myself."

"You mean you've given the admiral's commands and taken the fleet through Federation space? That must make you feel powerful."

"Not powerful so much as exhilarated. Moving ships through the vast, silent emptiness of space is something else." Stele paused when Xim returned and gave them both cups of tak. "I've made some good friends too. Questa and I have been spending time with the pilots in my pod."

Kian sighed and shook her head. "Oh no, not pilots. What about your drinking? How are you coping?"

Kian's question hit hard. Stele still remembered standing in front of her, in trouble for drinking and losing her trust. She had regained that faith, but the rawness of almost losing her mentor burned hot.

"I'm not drinking at all. I'm tempted at times, and I don't think that will ever go away. I just have to continue to control it. Dash is in my pod, and she's taken me under her wing. She's the lead pilot of one of the squadrons, and I told her up front I didn't drink." This was beginning to feel more like a discipline meeting than a friendly meal, but Stele understood Kian's concern. "Questa doesn't drink either, which helps."

"Mm. Having both must be helpful," Kian said.

"Questa and I stay away from anyone who's drinking. But they're crazy when they're sober too. They'll bet on anything. They play a card game called Zot, which I can't work out, so I always lose money whenever I play. But not as much as Questa. They're true to their empathic rules and switch everything off to play. But of course, they have no experience of reading people with none of their usual attributes, so they fail miserably. And quite happily too."

Stele stopped again when Xim came to their table loaded with a number of small plates each holding enough for two. One plate held a bright yellow sauce decorated with flowers. She breathed deeply and her mouth watered. If the food tasted as good as it looked, she was in for a treat. There were several plates of meats, some in sauces, some just meat cooked over fire, but it all looked and smelled heavenly.

"But it sounds good fun, and you seem happy." Kian handed the flowery yellow plate to Stele.

"I am." Stele nodded. She closed her eyes and took a deep breath, the truth of her response settling in her mind. *I am happy*. Was it the first time in her life she could truly say that? Having Ariane beside her would make it perfect. But that possibility seemed so far away right now.

"I understand there's a chance the marines will be deployed next time the Dartington goes out," Kian said, "which means I may get to travel with you and, who knows, maybe see some action."

"That would be great. I'd see you every sun cycle?"

"Yes, on board, but it could be brief because we'll be dropped off on different planets as part of warfare exercises. Meet-ups are likely to be fleeting." Kian had a bite of her food before she continued. "Sitting around here with my marine squadrons has done little for morale. I spend all my time encouraging aggression in my troops and punishing them when they're threatening and violent with each other. A good deployment will give them a little self-worth and a chance to let it all out."

Stele's heart missed a beat when she thought of war plans involving ground troops. They were a big hole in the work she had done so far, both in the academy and since. "I could use the practice too. I haven't had the opportunity to use fleet protocols involving ground troops. It'll be good for me."

CHAPTER NINE

STELE WAS HAPPY that her work was so involved and that she had good support from friends. She had spoken to Ariane just that morn and although she missed her more with every passing sun cycle, being busy meant that she hadn't had time to get too blue or despondent. Their conversations these days were about missing each other, about living their lives separately and how they wanted to be together. Ariane's hologram purple sparkling eyes always took her to another plane.

One of her conversations with Ariane recently had been about Jasper Sloan, Stele's nemesis. Ariane had put her arms around herself as if to protect her from the man Stele considered an epo that slithered out of his dark lair to create mayhem.

"Jasper Sloan has continued his vocal vendetta against starburst eyes and been loud, particularly against your black eyes. Even though you're no longer on Nero, Sloan has been bad-mouthing your parents for giving birth to you. He calls you a deformity and a slight against the people of Nero."

Those words still cut through her. She had heard the same sentiment so many times and despite being away from Nero, it still hurt. "I thought he would have given that up once I'd gone. I don't understand why he's doing it."

"I don't understand either, especially as lately he's been picking on me. Of course, as a major singer and composer, I'm news and it's making him a news item too. His latest is ridiculing me for being a friend to you and spending time with you, a violent outcast who didn't fit." Ariane had tears in her eyes. "Our parents have been talking to his parents. As members of the Ruling Council, they've done their best to negate Sloan's words but quite a few people believe him."

Stele's face heated up, and she recalled once again standing in the Coliseum and being banished. She clenched her fists. He was hurting Ariane, and she wanted to hurt him in return. "But I still don't get it. What have I, or you, ever done to upset him?"

"Our parents discussed this, and they've come to the same conclusion that we have: because Sloan has blue eyes and not purple, he can never join the Ruling Council. He's jealous of both his older sisters who are likely to be made members in the next few seasons. For the same reason he can't head up the Healers Guild which your mother happens to be the head of. So, he's going to continue being a thorn in our side."

Stele was still too far away to do anything that could help Ariane. "I want to do my best to ensure he doesn't hurt either them or you, but I don't know how I'm supposed to do anything from out here. I don't want to sit by while all these things are happening to you."

"They're only words. They haven't been a problem yet. He made a strange comment to me though the last time I saw him. He was ranting about you as usual and how I must be more than your friend for wanting to be associated with you. He said that when he finds the black gems from the legend, he'll be as successful as you are worthless."

"Black gems?" Stele gasped. "Jasper Sloan was talking about black gems?"

"Yes. Are they important?"

Sloan knowing about black gems was too much to process. Stele clenched her jaw. Maybe this legend was something different to Weller and Domino's hoard on Weston. It would be too coincidental that Sloan knew what black gems were and what they were worth, if, in fact, there was any truth to it at all. She willed her body to relax. "I'd like to know how he found out about black gems and what the legend is. They're likely to be valuable, perhaps more so than the lighting crystals. My friend Domino introduced me to his sister who's done some research, so I already knew about the theory. But she hasn't told anyone about it as far as I know. Have you got that black tear I gave you?"

Ariane took it out of a zipped pocket in her jumpsuit. Knowing about the importance of the small rock could make life difficult for Ariane if anyone found that she had one in her pocket, but it would be even worse if Ariane didn't understand what she had.

"That's what they're looking for. These are the valuable gems."

"My Stele tear?"

"Yes, I showed my tear to Weller, and she confirmed it was the same type as the black gem she had tested. Hold yours close and make sure

Sloan doesn't ever see it. Who knows, maybe there's some truth to the legend." Stele's face flushed as she looked at Ariane. She was so beautiful. Ariane put the tear back in her pocket without removing her gaze from Stele's. The thought of her body, warm and soft, nestled alongside hers made Stele's heart race, and her body... Stele smiled at the memory of them together on that small bed on the Vanguard and let out a sigh. Hopefully they could be together again soon.

***

The Fleet was on the move, and Stele felt an unusual edginess that she attributed to excitement, adventure, and heading into something new. The stay in port and working with Command Central had been both nerve-wracking and inspiring at the same time. Admiral Simpkin, Captain Harmer, and the command captains and staff officers had all insisted that she sat in on their strategic meetings and often asked her point of view. Kian had told her that it was rare, and Stele realized that she had been afforded a great learning experience.

Stele had invited Domino to a meal because she hadn't seen much of him despite them being on the same ship and wanted to catch up. She sat on the transom just off the main gangway of the Dartington as he came into view. He strode toward her, taking large steps and looking the part of an ADF career officer as he took the salute of a couple of crewmen. He looked different...older and more mature than she remembered.

"Hey, bud, you were lucky to catch me. We've been loading the squadron armaments and I'll have to go again shortly. I've been moved to Dash's squadron as her gunner, and she's given me a couple of hours' leave." He tilted his head and smiled. "Did you say you were buying me food?"

She laughed and nodded, glad that he hadn't changed *that* much. "Yeah, I did promise that," she said. They walked together to Xim's warehouse. "Good news about moving to be with Dash. You must be doing something right if you get to be shooter for the lead pilot. I've got a couple of questions for you, and I've missed you and your chattiness." She recalled the way he gave a narration to their lives together, struggling to stay quiet and tripping over his sentences as he pushed out everything he wanted to say.

"I'm glad you missed me, and I want to discuss something with you too. Is the colonel coming along?"

"She said she'd be here later...maybe in time for dessert," said Stele.

"Well, let's get a tak in and order. As much as I might like a Gandon wine, I'm on duty so will stick to drinking a tak with you."

They ordered and settled down into catching up on their lives which had been so closely entwined through their months of training. Now they saw each other much less; the Dartington was like a city, and they were a long way apart. But it was a friendship that would be hard to break; they'd gone through considerable stress and angst together.

"What's big, and red, and dangerous?" Domino asked. "Shimo's girlfriend in that bar when we had our fight."

He laughed wildly at his own joke, and Stele relaxed into the comfort of being with him again.

"That's one of the low spots of my studies at the academy, bud. The headache the next morning and the look of disappointment on the colonel's face will last me a lifetime. Don't ever let me near—"

"Shimo, her girlfriend, or alcohol?"

"Stop looking so innocent, Domino Gratis. All three are poisonous to me and you played a hand in it." Civilians couldn't understand that sense of family that the ADF, and particularly the pod system, encouraged. Stele had missed Domino terribly once they had finished training. He was noisy, rarely stopped talking to draw breath, and had a terrible sense of humor. But she missed his honesty and his unswerving loyalty. What he lacked in stature—coming in well below Stele's shoulders—he made up for with heart.

They continued their verbal sparring until Kian arrived, as Stele had predicted in time for dessert.

"Ah, just in time for something frozen, hot, and sweet," Kian said. "Have you ever tried frozen tak spread over hot chunks of solidified Nooller milk? It's delicious, and I suspect it's expensive enough and rare enough that neither of you've ever had any."

Stele looked at the menu and saw the price in credits. She sucked in a short deep breath and tried to figure out how she could *not* order the ridiculously priced delicacy.

"Don't worry about the price because I'm buying," Kian said.

Stele bit her lip. It was as if Kian had read her mind. "Thank you."

Domino echoed her gratitude.

"Domino, have you been home recently?" asked Stele.

"Yeah, that's what I wanted to talk to you about," he said.

"Kian and I were wondering about Weller's research. Ariane believes that at least one group of people outside the Ruling Council on Nero are looking for black gems. Is it public knowledge now?"

Domino raised his eyebrows and sat forward in his chair. "That's interesting. It hasn't gone outside Weller's research circle. I'll tell you the whole story." Domino leaned back in his chair and took a gulp of his tak. "While you're both here, I want to tell you an old story that relates to Weston and its relationship with Nero. As you know, we arrived here in spaceships that originated from Earth, and that each of the different ships settled on different planets in the Federation. The people settling on Nero were pacifists and wanted to stay away from the rest of the Federation. But they needed many items that they couldn't produce themselves, so they decided to trade their clear gems to provide planets' lighting needs. Over the years, the Neroian Ruling Council has had little contact with the Federation other than to order goods in exchange for another tranche of clear gems. These are now traded into the Allied Nations and further afield. They also use them to negotiate the relocation of banished Neroians. Hence Weller's frustration about having no black gems except the small one she found—"

"Yes, Domino, we all know that. Get to the point," said Stele, not having the patience for Domino's drawn-out way of storytelling.

He shook his head. "Patience, Stele. As children, Weller and I played a lot in the grounds of the Weston Science Academy where our family worked. There was a formal garden in one corner looked after by the Allegra family. In the center of the garden is a heavily wooded area, and we had a hideout in the middle of it. We had to sneak in and out so we didn't get caught." Domino laughed as if recalling the memory. "The trees were a thick belt of granta, you know, those ones that sprout in all directions and make natural fences. Our hideout was a cave with a broken boulder across the front. We climbed over the rock and found an absolute treasure trove inside. We had great fun in that cave; we were often caught and banned, but we always found our way back. Between there and the basements of the Academy, we had a wonderful playground full of forgotten objects—"

"I agree with Stele, Domino. Where are we going with this?" Kian asked.

"Nearly there, colonel. In one of those explorations, we found a big piece of black rock that we thought was a rocket. We used to sit on it and pretend to fly around the galaxy. We found lots of jewelry too that we imagined was buried treasure. It was full of black gems surrounded by colored ones. When you told me about the shards, Stele, I got to wondering if our black rocket was actually one of your shards, since it was exactly the same shape as you'd described. Weller went back to look at it recently to experiment with it, but she wasn't able to cut into it. She did find the jewels we played with, and that's where she got the black tear like yours. She didn't dare to speak about it because, well, we shouldn't have been there in the first place—"

"But someone knows," Stele said. "Ariane told me that Jasper Sloan on Nero was talking about looking for black gems. Perhaps you can ask Weller if she's told anyone?"

"Yes, sure. When I got home last time, I spoke to Weller about the rocket, and we went to see if we could find it without getting caught."

"Naveh, Domino! Did you find it? Who are the Allegras to Nero? Why would there be a Neroian shard hidden in a building on Weston? They're all in the Coliseum on Nero." Stele crossed her arms and bit her bottom lip. Things were happening that seemed beyond her control, and they were making her nervous.

"I've no idea, my friend. We found it again, and I think that it's a black shard; it's tall, almost as tall as you, like you said the ones in the Coliseum are. And what that means, I don't know. I thought I'd best tell you in person rather than trust it to the Mesh. I told Weller what I think it is, and she's not going near it again, but only because she doesn't exactly have legal access to it. She's been experimenting on the jewels which could get her in trouble too."

"A wise decision," said Kian.

"But a black shard? It's impossible. Why would one exist?" Stele asked. There were only the usual color shards to match Neroian eyes. There had never been anyone with black eyes before so why would there be a black shard? They were probably mistaken, and it wasn't a shard but just a piece of Neroian rock that was worthless. But if it was a shard, what was it doing on Weston? The thought made Stele's heart race and her mind was moving at a similar speed. It showed her thoughts in picture form like an electrical storm, flashes of one thought after another at frightening speed. They included rites of passage with a black shard for her and the banished, and the Ruling Council banishing them again. The worst flash was like a premonition of the black shard being a death shard to rid the universe of abominations like her and the starburst. She gripped her chair and only half listened to the discussion.

"Could we get it here to investigate it?" said Kian.

"That's what I'm thinking. Colonel, is there a way we can transport it without attracting attention?" asked Domino.

"What else is in the cave and the basements under the academy, Domino?" Kian said.

"Things like the materials used in Founder's Sun Cycle celebrations, including mini spaceships and things like that. The sort of thing we had fun with when I was young. Actually, I could quite happily have fun down there even now. Stele, you'd love—"

"Weston could lend Alton some of those for our next celebration, and we can move the black rock at the same time, boxed up and out of sight," said Stele.

"I'm ahead of you, Stele. I'm the Military Liaison for that festival. It's a boring job but it has to be done, and if I ever want to make General, I have to do it. Naveh, the endless committee meetings… But I can make a bit of a show this year if the military have some different materials. Domino, can Weller let me know who to talk to about getting the mini spaceships and anything else that will work in the festival, and will she help box up the rock?"

"Yeah. The test will be getting the rock out of the cave without the Allegra family being aware. They're careful that no-one impinges on their garden. I think some moonlight work will be necessary. I'll talk to Weller. We've created a code just in case anyone is monitoring us so that it seems like part of our regular chat," said Domino.

Their desserts arrived. There was silence as Stele savored every mouthful of the frozen tak and hot Nooller milk desert. The icy yet scorching, sharp and milky taste left her mouth mellow. "Wow, that has to be the most delicious dessert I've ever tasted. Thanks for spoiling us." Stele sat back in her chair and savored the moment. The lightness in her mind having spent time with friends was irreplaceable. It didn't matter what the black shard meant, Kian and Domino had immediately been there for her working out the best way forward. In the past, having friends was a dream. But now, here she was, living that dream.

***

Stele and Questa laid on Stele's bed as they discussed their time in space dock. Stele had told Questa about her meeting with Kian and Domino.

"I would like to try that dessert. Stele, settle down. Why are you constantly moving? It is like sitting next to Dash. Are you sure you do not have Sutton snapes in your clothing? They are known to make people itch," Questa said.

"Hah! I'm just looking forward to some real work, and I'm anxious. I've been sitting in meetings making no real contribution, and I need something practical to do. I had to tell the flip story so many times and while a lot of people were impressed, a number of senior officers didn't believe it was possible. It was frustrating."

"But you did it. There is evidence."

Stele shrugged. "A group of officers are saying that my training run was a fluke and wouldn't be possible in a real battle. I've got to be careful around men like them. They're in line for fast promotion and years ahead of me on the ladder. I imagine they feel me snapping at their heels as I come up behind them with these good ideas. I struggled to stay calm as they looked at me like the people on Nero did…half frightened, half angry."

"But they are wrong, are they not? From what you say, it *is* possible to flip a destroyer?" said Questa.

Stele reached out and put her hand on Questa's arm. She wanted to feel the support that her friend was giving her. "Thank you for making me see the positive instead of always being negative. Yes, it's possible, and I've realized that the only way to counter their disdain is to carry on regardless. If ever the admiral has to flip the Dartington, they'll see that I was right."

"What other problems have you got?"

"Well, the reason for my anxiety…" Anxiety was an understatement. She was about to be tested to the max and that left her feeling sick, physically sick. She'd been to the head and lost her breakfast already. "As you know, flipping a ship means that we need a new battle-ready state. It's complex because it means that everything in the ship has to be tied down, fixed, and in place." Stele stood and started pacing. "It's been a major effort to work out the logistics of trying it with some of the bigger frigates and destroyers. They've set the first demo of the flip using one of the smallest ships in the Fleet, the ADF Oboe, and I'm being transferred there in a few crons. I need to demonstrate it'll work." Stele's heart rate sped up and she wiped the sweat from her forehead.

She rubbed her hands on her trousers and took a deep breath. "And while I'm grateful to the admiral for giving me the opportunity, I'm seriously twitched it'll fail. I've been over the figures a thousand times, and I've tested it over and over to find the failure points, and I've checked and re-checked my calculations and—"

"Stop it, Stele. You are making me feel nervous and sick as well. You have this under control."

Stele was silent for a moment. She sat down and ran her hand through her hair as she went through the figures in her head yet again. "I need to make sure that the crew are safe and able to do their duties. And that means that although things are normally tied down for battle, they'll have to be checked and stricter rules applied when the ship turns upside down and is catapulted across space."

"Take a deep breath, my friend. Think that this is the same as a normal sun cycle at work. You are still being tested."

"My transport's here. Thank you, Questa, for being here. I needed you."

Questa's blue skellen waved as they nodded to Stele. "You will win this," they said.

Stele headed out with her mind already on the work she had to do.

***

"So, how did it go?"

It only seemed like a few moments later, although it was the next sun cycle when she and Questa were together again. They were sitting in the Officers Lounge with a glass of iced tak.

"It went okay, I think. No," Stele said and grinned. "I know it went well." She smiled and held her glass in the air, swirling the tak around as she stared into the blue liquid, remembering the epic event. She had a wonderful sense of elation, a warm, bright feeling that was new. She hadn't had many of those feelings in her life and none on Nero.

She described the maneuver to Questa in detail, moving her hands to illustrate the flight of the Oboe as it turned and was propelled with force across space. "The flip works! Questa, it works! There are some small problems, but my theory is first-class. The ship itself behaved as we predicted, and the trajectory was as expected. The crew were eager to show that Oboe was ideal as a trial, although having the bridge with all around vision was problematic. The comms guy couldn't cope and had to be taken to sick bay. They can fix that with medication so it won't happen again. There were also one or two minor injuries caused by things such as a forgotten cup of tak hurtling around a deck. More difficult was a loose electrical repair tool which became a mini missile in engineering as the ship flipped."

"So, most of the problems were caused by the crew and not by your idea?" Questa asked.

Their skellen were bouncing about, and Stele could see their excitement vibrating through their body.

"Yes, the admiral called it successful, and they're going to use it in the Fleet. But he wants to use it well away from prying eyes, and he'll only use it in exercise when there's no chance of it being seen. He realized that the flip was such a celebrity move that it would be discussed throughout the galaxy and people like the pirate, Rudd, would hear about it. However, it will need a fine mind to handle the maneuver and a detailed understanding of the speed and thrust capability of the ships involved, and maybe some retrofitting of thrusters."

Questa raised their glass. "To the Hosun Flip! Remember me when you get famous!"

"Unlikely. But I won't ever forget my family, and you're family. We'll always be family. Of course, everyone knows this as we look so alike."

CHAPTER TEN

WITH THE DARTINGTON travelling through Federation space conducting exercises with the rest of the fleet, Kian, Stele, and Domino had spent little time coordinating the move of the Neroian rock and other items from Weston to Alton.

On the bridge, Stele had her hands full. The work was exhausting: long periods of concentration with intense tension accompanied by instant decision-making. Her time messaging with Ariane was minimal as her workload on the bridge had ramped up. Ariane was understanding, because sometimes they were kept from talking by her commitments to rehearsals and singing concerts. Admiral Simpkin had increased the pressure, testing Stele continually and she needed to have her best game.

Captain Harmer dropped into his chair. "Hosun, I've been killed in action. You're to take command of the Dartington. Inform the admiral and the rest of the fleet."

Stele opened her mouth, but no sound came out. This was her moment, and she needed to step up. This kind of thing didn't usually happen to someone so early in their service, and she needed to succeed if she wanted to keep the forward momentum of her career.

"For exercise, for exercise, for exercise. The captain of the Dartington is down. Hosun is in charge. Continue as you were and await further instructions," said Stele, her training kicking in, allowing her to find her way.

"Hosun, move the Dartington into position using Fleet Pattern six and get the rest of the fleet to ensure the security of Alton artillery using the Marines," said the admiral.

Stele spent the rest of the exercise in command of the Dartington as well as doing strategic maneuvers for the admiral. She disembarked the marines at the gun placements. It went well, but at the same time she was being tested and pushed to identify errors in the admiral's judgement. It became apparent that the marines were meeting overwhelming force as part of the exercise and were struggling not to retreat. The admiral did nothing, so she dispatched Dartington's Sprint and Lightning attack fighter squadrons and smiled at the thought of Dash and Domino coming to the aid of Kian and her marines. They made good headway, and the attack fighters inflicted serious casualties on the exercise enemies. *I'm doing this.*

"Hosun, I want an emergency withdrawal of all our ground forces. Expedite," said the admiral.

"But, sir, we're just getting somewhere. The attack fighters have given us—" said Stele.

"Agreed, but what else do you need to consider?"

Stele realized she'd made a major error and had neglected the rest of the fleet whilst concentrating on one arena. "I've left the rest of the fleet exposed and if someone like Rudd appeared, I wouldn't have been ready," said Stele as she started to move the ground forces in an emergency withdrawal and at the same time, watched as the admiral moved several ships around.

"You understand what you did wrong?" the admiral asked.

"Yes, sir. It was a stupid mistake to make, and I'm cross with myself for making it."

"Good," said the admiral. "It means you're unlikely to do it again. You're here to learn, Hosun, and you can glare at the chart all you like. Recognizing your strengths and weaknesses is part of the exercise."

Stele clenched her jaw and grasped the back of her chair. She'd messed up and let herself, and the fleet, down.

The admiral turned back from his discussion with Questa and looked at Stele. "Calm down. I can see the white of your knuckles. Take a break and work out a different way to achieve the same results without leaving big holes in your strategy. There's an easy way which you'll see when you calm down."

Stele nodded, released her grip, and flexed her hands out as she left the bridge. As she walked toward the officers' mess she stopped still. Simpkin had a Fleet Pattern to deal with this whole scenario, but it was one she hadn't yet seen. She'd made a rookie error. She should have realized there was a Fleet pattern and, if she didn't know it, she should have asked. A good lesson indeed. She also recognized that being angry with herself had blinded her to the swift solution and that she'd been too quick to praise herself...she needed to keep her ego in check.

She returned to the bridge, calm and ready to learn the next lesson that the admiral and captain threw her way.

***

Stele met with Kian at their favorite tak house the next time the Dartington pulled into the docking bay on Alton.

Kian looked around, ensuring they were out of anyone's earshot. "I've been to check the objects that have arrived for the Founder's Sun Cycle celebration, and they're everything that we expected. The large box is also exactly what Domino thought it would be," said Kian with an almost unnoticeable wink. "In some respects, I'd hoped that it would just be a lump of random rock. I don't understand why a shard would be stored there."

Stele couldn't move. The rock *was* a black shard. She'd avoided thinking about it, because she didn't want it to be true, didn't want to think about what it might mean. Her hope had been that it was just any black rock, and things would go back to normal. But a black shard meant she'd been denied her rite of passage. It meant she wasn't the freak she'd been programmed to believe she was. *Naveh!*

"Stele, you need to consider this and what it likely means. You have black eyes…this black shard is effectively yours. The Neroians have obviously gone to great lengths to remove it from their planet. Did you hear anyone talk of a black shard when you were on Nero?"

Stele had had enough talk of shards and Nero. She didn't want anything to do with it. She'd been denied her rite of passage, but maybe the shard had been hidden for a good reason. "No, I never did." She rolled her neck and looked beyond Kian to feign boredom. "So, there's a shard. I'm not getting involved in Neroian affairs." She shrugged and held up her hands. "It has nothing to do with me. I was banished from Nero, and they were *very* clear that I'm nothing to them. Leave the rock in its box, and let's enjoy our tak."

Kian shook her head and put her hand on Stele's shoulder. "I think you're wrong. I suspect that this shard is of vital importance to you and the reason you've been denied your rite of passage. You're important to the planet and its people, whether you like it or not. The Ruling Council have hidden this for a reason." She released Stele's shoulder and paced for a few moments. "On the hierarchy of eye colors, you're the only one with black eyes. You have strategic and leadership skills off the scale already. Perhaps you're a Neroian leader-in-waiting."

Stele scoffed. "You're grasping at a snape in the wind, Kian. I don't belong on Nero. It's not our planet anymore. They didn't want me, and they didn't want you. I'm too violent for their world. That's probably why they concealed the shard. They don't want me as their leader. And what about you with your starbursts? Are you to be my second-in-command?" Stele laughed loudly, amused by the fanciful change in their leadership roles. She put her hand on Kian's forearm and squeezed it gently. "Please. Let's just forget about the shard and eat." Her throat constricted, making it difficult to eat as she thought about pushing Kian away. There was something about Kian's words that hummed in her mind. There was a rightness to them, but Stele couldn't afford to believe them, otherwise she would be lost. And what of Ariane? How would all this change her relationship with the woman she loved? Stele felt her heart nearly explode. *My Ariane.*

***

"Questa, why do your parents want to see me and Colonel Ray this visit? I know you must have some idea." Stele's nerves gave her a sour taste in her mouth. She couldn't lose Questa as her friend. She relied on them for support, both emotional and for the happenings of her life.

"I have no idea, Stele. Perhaps they are impatient with you leading me astray with the rest of the pilots and wish to have words?"

Questa's words seemed to agree with Stele's concerns. "Don't joke, Questa, there could be some truth in that. We've been in several situations recently that could make them worry. Like that time we both ended up in the back seat of one of the flight trainers and got taken out on maneuvers. Naveh, that was bad." Stele could still remember the feeling she had in her stomach after the flight.

They stood in the spaceport reception area waiting, and Stele couldn't stand still as she worried about this visit. The fact they'd asked for Kian to attend had Stele's nerves on edge. She wasn't quite sure how she'd managed to get in trouble, and with the Pargent of all people, but she guessed the ride had to end somewhere. They were important to the

Federation and the Allied Nations. One word from them and her career could be over. *Breathe, Stele. Long and slow.*

Kian appeared from the direction of the Dartington just as Questa's parents arrived from across the spaceport. Xian Quess bowed to them all before hugging Questa, who was enveloped in the arms of Lai Quess. None of the trio spoke, but their blue tresses turned green as they communicated with each other. Xian and Lai turned to the rest of them as their skellen returned to its normal blue.

"Thank you for meeting with us," Xian said. "I know you will have had to lose some leave to do this, but we hope that you will realize the importance by the time we depart. I have booked us meeting room accommodation in the spaceport. Please follow."

Stele looked at Kian and raised her eyebrows. Kian put up both hands and shook her head. She was obviously in the dark here too.

Once they were all settled in the Pargent accommodation with an iced tak and an array of sweet bites, Questa's parents inquired about their health and careers. The small talk did nothing to calm Stele's racing heart, and she smiled nervously at Questa. *Please tell me I'm not in trouble.* Stele hoped that none of the Pargent had stolen a look at her fears. Their skellen would turn green if they peeked at her mind, but that didn't mean her fears weren't leaking everywhere.

"I think I should first of all say that whilst this has everything to do with you, this has nothing to do with what I suspect are your fears, Stele, about leading Questa astray. You should understand that Questa tries to keep some things back when talking to us, but as you know they're still learning and are not always successful. We expect Questa to enjoy their learning experience with the ADF," Xian turned to Questa and nodded. "This is about history, and a number of events have been set in motion in the Federation that have meant that the Pargent have had to react." Xian stood and took some electronics from their cloak. They cleared their throat.

Stele breathed out slowly and leaned back into her chair. She started as she realized the Pargent knew all about their antics. Questa had told her about their thoughts draining out in small bursts when they talked to their parents, but this was the first time Stele understood the problem. Questa looked at her and smiled, their skellen waving. Stele smiled back but her stomach was still somersaulting. *Creff.* So there was no problem with their friendship. What was this about? Stele turned in her seat to face Xian.

"Many moon cycles ago, not long after the Federation settled these planets, the Pargent were tasked with creating a series of records after a rebellion on Nero. These records were only to be released if a number of events took place. Firstly, a black-eyed Neroian had to appear, and you, Stele, are the first one to do so. Secondly, the black shard hidden on Weston had to be discovered and identified as such. Your friend Domino completed that part. Finally, there needed to be something happening in the Federation that would affect Nero's future. We believe that the discovery of black gems on Nero and their potential use as power for spaceships is that event, and therefore the historic records are being released to you."

Xian's formality took Stele by surprise. She could never have imagined that Domino's discovery of the black shard could lead to some sort of… prophecy? What was she supposed to do with that? She'd spent years being ridiculed and ostracized, forced to believe she was an anomaly and not a true Neroian. Xian's words contradicted everything she'd grown to believe. She needed to hear this but at the same time, she wished she could be *anywhere* else.

"The records are to be revealed to whoever appears with black eyes," Xian continued. "The Pargent have given Xian and Lai Pargent the honor of revealing the details to you as they know you, and Questa is part of the Federation. They realize that you have the black shard, Colonel Kian Ray and that you are Stele's mentor. So, we are here to tell you what the records say and to show you the recording."

"Save any questions to the end when we will do our best to answer them," Lai said as Stele opened her mouth to speak.

"Please…I'd like a moment with the colonel," Stele said, standing and not waiting for permission. She crossed to Kian. "Did you know about any of this?" Stele could see that Kian was processing something, so she waited for a moment before asking, "You've realized something though?"

Kian blew out a long breath. "The shards in the Coliseum are lined in a row at the far end?"

Stele confirmed Kian's question with a nod, though Kian would know exactly what the Coliseum looked like from her own childhood on Nero.

"Each shard has its own pedestal. There are clear, blue, green, and purple shards and in the middle, the Zoccantus gem sculpture. What if the black shard used to be there instead?"

"Naveh!" Stele couldn't say more. Her stomach felt heavy, it hurt to breathe, and her throat was tied as if it were part of the gem sculpture itself.

"Maybe Zoccantus wasn't alive when Nero was first settled and the gems nests were found. What if the sculpture was added later?" Kian asked.

"No…that can't be. No," Stele said as if repeating the word could somehow change the facts. Kian's thoughts made sense and a fifth shard was a real possibility.

Questa moved alongside Stele and held onto her. Their proximity instilled some calm into the torrent of emotion battling inside her.

"Let us hear what has yet to be said and maybe it will all make sense," Questa said. "Come. Sit."

Questa took Stele back to her seat, holding onto her elbow to guide her. They poured her some tak and nodded to their parents.

Xian opened a packet in front of them and unrolled an ancient-looking parchment. "I, Cloud Chetto, Pargent, have been chosen to record the details of the events on Nero by the Ruling Council as an independent viewer. The attached recording is my true record. Signed and dated… Please bear with me while I get the recording to play," said Xian.

An image of a Pargent appeared against the far wall of the room. "This is a true record of the happenings on Nero from Cloud Chetto's observations. The population on Nero made many adjustments when they first settled and realized the power of the gems and shards. The clear gems provided light without an outside power source and so gave them currency to buy items from other worlds. Nero became wealthy."

Stele gripped Questa's arm and fought against the urge to flee from the room, partly because she unwilling to hear what the old Pargent had to say and partly because she was curious and hopeful that maybe she shouldn't be an outcast.

"There were five shards which were, over time, reflected in the eyes of the population. The clear-eyed accounted for over half, the green and blue eyes together around forty-five percent, and there were only a handful of Neroians with purple eyes. But over each generation, there was only a single person with black eyes. They were always the leader of the world and almost without exception, female. There were a number of Neroians with colored eyes with black starbursts in them, and they were all members of the Legion, Nero's defense force."

"No," Stele stood, and Xian stopped the record. "I don't want this. It can't be." The walls and the ceiling were closing in on her, and it was as if gravity had doubled and was pulling her to the floor. She owed Nero and its people nothing. She couldn't be their leader; she hadn't even had a rite of passage. She turned and ran out of the room, struggling to see beyond the red of her anger and the white of her fear. The noise in her head beat in time with the drumming of her heartbeat. She ran. And she kept running.

Finally, the red faded, and the beating of her heart slowed. Stele came to a stop, aware she'd ended up at the end of the docks which she knew from her daily runs was twenty-five crons away. No-one seemed to notice or care as she slumped to the floor and leaned against an upturned metal box. Tears banged at the back of her eyes, fighting to escape, and she so wanted Ariane to envelop her in her arms and tell her everything would be okay. She could always make Stele feel better when her whole world was against her. She needed Ariane's warmth. She needed her touch.

She felt a hand on her arm and recognized the familiar scent of Questa before they dropped to the floor and shuffled up next to her. Questa opened their arms and Stele, after a moment's hesitation, rested her head on Questa's broad shoulder and wept. She didn't need words; Questa could feel her emotions, and she gave her full permission to them.

Her thoughts spiraled in different directions like a number of giant vortices in space about to collide. She just wanted to be ordinary, enjoy her job, and live her life with someone she loved. Part of her didn't want any of this. She was the misfit, the banished. How could she be a leader if what Xian said was true? Neroians loathed her and made sure she was removed. There was no way she would ever survive on Nero as a leader. Xian had said that a number of things had to be in place before this briefing. The future is always the unknown, but this future was getting close to being something expected. As much as she was in turmoil, Stele realized she didn't know enough or understand enough. She needed more information. If there was one thing she'd learned in her time away from Nero, it was that running didn't solve anything. She needed to face her fears.

Eventually Stele stood and pulled Questa up from the floor and into her arms. "Thank you. I needed that," she whispered. "Let's go back and find out what happened."

CHAPTER ELEVEN

KIAN STOOD BY the door as they entered. Stele sighed when Kian gently patted her on the back. There was a moment of silence as if Kian was wondering how to start the conversation.

"None of us can quite understand what this means to you, Stele, but let's listen to what the Pargent have to say. Afterwards we can discuss it and how it may affect you. Just remember, you're not alone. You have us all, along with Domino and his family. We're your adopted family, and we care about what happens to you."

Stele straightened. There was a pleasant pain in her heart. She had never had a close relationship with friends and their families, and this was all new to her. She wasn't alone. People caring about her gave her a warm feeling inside and she wanted to savor the moment. "Thank you. Thoughts of this future overwhelm me. I feel as if there's a black hole that's going to take me away on a tide of my fears. I revert to feeling alone just as I was on Nero, and I just can't seem to control it. I forget that I have a whole family of friends supporting me. It's good to be reminded."

Kian nodded. "We're all with you." She gestured to a chair. "Sit and have some tak."

Stele took a seat, nodding to the Pargent, Xian. Questa sat down next to her and held her hand. Stele felt Questa's calm seep into her and flood her. She put her other hand in her pocket and felt for Ariane's stone. *Relax and breathe.*

"Let us continue, if you are in agreement, Stele?" Xian said.

When Stele nodded, they picked up the parchment again.

"I am using Cloud Chetto's summary. The full details are on the recording. The clear gems had made Nero its fortune and the Neroian sculpture, art and music was valued everywhere," Xian said. "There appeared to be no end to the visitors that were going to Nero, taking their wealth with them and spending it there. Nero was the place to be in the Federation. I have to say that with Nero so shut away these days, this may be difficult to imagine."

Kian sank back into her chair. She looked as awed as Stele felt. Their home planet was once the hub of what was now Federation space.

"The leader at that time was a woman named Bellum Trace. She had black eyes and had completed a rite of passage, but instead of her rites inspiring her to lead for the good of Nero, something failed."

Stele bit the inside of her mouth. This was what she expected of her life, things going wrong. "Something failed?"

Lai looked at Stele and nodded. "Yes. No one knows what happened nor why."

"What we do know is that Bellum Trace was greedy for wealth and power and didn't care about her world." Xian tapped the table and shook their head. "Her greed was reflected in her personal life. She loved women and surrounded herself with them, most of whom she treated as slaves. She was ruthless and used her personal guard, the Legion, to force the people of Nero to be her personal workers. They had no value to her beyond the hours they worked."

Stele's heart pounded. Her home planet had treated women as slaves. She looked at Kian and her expression showed it was news to her too.

"This finally led to a rebellion which Cloud Chetto witnessed and recorded." Xian gestured to the ancient recording device.

Stele closed her eyes briefly and took a deep breath. "Xian, could I have a minute, please?"

Questa came to her side and took Stele's hand. "It is a lot to understand. You must take your time."

Stele remembered those times when Ariane had given her strength when life had been difficult. Just thinking about her helped. "I'm good. Let's finish this," Stele said and nodded to Xian, who continued.

"Bellum Trace was banished and imprisoned somewhere in the Alliance for the rest of her life. The Legion were also banished, and many settled on Alton, most joining the Alton Defense Force. The population of Nero as a whole voted to remove the black shard from the Coliseum and to replace it with a sculpture which signified the intertwining of the clear, green, blue, and purple-eyed population. It was agreed that all mention of black-eyed and star-burst people would be removed from the record."

Now everything became clear. This explained Stele's whole life and why she'd always been treated so badly. All evidence of black eyes had been removed, and she couldn't stop herself from wondering why she'd been born now.

"The black plinth that the Shard stood on was removed," Xian said. "It had roots deep beneath the surface, but it had somehow cracked at surface level and was easy to remove. It was replaced by a sculpture created by Zoccantus. The purple-eyed population took on a new role by creating a Ruling Council and forming a governing body that made the decisions for Nero."

Kian stood and circled the table. "That makes sense. I'd always wondered why that sculpture was so different from the rest of the shards."

"For your information, the Pargent first became involved when the Neroian way of life started to change. A rich, purple eyed Neroian merchant could see how the Nero that he loved was becoming different, and he didn't like it. He knew things were close to boiling point and asked the Pargent to record it for the future."

Xian and Lai's skellen turned from blue to green as they communicated. They nodded in agreement.

"The new Ruling Council, who still remembered the good black-eyed leaders of the past, realized that there may come a time when Nero needed a black-eyed leader once again, and therefore asked the Pargent to place the Shard in storage in a place known only to them and to ensure that the record would be released under a set of clear criteria. Hence the reason we're here this sun cycle," Lai said and bowed their head to Xian.

"I believe that is the basis of the record," said Xian. "The Pargent have no advice to give, nor should we, as we have always been impartial bystanders in Nero's history. We shall withdraw now and spend some time with Questa. The family will be here for the next three sun cycles. We've reserved this room and the attached living quarters for us all, so please stay and discuss anything you need to. If you have any questions, we will be here."

The Pargent withdrew, leaving Stele and Kian alone. Stele put her head in her hands and closed her eyes. It was just so much to take in. Neither she or Kian spoke nor moved for some time.

Stele eventually opened her eyes, turned in her chair and looked at Kian. She was staring at the blank wall in front of her. Stele cleared her throat several times before Kian looked at her. Stele recognized the look that Kian gave her as being the same as when she graduated from the academy. Love and pride. But Kian's lips thinned, and Stele noticed there was something else in her eyes that she'd never seen before. Was it fear? Stele didn't want anything she had heard this sun cycle to change her life. Yes, if she were a leader, she could perhaps be with Ariane, but Nero wouldn't accept her, so it was a moot point. Nero wasn't a part of her life anymore.

"Stele, this is a big thing," Kian whispered. "There hasn't been another black-eyed Neroian since Bellum Trace, and Naveh must have plans for you if everything we've been told is true. I think fate is foretelling that there will be trouble on Nero and the events are leading up to some significance for the shard. How do you read this?"

She sat quietly. If she didn't say anything, maybe all of this would go away.

"Stele, what do you think?" Kian repeated, her voice a little louder.

Stele rested her elbows on her knees and her chin in her hands. "I'm reading this like you, but underneath it my mind and body are screaming no. I'm not ready for this, and I'm trying not to run again." Stele shivered and folded her arms against her chest for both warmth and comfort against her fears.

"Why don't we head out for a walk and some food? We don't need to talk. I think we both need to work out what this all means, and we can discuss what we should consider doing. I've got some initial thoughts, but I think we both need some time. How does that suit?"

"I need to speak with Ariane. She's due to contact me in a few crons."

"Of course." Kian smiled and winked.

Stele rose and left the conference room for the privacy of her temporary accommodation. In an effort to forget all her problems, she turned her attention to Ariane, and her heart raced in response. She imagined herself wrapped in those arms, those arms of safety and warmth and home.

Stele switched her Mesh to discreet and waited to hear from the messaging experts on Nero, who would be homing in on her unique Mesh setting to give her a connection that was impossible to trace. From across the expanse Ariane came into view. She faded in and out, and Stele initially panicked that they wouldn't get to speak. In truth their linking this way was tenuous and sometimes like torture, but it was all they had and better than nothing at all. Luckily, this time the signal strengthened, and she could see Ariane's hologram clearly, though she looked pale and a little forlorn. "Is that my darling? You look more beautiful than ever."

Ariane looked away and giggled. "Jaz wonders if that applies to him as well?"

A part hologram of a Neroian male came into view. He waved briefly before disappearing.

"He's left us. We've ten crons before we'll be cut off...ten crons that will be over too quickly. I miss you. I need you to give me a hug. I've been hanging onto the thought of you to keep me going through my every sun cycle." She began to cry softly. "I miss you and need you."

Stele's heart ached and she had to fight the nausea rising from her stomach. Ariane was hurting, and she was powerless to do anything about it from so far away. Her anger rose from within, and she breathed quickly in and out. She was too far away to fix this, but she wasn't going to let it take over. She breathed out slowly, let go of the ties to her rage and relaxed her hands. Stele had to be positive about this so that despite the inescapable distance between them, Ariane had her strength. "Close your eyes. Concentrate on my voice. Imagine I'm in the room with you, standing close. Can you feel my love and the warmth from my body?"

Ariane put out her arms. Stele closed her eyes and reveled in the feeling of closeness that she missed. They'd had a sun cycle together, and she wouldn't have missed it for anything, but the agony of separation was more than she had ever imagined. "Pull me close. Just remember our time together, and you'll feel me there with you. I know things have been difficult but take some of my strength. You're not alone. I'm here with you. I love you." Stele opened her eyes and continued to speak softly comforting words, unable to do more than watch Ariane hug herself. When Ariane opened her eyes and sighed, Stele knew she had calmed. Her world began and ended with her thoughts of Ariane and this messaging seemed such a small thing in their lives, but it had such a large consequence in their souls. She would do what she could to get them together. She couldn't see a way it would happen yet, but she would never lose sight of it for their future. "So, my love, tell me about what you've been up to."

Ariane smiled. "Am I still your love, Stele?"

Stele blew a kiss to Ariane. "Of course, you're my love, just as you're *my* Ariane. You're my pillar of support in times of trouble, the one I desire above all others, the one I love. The one that I'm desperate to kiss, to hug, and to protect...my love." Stele could see Ariane hanging onto every word, mouthing the words after Stele said each one. Giving Ariane words of love and giving her the surety and security of their relationship allowed Stele's stomach to settle and her anger to deflate. Their togetherness would need her strength and confidence and didn't always need to be explosiveness and sparks. "Tell me how things are for you. I may not be able to help, but I can always listen."

Ariane stiffened and sighed. "Since our time together I've been blue, and I've been writing songs full of tears and loneliness, dark skies and storms. I look forward and see nothing. I'm writing about the agonies of no life beyond the current morn, and the loneliness of living a solitary life. I started repeating to myself what you say about being together again sometime, and we must keep thinking that. The last few sun cycles things have started to seem better. But I drift backward faster than a decko." Ariane smiled.

Stele understood. She would never forget her complete devastation as she hurtled away from Ariane after having spent that special time with her. The only thing that relieved the sharp, almost cutting feeling in her chest was the thought that she would be able to speak to her. "So have you finished any of the blue songs yet?"

"I've had all that new music in my head, which seemed to be stuck in there. When we met on the Vanguard it seemed I couldn't do anything with the music running around my mind. It's been like waking up from a wonderful dream. You know those sub-conscious thoughts were exquisite, but the memory of them disappears through your fingertips into nothing and you're unable to hang onto them. It was frustrating to know that whatever wonderful compositions I might have were just beyond reach. The rite gave me so much extra talent in composition, but I seemed to have a block. After we spent that time together and we talked of our love, it all started to flow, and the music is starting to come out. But Sloan's comments always get me, and I feel a little sad and lonely." Ariane hummed. "The long blue song is almost finished, and the loneliness comes through in the words. But you've just given me the feelings and words of something new… 'you bring out the best in me.'"

Stele settled into the sound of Ariane's voice and watched her beautiful face, and she could feel her love. She hoped that the look she gave in return was carrying similar feelings. Ariane mentioning Sloan again was unsettling. That man got everywhere and had Ariane firmly in his sights.

"What about Sloan? How are things with him?"

"He and his enclave of followers appear around me quite often. They're just a nuisance and have done nothing that I can complain about officially."

Stele had been pushed around and ridiculed by Sloan all her life. That hurt was still a part of her, the need to run and disappear still strong. Now Ariane had the same thing happening to her, and Stele was helpless to intervene. Another feature of separation to cope with.

"It does get to me when I'm not on top of my thoughts. By the way, he's still talking about black gems, although I don't know how he'll find any without going underground." Ariane laughed loudly. "And the black gems are as rare as the non-existent black shard."

Stele stood perfectly still. Naveh was playing with her. All this talk of Kian's about fate and here was yet another slice of coincidence. The need to tell Ariane the story brought to her by the Pargent fought with her need to keep Ariane safe. "I need to talk to you about that black shard." Stele clenched her fists at the thought of any danger coming to Ariane because of her. "There's a bit of history that's missing on Nero, and it relates to black-eyes and a black shard." Stele told Ariane a short version of the story.

"Oh, my love, that's a lot to take in and understand. How are you feeling?"

Ariane reached out a hand toward her, and she imagined she was holding it. Stele wondered how to tell Ariane her stomach was broiling, that the feeling of nausea kept rising within. "It's hard. I'm trying to live a normal life. Halfway through hearing it, I ran away."

"Was it like when you were on Nero? It just got too much?" Ariane asked.

She understood Stele's fears and anger and the panic that pushed her all those times she'd escaped. Running faster than the wind along alleyways and dark tunnels to peace, to the feeling of serenity the dark and jewel lit caverns brought her. There Ariane would find her and restore her back to life again. "Yes, just like that. I was angry and frightened." That raw fear that seemed to follow her through whatever life she was living, from Nero to Alton, from training to life in the fleet. "This morn I so wanted to hug you and for you to tell me it would all be better." Stele put out her hand toward Ariane's, still needing that feeling. "I had to make do with Questa, the Pargent. They did a good job, but they're not you." She dropped on to the bed of her temporary quarters.

"Oh, my darling, my love. I'm so sorry."

Ariane had called her darling and love before but somehow the sorry made it more special. *Ariane understood.* "But I have to face facts—the black shard isn't going away. I know that. I'm happy where I am, except for not having you here."

"I'd love to be there with you. We'd be together properly," said Ariane.

"If this story is true and it's something to do with me, I don't want the leadership on Nero. It may mean I could see you, but of course we could never be together. I'm sure no one on Nero will believe the story either, and they'll think I made it up to get back at them for banishing me." Stele sat and gripped the thin covering on the bed trying to keep her emotions in check. "I'm angry these things keep happening to me. I keep saying, why me? Now it's me that needs your arms about me." Stele swiped at her tears. Creff! She wanted to be strong about all this. And here she was like a child, blubbing at the first sign of sympathy.

"Oh, my dear heart," Ariane said, her arms outstretched toward Stele. "Know that I am with you. We're a strange pair. We seem to have everything going for us: good lives with exciting careers ahead of us. I've family and friends, you've adopted family and friends, and yet we are each, in our own ways, struggling to cope with life alone. I am with you dear heart, every step of the way."

"I'm going to talk to Kian later, to try to make sense of everything, and figure out what we should do about it. I don't think I want to do anything. But then, a black shard hidden on Alton means that we could try the rite of passage with the starburst Neroians and myself here. There's a risk though."

"Yes…what will it do to you? What power will you get from the shard? Will it kill you? And what might happen to the starbursts, will they die?"

Stele shook her head. "All we have are questions no one has the answers to. We'll come up with a plan. The Pargent may have clues about it in their records." She shuddered when she thought of the last person with black eyes. "I don't want to pick up where Bellum Trace left off."

"Oh, darling, our time is up. We must say our good-byes. We'll talk again soon. I love and miss you and need you. Be safe."

Stele squeezed her eyes closed. Their time together was always so brief. When would it be different? Could it be different? Would this black shard be the key to them finally being together? If that were so, Stele would do whatever was needed to make it happen, no matter the risk, no matter what the rite of passage might do to her. "My darling, I'm kissing you good-bye."

The connection ended, leaving Stele in a dark place both physically and emotionally. She was still full of the euphoria that the call gave her, but with it came the finality and the emptiness that being without Ariane always left her with. She rubbed her eyes with the heel of her hands. She was hollow and alone. Stele grasped the black tear-shaped rock in her pocket and gripped it tightly, hoping that Ariane was doing the same with hers. The resulting warmth surrounded her heart. It helped.

***

Stele re-joined Kian in the conference center, bringing two cups of hot tak with her.

"How was your young lady?" Kian asked.

"Beautiful, as always. And talking is good for me… like a warm hug. The difficult thing is saying good-bye. I'm empty when she leaves. She understands me like no one else, and I just want to take care of her. When she's gone, there's nothing. Only darkness and pain. I have to pull myself up every time." Stele took a long slug of her drink. "I can't think about our future and where this could go for us. I'm just surviving, hoping there will be a future for us someday." Hopelessness engulfed Stele as she thought about her future with Ariane, or worse, the lack of one.

"I can't begin to grasp how difficult this must be for you. I've never gotten over the devastation of being here in those early years, having left my love behind. I've never found Kallie's equal and believe me, I've looked."

Kian smiled and looked wistful, but there was a sadness in her eyes that Stele hadn't seen before. Unless she just hadn't taken the time to look. "Is that what you're doing…trying to replace your true love?"

She nodded. "I went everywhere and tried most women who would look at me. Inevitably, it didn't work. But I kept going, forever hopeful."

Kian chuckled and went red, staring at the wall as if she were remembering some of those couplings. Stele had been in the Strip and seen couples that were together just for the night or a couple of nights. There was little happiness amongst the men or women. "But I came to realize that I was trying to replace Kallie in my head, in my memories, in my heart. That was never going to work, but I didn't want to accept it. I didn't want to let the past go. I managed to speak to Kallie once, after I was banished. She'd moved on, gotten married. She'd let go, but I hadn't."

Stele had wondered if Kian helping arrange her visit to Nero was because of her past and this seemed to underline it.

"I'm beginning to think I might be there now, after all these years. I need to start again and find someone I can take care of and who'll take care of me. I've watched you with Ariane and realized I've been trying to find someone who matched Kallie on Nero from all that time ago. Maybe having someone I could talk to would be a good place for me to start." Kian stood and rubbed her hands together. "Let's find some food. I'm hungry."

Stele was so glad to have Ariane, even if she couldn't get to see her. Ariane knew her inside and out, had stood by her through a lifetime of humiliation and anger and seen something in her all that time ago. Stele wasn't going to let her go, she didn't want to be like Kian forever looking and searching for something.

After dark-meal, Stele and Kian returned to the conference room and settled into their chairs. Despite her exhaustion, Stele was too emotionally charged to go to bed. She lounged across her chair, sitting sideways with her knees hooked over the armrest.

Kian took a sip of her tak. "I believe you're some kind of catalyst, Stele. You've set a variety of things in motion. How we're going to deal with all these things is interesting. It feels like we're all acting our parts in something already scripted, something beyond our control. There are a number of directions we could go, as if we have free will, but each of them has already been played out in the script and the universe knows exactly what's going to happen."

Stele didn't want to be a catalyst for anything. She certainly wanted no part of a future that was already written, particularly if Ariane wasn't a part of it. She didn't want to make waves that could affect thousands, if not millions of people. Naveh! It wasn't so long ago she was drunk under a table, a banished nobody. She pulled her knees up to her chest and hugged herself.

Had her whole life been leading to this moment? Was Kian fated to find her and enroll her in the ADF? Perhaps neither Stele, nor Kian, had made any decisions at all. Was she being guided? If so, who was doing the guiding? Stele pulled her knees in tighter, as if to create a barrier between her and this...future of which she was this catalyst. No matter how much she thought about it, all she had were questions. *So do nothing.* That could be the answer, but was it even an option? What would happen if she did nothing? The shard would stay boxed up, she would continue her career, and life would still be good. There was the question about Ariane and whether life would have meaning without her. Could she conceive a life without her? Stele didn't want to consider the alternatives though Kian was pushing her into weighing up the options, to make an informed decision instead of her usual go-to of anger and running away. But just thinking about what may be expected of her got her riled, and she worried that she would explode.

The following morn, Kian and Stele met up to work out the way forward. Stele had managed a little sleep but knew she must look as washed out as Kian, pale-faced and dark around the eyes.

"Did you get any sleep?" Stele asked.

Kian sighed. "Not much. I was asking the what ifs? I ended up going around in circles in my head and staying awake."

"I'm sorry, Kian. I did manage a few crons. Like you, I went around the what ifs. Most of my questions are about how the shard will work on us and, of course, what this will mean for me. I'm also worried about how this may affect my relationship with Ariane. I don't want it to change me. Bellum Trace wasn't the sort of person I want to be. That's the thing that kept me awake most of the night. And it was my first thought when I woke."

"I was wondering about the rite of passage too. Will it work? If it works, what will it mean for us? I worry that it may be dangerous for us, and we need to be able to say no. What about the other starburst people? Do they get a choice?" Kian asked.

That was another of Stele's major concerns. There were two hundred and thirty-eight starbursts in the ADF, and they had a right to either accept or reject the shard.

"If we manage to do a rite of passage, does that mean that we'd be free to return to Nero? I suppose that's a whole new issue. I wonder if the Pargent have records about how the shard worked when it was in place. That may help us answer some questions. The rest we'll have to leave to your fates," said Stele.

"Let's see how we feel after a large tak and a couple of chun milk biskits. Do you want your tak hot?"

"Yes, please," said Stele. She thought about Ariane and how this would affect her. She expected that Ariane would tell her to go with her instincts and that she and Stele would work it out. Stele got sidetracked into thinking about Ariane leaning over her naked.

"That must have been a hot thought, I can feel the heat over here. You didn't hear or see me."

Stele opened her eyes to Kian leaning over her. "Guilty."

"Leave her be and eat morn meal with me," said Kian.

The good thing about all of this was that with Kian and Ariane behind her, she would work something out. Even if it was something later rather than sooner.

***

When Stele and Kian got to the conference room, the Pargent stood.

"Good morn, everyone," Stele said. "Kian and I have a number of questions. We don't want to create any problems for you, but there are one or two areas we think you may be able to help with," Stele said.

"Good morn, Stele. Kian," Xian said. "The Pargent expected you to have questions, so please ask them."

"I think the most important question to both of us is what the rite of passage will do to me and what will it do to the starbursts like Kian? Is it dangerous? Are there risks?" asked Stele. "I have no special abilities, and I don't want to end up like Bellum Trace, enslaving a nation." She paused, conscious of Kian's warning glance toward her. Stele took a breath and nodded toward Xian. If she wanted answers, she needed to let Xian speak.

"Before Bellum Trace, the rites of passage were the same for everyone, and their abilities and talents were enhanced. The starburst Neroians all appear to have been given different abilities. The clear-eyed Neroians are usually peace-loving people who work hard and are content with their place in the world. Clear-eyes with starburst in the past found that they were given the basic ability to attack and defend, which today could make them a marine. Clear-eye starburst Neroians in the ADF in the present are used as low skilled chefs and maintenance workers as they show no aggression. This could change if they undergo the rite, as they are likely to become a fully functioning ground trooper, marine, or other combat personnel.

"For people such as you, colonel, your leadership skills will be enhanced. You will find you are stronger, able to think quicker, find the right words to lead, strategize easily, and we suspect you would become a general quickly. So, you can see how this works, yes?"

Stele bristled. She had no abilities to enhance. She didn't excel at armed combat. She felt small next to Kian with her abilities, and her generosity, and care for her fellow banished Neroians. She was nobody on this scale. A problem. Perhaps she *would* become like Bellum Trace. Another reason not to push this forward. There was nothing to be gained if all she could do was become a power-hungry leader...*if* leader was her destiny. Maybe drinking and disappearing into the bars of Alton would be the best solution. This could affect Ariane, and it could change their relationship as well as Stele. "Where does that leave me? I have no skills to enhance. I'm trouble. If that's considered a skill, and that's enhanced, I would become another Bellum Trace. We should stop this now. I don't want that future." She looked at Kian. "*You* shouldn't want that future."

Kian shook her head. "No, we have faith in you, Stele. I'm certain that fate didn't encourage me to pull you out of the gutter to let you disappear back to them. They...I...want a lot more from you yet."

Questa nudged her gently. "I'm not following you around the bars of Alton. Our one trip together was enough, thank you. The look on your face the next morn. Never again."

"Stele, I would expect a black-eyed Neroian to receive enhanced strategic skills, perhaps with abilities beyond our current comprehension. You are likely to perceive things that even we cannot. You will be mentally quicker than some of the machines we have developed. Apart from Bellum, all black-eyed Neroians were leaders, and they were good. They developed strategies for Neroian and Federation peace, and they encouraged stability. They were always women and took partners for life, mostly female. Their progeny was often, but not always, black-eyed. A number of black-eyed leaders also came from parents with a selection of eye colors, just as you have," said Xian.

"That makes sense," said Kian. "You're already fast, and you have tactical and strategic ability beyond that expected for your age and background. Don't dwell on the negative parts of your life, Stele. That was your past. This, the shard, your rite: that's your future."

Stele ran things through her mind. There were risks on a personal level. If she moved things forward, it could affect her personality and thus her love and care for Ariane could be changed. It could seriously affect her career, which was going well. Finally, well, she could become another Bellum Trace.

But if she did nothing, her relationship with Ariane would probably suffer if all they could do was talk through space. Who knew when they could meet up again? The thought that Kian could be disappointed in her for doing nothing, for not making any decision, was also a big factor.

That didn't include her thoughts on the other banished. If Stele did nothing the other banished would also do nothing, and Stele was aware that she wasn't giving anyone the opportunity to complete a rite of passage. She'd not given them a choice, and she knew that if they wanted to, they could overrule her. They were deferring to her, and she'd let them. But there was no emergency. Nothing had happened on Nero or elsewhere. Whatever fate had in store was far in the future. It could wait.

"Thank you all for spending this time with me, particularly the Pargent for coming all this way. I've enjoyed seeing you all again." Stele nodded to them. "I've made my decision, and I don't want to do this. There's no need for things to change. We're the only people who know about this and even if the Pargent, or you, Kian, believe that fate has something in store for us, nothing has yet happened. I just want things to stay as they are. I'm happy at last. I have you, and my friends, and my life is good. Let's leave it at that." Stele left the room quickly so that no-one could try to change her mind.

The resolution of the matter gave her focus for the future, and she returned to the Dartington with a new sense of hope.

CHAPTER TWELVE

STELE HAD MADE the decision, and she was going to do nothing. It didn't end there though. It didn't mean that the shard, its story, and the Pargent left Stele's mind. They were all part of an endless spiral in her thoughts. Awareness of the future and how she could get to be with Ariane battled with all the others. She worried that she'd made the right choice, especially as it would affect all the starburst on Alton, including those who came later, and what worked for her was perhaps a detriment to them. The pressure on her was relentless as thoughts around the shard and the rites of passage filled her head like an invasion of kret buzzing continually.

Outwardly Stele presented the same demeanor, and no one would be able to see that her head ached with the thoughts. The medic smiled when she came to him nearly every sun cycle with a headache and he had the spray ready to give her some relief. His advice to her each time was to do something to relieve the stress and consider taking a break before he had to give her an enforced rest.

Relief appeared to be at hand when Kian had invited her to her home for the first time. "Now you've completed your training and have your own career, I think it would be nice to meet at my place. Perhaps you and Questa would like to come visit for dark-meal and stay over a couple of sun cycles? You could even ask your friend Dash if you like? I'll get hold of Domino to see if he has time to join us."

A trip somewhere with her family of friends was just what she needed. Her body began relaxing already with the thought of a break. It was a surprise that Kian lived anywhere other than on the base or onboard ship. "You've a home here?" Stele asked. She didn't know much about Kian, but her mentor knew everything about her.

"Yes, I've been here long enough to accrue good allowances, and I'm a high grade so I can afford a nice place."

Kian was the most senior Neroian, so had to have been on Alton many seasons. Few serving ADF starburst could have been on Alton longer than her, except maybe Harlen Sloan, Jasper Sloan's older brother, who was older than Kian and about to retire. "Where is your home?"

"I'm not telling you. I think it'll make an excellent surprise. Be here at high sun with whoever can make it, and we'll have some fun. Pack dark gear and anything you might need for outdoors."

Stele couldn't wait to get Questa and Dash to come along for the trip, and the distraction meant that she was able to take her mind off what was happening on Nero. Kian would undoubtedly want to talk about it, but Stele was grateful that, for the next few sun cycles, there was nothing she could do.

Questa, Dash, Domino, and Stele waited at the end of the dock at the appointed time. Dash had been surprised to be included in the group's invitation but had been willing to come along. Dash had often asked her about Kian and vice versa. Stele made the introductions when Kian appeared in a small ground hover.

"In you get. It'll be a squeeze with your kit, but it's not a long journey. Good to see you again, Dash. Please don't look too closely at my flying and don't be tempted to try and take over."

"Stele has let loose a number of your secrets. And I promise to keep my hands to myself, at least until we arrive."

Kian's face turned bright red, but she smiled. "Call me Kian while we're off duty."

"Yes, ma'am—Creff—Kian. I'll work on it."

Kian took them over the surface of a large stretch of water which she told them was Founders Lake. Stele knew there were a number of lakes on Alton but had never managed to see one. She put her hand to the window of the hover as if it would hold the picture held within the window-frame and keep it there longer. Stele looked around and saw her wonder reflected on the faces of her friends.

Kian opened the windows and the air rushed in, warm and exhilarating. It smelled like the moist air beneath Nero in the gem tunnels and took her back to the time she had spent underground. She shook her head to rid herself of the flashback, determined that she was going to enjoy what the next sun cycles had to offer and create new memories for herself. At the far side of the lake, nestled in between two rocky outcrops stood a flat, single story building fashioned from the local crafted green Alton stone and blue metal.

"Home," Kian said. "Welcome."

Kian parked the hover in front of the building, and everyone disembarked silently, while Stele continued to stare at the expanse of water they had flown over.

"Come indoors. We'll dump our luggage, sort out some food, and we'll return so we can spend some time in the water."

"In the water..." Stele had never seen such an expanse before and to go in it made her heart race and gave her a rush of anticipation. After a few moments of shared silence between the group, Domino put his arm around Questa.

"Come on, my friend, let's get unpacked so's we can experience the wonder that is Founders Lake."

They followed Kian indoors leaving Dash with Stele, still looking at the view.

"This is going to be a fun couple of sun cycles. I need this break," Dash said.

Stele smiled, feeling something like happy for the first time in what seemed like forever. "Me too. I need to get my thoughts into perspective, and this looks like the perfect place." The thoughts of Ariane and their future together, the shard history and what she should do about it now had been spiraling out of control, and they needed both an anchor and a safe space. Maybe she could find it here. "You ready to come in?"

"I'm with you," Dash said but failed to move. "The lakes on Bacton are all frozen. I never imagined how an *unfrozen* one could be so beautiful."

Stele had only seen vid pics of Dash's home planet and was about to say so when Dash quickly turned and sped off indoors. Dash's unusually still and reflective moment was clearly over, and Stele couldn't help but laugh at Dash's two speeds of fast and stop as she followed.

"I've only three guest rooms, so I've had to give you the storage room, Stele. You're family, so you'll have to put up with the worst space," Kian said and laughed. "I hope you won't be too uncomfortable amongst my clutter."

Stele looked at Kian and felt as if her heart would burst. *Family.* She belonged here. Her eyes teared up, and Kian held out her arms. Stele moved into Kian's hug and for a moment, complete happiness enveloped her. Contrary to her prior beliefs, it didn't feel like weakness to submit to the comfort of another person. Rather, it was enabling and peaceful in ways she'd never imagined. Stele coughed, pulled out of the hug reluctantly, and turned over the cuffs on her jumpsuit. "As family, I'd happily sleep on the floor. Thank you for this. I need the break and to be here with my friends is just perfect."

"I want you to have time and space to adjust to everything that's happening without the pressure of the Pargent, Neroian history, and both your own and everyone else's expectation. Let's have some fun, and you can worry about the rest when we return. By the way," Kian shoved Stele's shoulder playfully, "when are you due to talk to Ariane again?"

Stele's heart jumped with anticipation. Ariane was working hard for her next concert, and they'd both been busy so it would be good to speak to her and see what she was up to. Stele wanted to see how Ariane was feeling about the Pargent story, along with Stele's decision. "I should be hearing from her after dark-meal," she said, and a warm flush enveloped her body.

Kian looked across to her. "So, let's go find the others and we can work out what we want to do for the next few cron, apart from getting in the lake."

After their dark-meal, Domino, Questa, and Stele were outside lying on the sandy lakeshore enjoying the dark air and looking at the sky full of stars and planets. Domino invented a game for them all to try to identify worlds including their own.

"Pargent is not visible from here. It is too far away," Questa said.

Stele wondered about not being able to see her home planet. "Does it feel strange, being so far away?" Although Stele only thought of Nero because Ariane was there. It didn't matter how far away or close it was, it was still out of reach. But even as a banished member of the population it gave her a sense of place, an anchor. "We're all a long way from our homes, but at least we can still see them. Even if Kian and I no longer have a home, our original planet's up there."

"My home is just up there as well. It is through the jump gate and in the Allied Nations space, but it is still just up there. Or that is how I feel." Questa lay down flat on the ground looking up at the sky. "I am not likely to go back to my home world for some time. I have to complete my career and will only go back when it is time for me to partner and produce Pargent. But that is a long way ahead."

"Lots of little Questas running about causing trouble. That'd be a sight to see," said Domino.

Stele lay between Domino and Questa and held on to their hands. "I hope your 'long way ahead' is as long away as I hope." She needed her friends, now more than ever, to help her deal with what was happening.

Questa turned on their side and propped themselves up on their elbow. They looked at Stele and nodded, their blue skellen slowly waving as if there were a breeze. "I am here for you, friend. I still have much to do with you and more trouble to get into before I have to leave."

Stele checked her watch, hopeful that Ariane would still be able to chat with her. "I'm going to find a private spot to talk to Ariane."

"Please tell her that I wish her well," said Questa.

"And from me," said Domino.

"I will." Stele walked a little way off from her friends toward a rocky outcrop that pushed out into the lake.

Stele sat on a stone and wished Ariane could share this beautiful sight with her in person, but the Mesh would have to do. She thought about their love and their short time together. The warmth of Ariane's body and the soft feel of her skin, the way she'd been unable to speak with the depth of her emotion, and her delicate cries as she orgasmed. The ache between her legs, missing for most of the sun cycle, was now back. The air was still warm, and a slight breeze had come up and caused the water to have little wrinkles that reminded her of Admiral Simpkin's face.

She'd enjoyed the sun cycle and felt more rested. And although she still worried about her decision, she felt more in control than she had for some time. That said, there were still too many unknowns and they nearly all affected her and Ariane and their life together. Life had, in the past, a habit of giving her a world full of decko dung. She still wasn't free of it. She put her hand on her ever-present tear drop rock and thought of Ariane. Her Mesh burst into life and with it, Stele's whole body buzzed. The excitement of seeing Ariane caused all other thoughts to flee.

"Stele?"

Stele frowned. "Jaz?" She gripped her tear-drop rock tightly. *She's coming. She's just been held up.* Stele swallowed hard against the onslaught of fears creeping up her throat.

"Yes, this is Jaz. I'm sorry…" His hologram appeared in front of her as he shook his head and ran his hand across his angular forehead. "Nero's been invaded by pirates. The pirates are holding the Ruling Council and their families as hostages, which includes Ariane."

"NO." *Ariane.* Time stopped, and Stele fought to breathe, as panic gripped and paralyzed her, mentally and physically. She struggled against fear, desperately trying to control it. She forced deep, slow breaths. She needed to believe Ariane was safe. She had to be safe. Stele could no longer hear her heart beating. Nausea gripped her stomach, and she emptied her dark-meal onto the rocks below.

"Stele!"

She looked up to see Domino and Questa running toward her. "The pirates. Invaded Nero. They have Ariane. What can I do?" She screamed as she jumped down from the rocks and turned in circles, unable to focus. "How can I get there? I have to find her. I have to get to Nero."

"Shh!" said Questa. "Stele, concentrate. Let the messenger talk."

Stele stared out over the lake and tried to get some semblance of order to her random thoughts. Ariane needed her to be together for this. She put her hand in her pocket and rubbed her lucky gem. She breathed out slowly and nodded to Questa.

"Sorry, Jaz." *Ariane needs you. Listen.* "I'm recording you."

"I know this is heart-breaking," Jaz said. "I'll tell you everything I know but I'm warning you it won't be easy listening." He looked over his shoulder. "And I need to keep it brief."

Stele stood between her friends, glad of their support. Questa gripped her hand tightly.

"The first I knew of anything was when I heard a lot of heavy ground hovers landing. I heard a lot of loud bangs like fireworks. I ran toward the sound and as I came to the Square, I saw soldiers pulling Neroian bodies onto a grotesque pile outside the tak shop. They'd shot them." Jaz's voice had gone up an octave and he looked dazed as he spoke. "I counted at least twenty." His eyes widened, and he rubbed at them with both hands as if he were cleaning away what he was seeing.

"You mean they shot ordinary people? People we know?" This all seemed like a bad dream.

"Yes. Shot dead. I hid around the corner. I know that was cowardly, but there was nothing I could do. A loud horn sounded outside the Coliseum and armed soldiers rounded everyone up. They searched buildings and marched our people from the Square to the Coliseum. I stayed well back and by using the tunnels managed to keep out of the way. I could see the

Ruling Council with their families on the platform in front of the Coliseum from my hiding place; they were under guard."

"Was Ariane with them?" She could think of nothing and no one else.

"Yes. I had been there a few crons waiting to see what would happen next, and to be honest, I was too frightened to move. A fat humanoid male with a green tinge to his skin and a long beard appeared, walking alongside Jasper Sloan." Jaz waved his arms at Stele. "Jasper is in with the pirates. Naveh, Stele. What has he done?"

"I've no idea, but I promise if he's part of this he'll pay." Stele clenched her fists, hardly able to breathe.

"The man said his name was Rudd and he was our master. He told us that any resistance to him, his men, or the new union party led by Jasper Sloan would be met with force. Sloan, who'd been surrounded by a group of his friends, made his way to the front of them. Stele, I knew there was a reason I didn't like him. Creff. He even has his parents and sisters held hostage."

The thought that Jasper Sloan, who had been a thorn in her side all her life and who treated Ariane so badly, was now doing the same thing to his own family was overwhelming. She was going to make sure he paid for what he was doing. Sloan and Rudd together was a new development, and she couldn't understand the logic to their partnership. She remembered the way Rudd had looked at her on the bridge and shivered.

"Rudd told us he was holding the hostages to make sure we behaved ourselves. He was looking for people with a number of skills but in the meantime, the rest of us should carry on as normal. He told us to treat Jasper's orders as if he'd made them. The soldiers that were around the crowd beat their guns with their hands cheering Rudd, who left. The guards surrounding the hostages led them away into the Healer Center. The pirates are using it as their base."

Jaz raised a fist, and the comms signal went in and out for the second time. It went dark but came back almost immediately.

"You there, Stele?"

"Yes, you disappeared briefly, but all good here." Though there was nothing good about any of this.

"So, Jasper starts speaking. He got all the miners to report to the Healer Center and told everyone else to leave the Square and go about their normal business." Jaz looked away and cleared his throat. "That was the last time I saw Ariane. I've managed to hack into the Healer Center camera system. Ariane and her parents are alive and well, as are the other hostages. That includes your parents, Stele."

Stele took in a deep breath and counted slowly, trying to stop a panic attack.

"The pirates don't know I can send messages, and I'm doing everything to stay hidden. Please, get this message to the Federation and tell them what's going on. We need their help."

Stele nodded. "I'll work it out. Leave it to me." There was no point telling Jaz that she'd no input to the Federation. She'd get Kian to help her tell the right people.

"I have to go. I'll try to call again at the usual time in the next sun cycle to keep you updated. Jaz out."

The comm-call ended. Stele remained motionless though she could feel Domino's arms around her. Questa held her hand tightly. Stele thought she'd known what despair was when she was banished, but this was a whole new level. She looked across the shoreline to see Kian and Dash running toward them.

"What's happened? We heard yelling," Kian said.

"Nero has been invaded by pirates. The Ruling Council and their families have all been taken captive, including Ariane," Domino said. "That's all we know. The message guy, Jaz, is going to call Stele in a sun cycle—"

"Oh, Stele, I'm so sorry." Kian pulled Stele into a tight hug. "Come, let's all go inside. We all need a hot tak, and we'll figure out what we're going to do about it."

Stele shivered. Ariane was in danger, but she would fix it, whatever it took. She followed Kian inside.

They sat in the main room, and Kian handed around hot tak before sitting. "We need to inform Command Central about this, and I suggest we should let Admiral Simpkin and Captain Harmer know, Stele."

Stele shut her eyes tightly, struggling to understand what Kian had said. The thought of Ariane in danger, of her being scared and held hostage, made all the old rage she'd managed to control begin to rise to the surface.

"Stele, are you with us?" Kian asked.

Stele opened her eyes and concentrated on what Kian was saying. "Yes, sorry."

"Are you onboard with what we need to do? I think you're still in shock," she said.

"Yes, yes, of course. I'm not in shock. It's difficult to concentrate on anything though. I want to tear those bastards to pieces."

"I expect they'll want to de-brief you themselves. So, it's probably best if we go back to the spaceport straight away. You pack up while I do the comms," Kian said.

"I will help you, Stele," Questa said before they turned to Kian. "I can feel her despair and shock, but Stele will be ready when you are."

***

The meeting took place in the main briefing room at Command Central, with about thirty officers around the table. They wanted to know everything that had happened in the call from Jaz and asked a lot of questions. Stele replayed the comm-call and as she listened to it, the rising nausea caused her to keep swallowing like a gawping venu.

At the end of the briefing Admiral Heddin stood. "Thank you, Hosun, for your honesty. We'll take it from here. We can't make decisions about what can or cannot be done: that will be up to the Federation. If the pirates take over, the power sources that Nero provide the galaxy are in jeopardy. That may make the Federation's decision for them. But we can start planning in case they approve action. I know you won't want to hear this, but I'm not hopeful as to how much help will be forthcoming. Nero, as you know, hasn't signed up to the Federation. But we do need to look into how Rudd has managed to get enough forces into Federation space to invade Nero."

"Hosun, perhaps you can help me with that," said Admiral Simpkin. "I'll meet you on the Dartington in thirty crons. We'll get to the bottom of this."

"Good," said Admiral Heddin. "Dismissed."

Stele nodded to the room and left with Kian. They went to the Dartington lounge before she had to report to the bridge. Stele poured them both a hot tak, before sitting in her customary sideways position on one of the lounge seats. Her left arm hung over the back of the seat and her long legs hooked over the arm.

"How are you feeling, Stele?" Kian said.

Stele blew out a breath. "I don't know what to tell you. I was still reeling from the Pargent and their story about black-eyed leaders. With this on top, I'm lost. I don't know where to start or what to do first. I feel like I'm headed toward a black hole that's going to swallow me up."

"There's little to do, and you need some sleep. But maybe it's as well to keep busy for the moment," said Kian.

"All I can think about is Ariane on Nero." Stele quickly stood and started toward the door to go to the bridge. She thought about all Kian had done for her during the sun cycle and turned. "Thank you for all your support today. It's good to have family behind you when things are hard."

Kian gave her another hug. It was just what Stele needed to help her gather herself and to ground her.

When she arrived on the bridge, she took a deep breath. She was on duty now; she needed to be professional.

Admiral Simpkin pointed to the visual of Federation space ahead of them. "We need to work out how the pirates got to Nero undetected. Command Central will be working on that, but I want to get ahead of their thinking. That's why I volunteered us. I know you and Quess are a good team, so perhaps you could work together on this.

"There were other ships in that space quadrant. Some of them were fleet ships, some were trading ships, and obviously, there were pirate ships, but we had no reports. I want to know the names of all the ships present and who else was there. Haven't we got a number of fleet ships patrolling the main trade routes through the Federation as well?"

"Yes, sir, I'm on it. Quess is on their way." Stele messaged Questa, who was in their pod. "We'll give you a full list, call signs, and current status in a few crons," Stele said.

She and Questa soon created a timeline view of Federation space. Stele linked all the reports of ship movements over the last month. They messaged a number of ships that had been close to Nero during their passage, requested extra information, and plotted everything they had.

The pirates had been clever, but this was something she should've seen at the time. Her arms were heavy as she tried to move the timeline forward. Her thoughts spiraled. Her neglect had let everyone down. Her happiness and the hope that she had for the future wouldn't last. She banged her hand against the console.

"Come back. I can feel you and your thoughts. Concentrate on this task. We can discuss what has gone wrong and why you seem to think you are responsible when we have finished," Questa said.

"You're right, as always." Stele dragged her thoughts back. "Questa, are you seeing what I'm seeing here?"

"Yes, but how did they do it?" Questa asked.

"They've been able to create a mobile jump gate and remove it, and we just haven't noticed what's been happening. Mobile jump gates are illegal in Federation space, so we haven't been looking for one. We've been stupid. They couldn't get away with using one in the middle of Federation planets, but out on the rim, no one would notice. We should do some quick research and find out what we can about them. Let's look in the Allied Nations... Remember Rudd playing with us? What if he was actually testing us all along?"

Stele had been more concerned with the way Rudd looked at her than what was happening operationally. "We may have been monitoring ships coming through the established jump gates, but we haven't noticed the pirate movements because they've been clever. Rudd knows all our weak spots and has exploited them well. There aren't any beacons on the far side of Nero, so we would've been blind. That and the fact that Nero isn't in the Federation, and it hasn't mattered before. That has to be the way that ten ships could instantly appear in Neroian space and for no one to be aware of them until that moment."

"Clever...and disastrous for Nero. Let's brief the admiral," said Questa.

Stele clawed to control her emotions. She could have—should have—done so much better monitoring Rudd and his fleet. He'd probably been laughing at her naivety, knowing that he could easily fool the admiral's newest protege. Stele shook as anger and embarrassment fought for the upper hand and warred with her worry and fear for Nero and her parents, but most of all, for Ariane. She couldn't lose her. The thought almost stopped her heart. Not now they'd finally come together.

She had to admit her failings to the admiral and explain how the fleet had managed to miss the pirates. Command Central was usually monitoring space movements, but she should have noticed.

"Admiral, I'm so sorry," said Stele.

"No, Hosun. Command Central didn't pick up on it, and it's *their* job. Now that we know how it happened, we can fix it. I'll brief Command Central. Well done to both of you." The Admiral rubbed his hands together.

"What I can't understand is the why of it all. What does Rudd want with a planet like Nero?"

Stele's stomach dropped as the realization hit. Kian had talked of the fates and things being predetermined. This invasion was on her timeline, and Stele had screwed up because she hadn't wanted anything to change.

Creff! Weller thought the black gems were powerful, and she'd said as much. Somehow Rudd had found out about that too, and if he got them at source, he'd control the supply. And without knowing just what the black gems could do, it could be even worse.

She'd been thinking of herself and the black shard and what it would mean; it hadn't occurred to her that someone knew about the gems, although she should have paid more attention when Rudd had been so interested in her. Weller had worried she was being watched, and maybe she was right. Perhaps Rudd and his pirates had been watching Weller. It still didn't answer their question as to how they knew she was looking at black gems, but if they were as powerful as Weller thought, then Rudd might well know what he was looking for and why. Stele had been so naive. "Sir, I think I know why he's invaded Nero. We need to meet with Colonel Ray, and we can tell you what we know."

Stele wanted to run and hide. This whole situation was likely her fault. Kian would tell her to stand and face her fears. Maybe with Kian beside her, she could.

CHAPTER THIRTEEN

STELE ENTERED HER Pod in darkness. She lay on her bed but couldn't relax. Her mind rolled as if in a whirlpool, with continuous thoughts of Ariane and what was happening on Nero turning over with thoughts about the black shard and rites of passage. Ariane was in trouble, and Stele couldn't do anything about it from where she was. She didn't know if or how she could convince the Federation to help. She should have tried to put her own force of friends and the starburst together to rescue the hostages.

If she were the leader on Nero, maybe she could be with Ariane. Nero in the days before Bellum Trace allowed women to love women. But modern-day Nero didn't allow it, and if she were there, she couldn't *not* be with her. Maybe she'd made the wrong decision by having nothing to do with the shard, and she'd forced these circumstances. She wavered between thinking she should accept the shard and all that it meant about becoming a leader, and renouncing it. She couldn't be a good leader. She had neither the temperament nor the ability to control her aggression.

She needed to talk to Ariane, but she was no longer there at the end of a comms link. Stele loved her with everything she had. She needed to hear Ariane's soft and gentle melodic voice, her words of love, and the sense that she gave to Stele's wandering thoughts. Without Ariane as a sounding board, she was on a downward journey again.

Ariane had to be safe. Stele didn't want to think about Rudd and what he might do with someone as gorgeous as Ariane, especially if Sloan felt it would be good to be rid of her. She hoped he wouldn't want Ariane for himself. Ariane was a celebrity and a singer and beautiful. The thought of her held captive by Rudd made Stele shudder, and her anger and fear were overpowering. Maybe if she'd moved forward earlier, Ariane would be safe now. She stood and leaned against the bulkhead, banging her head against it. She was powerless. *Naveh.*

She could never be the leader Nero needed. She'd start with what she needed: a drink.

Stele hadn't been in this bar since the night she thought she could control her need to drink. How much of a failure had that proved to be? She had no such control. But now it wasn't a case of restraint, now she just wanted oblivion. When Stele had left her Pod, she'd run, anywhere, once again trying to run out her worries. She'd ended up in the bar.

She had so many questions. So many what ifs and whys and most importantly, hows. If the Federation chose not to help a world that had refused to join it, it would be down to her to rescue Ariane. Despite knowing Nero well, she was only one person. How could she mount a rescue on her own? How could she find a ship to get her there? She didn't owe the people of Nero anything, so she didn't need to help them, did she? Her first answer was that she shouldn't, but deep down, she was incapable of inaction. She couldn't leave her home world to a life of captivity.

The bar was empty which wasn't surprising given that it was the middle of dark and most people would have just finished for the night. She sat at the table she and her friends had been sitting at that night. She remembered the bravado the alcohol had given her. She needed that now. She turned to order a drink.

"I knew I'd find you here," said Kian.

"The errant child is behaving true to form you mean." Stele was being unreasonable, but Kian couldn't understand the position she was in. "You just don't get it, do you? I want to be the same as everyone else. Why should this happen to me? I don't want it. I was happy. I had friends and a new family. Life was good. No one expected me to do anything. Now I'm back where I started, where people on Nero will hate me, and I'm likely to fail." The familiar rush of adrenaline surged through her body, making her rigid with anger.

Kian stood quickly. "Come with me, Hosun. NOW."

Stele responded to the command. This was her colonel talking rather than her friend. She followed Kian out of the bar and ran to keep up with her as Kian strode back to the base. She went into the training wing and Stele followed her into one of the training rooms.

Kian locked the door. "Take off your jacket." She removed her own. "Come on, stop wasting my time. You've been given a command. Obey it."

Stele tossed her jacket to the floor. She froze, unable to speak and jammed her hands into her pockets. She'd never seen Kian like this. She looked both imperious and deadly.

"You think you've had it hard? I think you're just scared and like always, you'll run away. Well, I'm stopping you from running away, you insignificant snock dung. Let's see what you do when the chips are down."

Kian punched her and knocked her head backward. Her heart pounded, and her vision edged with red. A rage stronger than anything she'd ever had before coursed through her. No one had ever understood her, and now Kian had shown she didn't understand either. She moved quickly, just in time to dodge another punch, but Kian's follow-up slammed into the side of Stele's head as she tried to slide away. It knocked the breath from her, and her whole body vibrated.

Stele threw a sharp right jab into Kian's face and added a left hook to her gut. Kian grunted. Stele threw a series of punches, her mind overflowing with rage. One of her punches connected with Kian's head, and she stumbled. Stele's confidence grew. *I can beat you.*

She moved in closer and threw a few more blows to Kian's head. Yes. She was going to win this.

Then, there was a crunch to her face, horrendous pain shot through her nose, and there was darkness.

***

"They should call this room the Stele Hosun recovery suite," said Kian.

Stele was momentarily unable to open her eyes. Her head ached and although the pain was dull, it was exhaustingly present.

She forced her eyes open and looked to find Kian. "Did I hurt you?" Stele asked.

"No, Stele, I have a few bruises, and I certainly look as if I've been in a fight but nothing serious. You wouldn't have been so badly hurt if you hadn't run forward with such force on to my fist," Kian said and laughed. "I know that's what they all say, but in this case it was true. Your rage completely took over, and you were blind to anything I was doing."

Stele face ached and her side throbbed from Kian's battering. Emotionally though, Stele recognized that Kian cared for her and had stopped her from destroying herself—again. "Thanks for being here for me. I know I haven't always deserved your support. Thanks to you, I haven't drowned myself in Gandon wine."

Stele slumped in the bed. She hurt for what she'd done to Kian, the person who had shown her nothing but understanding and family love. Kian had supported her even when she was being stupid and causing trouble. "I'm so sorry. I was like one of the ship's torpedoes. I was on a journey that was never going to be changed, and there was always going to be a final explosion." Stele pulled herself up in the bed.

"I encouraged you. I needed you to lose the feelings that were poisoning your mind. That rage was paralyzing you, and it was going to send you spiraling downward into drunken oblivion again. I knew if you lost your anger you'd see clearly and realize that you, and only you, are in charge of your destiny." Kian sat next to her on the bed and held out her arms.

Stele leaned into the embrace and relaxed. She put her head on Kian's shoulder and settled into the safety that had always been missing from her life.

"I'll see what Questa is doing later. Perhaps you'd like some company other than me, though Dash is only on duty until high sun," Kian said as she released her.

Stele missed the closeness. "You seem to know a lot about Dash's movements. Are you going to come clean and tell me about what's going on between you?"

Kian sighed. "It was a sudden thing and it's rather nice."

"Nice? That's not enough. You're family and Dash is almost family… and whatever you're doing is nice?" Stele could almost feel Kian blush. "So how did it all happen?"

"I've seen Dash from afar since before you started to strike up a friendship with her, and I thought she was attractive. We spoke a couple of times, and she was quite insistent that she wasn't too young for me. So I thought, why not? She's not Kallie, and that's okay. She doesn't have to be."

"So, you leapt on Dash?"

"No, it was the other way around. I let her take the lead. *She* leapt on me," she said and laughed gently. "While you, Domino and Questa played in the lake over at my place, Dash and I had a number of conversations about our lives and our families. I wouldn't have done anything at all because, well, with you as a mutual friend it could have been difficult if it went wrong. But while you were all star-gazing after dark-meal, she put her arms around me and kissed me."

"And?" said Stele. "You can't leave me there."

"And I melted. We were just beginning to enjoy each other when you yelled. The rest is history, as they say."

"I'm sorry about that." Stele held Kian's hand. "My timing sucked. Now, Ariane needs me, and it's time that we discussed how we can influence the Federation." Stele sat upright. "Unofficially the Federation said that Nero is on its own. They don't contribute to its defense and therefore the Federation should do nothing to help them. Sure, they provide our power crystals for light, but if we can't get them from Nero, we'll find some other option. Is it possible that we can present a case to them to see if we can get some help for Nero?"

"I don't see why not." Kian stared into the distance, obviously deep in thought. "I met Councilor Elodie Dann, from the Federation, a short while back when she visited the marines. She was interested in Nero and the Neroians. I'll message her now and see if she will speak with me. It's worth a try," Kian said.

"Good idea. We need someone who knows how these things work." Stele waited silently while Kian used her Mesh.

"Done. I know you've been wondering how the black shard and the skills it will give us are important to what's happening on Nero. In your mind, the rites of passage probably aren't important to either the pirate invasion or rescuing the hostages. They may be two separate things, but I still think Nero and the shard are your destiny," Kian said.

Stele shuddered. Her destiny. She somehow couldn't separate the two things, they kept coming back together. The pirates and the shard, gems and hostages, rites of passage and legends, her and Ariane.

"The most important thing is getting to the hostages and getting them out of the hands of the pirates without losing any lives," Kian said.

"Domino would want to go in and blow everything up." Stele smiled, and it seemed to transform the worried frown on Kian's face. "We need the Federation to agree to an ADF strike force to help us mount a rescue. I need to think my way through the tunnel layout and put some kind of map together. I think I can make those tunnels part of any hostage rescue plans. I probably know them better than anyone because I spent a lot of my life down there." Stele could already see the map in her mind.

"Talking of tunnels, the bad news is that the shard will need to be taken to Nero and replaced in its position in the Coliseum for it to have any effect. It's now arrived from Weston, so I went to the Founders Day equipment store and put my hands on it, but nothing happened," said Kian. "If, as I think, it's the correct shard for me and all starburst, there would have been something like a power surge through my hands. I took a chance and tried it. There was nothing," Kian said, putting her hands out flat in front of her as if laying hands on the shard. "I wondered if there were a special set of words I should've used, but I spoke to Lieutenant Chumo who serves with me. His family are involved in the ceremonies on Nero. He told me that the words and pageantry are about creating a feeling of loyalty to Nero and the community, and none of it is related to the shard. Its powers come from within and happens quickly and only once. I think it's tied to the planet, and it won't work unless it's there."

Another piece of the puzzle to solve. They had to get the black shard into the Coliseum on Nero to conduct a rite of passage ceremony for themselves and those of the two hundred and thirty-eight starburst that wanted it.

Stele sighed and tried to look at Kian, but the enormity of what they needed to do caused her to stop and stare into the wall above her head. She was expecting too much. How were they supposed to manage all this without losing lives?

"Wait. Councilor Elodie Dann will meet me now if I go over to her office. I'm surprised. I didn't expect her to remember me," Kian said.

Stele raised her eyebrow. "You didn't expect her to remember a handsome, single marine colonel? Please, Kian."

"No, honestly, I didn't expect it." Kian smiled. "But it proved useful as I can get to talk to her. We need all the help we can get."

Maybe Naveh was listening. A little help from that direction could make this all work out.

CHAPTER FOURTEEN

STELE LEANED BACK in her chair and closed her eyes. She'd mapped the tunnels as best she could. No plan existed for the tunnels beneath the whole of Nero and even the Master of the Miners only knew of patches that gave the best results for finding gems suitable for sculpture.

The creation of a strategy had been mentally draining, not so much for the work, but because she had been sucked into the world she had left and to her memories of Ariane. Thinking of tunnels on Nero reminded her of the time of Ariane's first concert and how she sneaked through them to wish Ariane luck. The glow of warmth spread through her as the first notes Ariane sang slid through the dark, wrapping her in a tender cocoon of sound.

Stele forced herself to stop reminiscing. Yes, they may use the tunnels to rescue the hostages, but these thoughts only served to give her ever more internal pain and anxiety. Stele was exhausted, but finally, she had a plan. It was a good operation, except for the lack of space support. Whichever way she looked at it, the space force support was vital to distract Rudd and his pirates. The pirates had ten heavily armed ships, at Jaz's best guess.

Her blueprint for an attack was only an outline, and the biggest problem was landing on Nero and getting into the tunnels without being detected. Any ships would be spotted by Rudd as soon as they left the main shipping route and came anywhere near Nero. Even a diversion on the planet's surface wouldn't take enough attention away from space and the automated alarm systems that would be spread planet wide. A mobile jump gate would be the answer to enable a rescue team to jump to behind Nero and outwit the pirates, but Stele had no idea where she could source one.

Are you on board and free for a tak...and can I bring a friend?

Kian's Mesh message forced her to return to the real world: a world in which she had friends and a chosen family. *Together*, they would rescue Ariane.

Stele got to the lounge before Kian and Dash and threw herself in her usual chair. She couldn't settle, so stood up and walked around to lose the twitchiness in her legs.

"Stele, you'll wear that floor out. Have you been taking lessons from Dash?" asked Kian as they entered.

"While you've been gone, I've been busy. I've put together an attack plan both for the Fleet and the underground force rescuing the hostages," she said.

"I've been busy too," said Kian as she sat down next to Dash.

"I can see," Stele said, looking between Kian and Dash with a low stare.

"I met with Elodie, and she'll help us," said Kian. "I went to Merton's lakeland sector of Alton Federation HQ."

"She's from a water world?" Stele asked.

"Yes, although Elodie's what they call a lander and lives on the water and not in it. She's a small humanoid woman with pale skin like all Mertonians but not transparent like those that live in the water. Most of the population on Merton live in the water permanently."

"Will she help us?" Stele sat and leaned towards Kian.

"She's particularly interested in the ADF and the defense of this stretch of the galaxy because Merton had trouble with pirates not so long ago, and they're eager to see we're all well defended," said Kian.

"That's good news for us, isn't it?" Dash asked.

Kian nodded. "She'll be an advocate for us. She told me that the matter of Nero has been tabled for later this dark and that she'll request that we are both allowed to speak. She's not confident about anything being done for the 'Nero problem.' There are too many representatives who believe that a planet should only get out of the Federation what they put in, and Nero contributes only the power crystals, which they're well paid for. Now that Nero needs help, they say that the Neroians shouldn't expect the Federation to come running."

Stele agreed with Elodie's summary of the current situation. "It's true. Nero has given the Federation nothing except the people they banish. They expected the Federation to take them in without giving anything in return. Even I'm wondering why the Federation should care." Being unwanted was never far from her mind, despite everything that she had on Alton. The support, caring, and yes, she could call it love, were all tangible, but she still had doubts about herself and was sure that she could end up in major trouble again.

"I have those feelings of being unloved too, although perhaps not so obviously these days. I think that being banished gives you a feeling of inadequacy that comes from being different to everyone from the beginning of your life. But we all have family on Nero that we may still care about in some way or other."

Kian's words echoed Stele's thoughts.

Dash leaned over and took Kian's hand and held it against her cheek. "I care about you, and I love your difference." She released Kian's hand and did the same with Stele's hand. "You've become a special friend, and I care about you too." She laughed. "Obviously not in the same way as Kian. I don't want to rip your clothes off."

The three of them laughed.

"Back to the serious stuff," Kian said. "Elodie will message me a time, and she said it would be soon. We need to prepare what we're going to say. We should tell them about the black shard too."

Stele grimaced. This was the most contentious of their issues. "I wasn't sure they needed to know, and it could be difficult trying to explain it. But I think they need to understand the powers that a black shard can give to us and the starburst, and why Rudd might want it."

Kian nodded. "Yes, you're right. Jaz is due to call if he's not been discovered and captured. We can finalize our ideas after we've spoken to him," Kian said, just as Jaz's call came through. "You're sharing the call with me?"

"Yes, all done," Stele said.

"Hello, Stele."

"Hello, Jaz. I have Colonel Kian Ray from the ADF marines sharing the call."

"Hello, colonel. I think my mother has mentioned you. She knew you before you were banished, but we can catch up with that later." He smiled and rubbed his chin. "I've managed to stay hidden but can only speak for five crons to ensure the pirates can't monitor anything I'm doing."

"Okay, we're listening." Stele tried not to let her impatience come through. They had no time for pleasantries. Ariane's life was on the line.

"Firstly, Rudd has all the miners and a number of sculptors looking for black gems, but no one has ever seen one and they don't know what they're looking for. The miners are being accompanied to all the places in the tunnels where there are known to be gem nests. Secondly, Rudd is using the Healer Center as his HQ."

"What about the hostages?" Stele tapped her fist on the table.

"They're in the Healer Center. As you know, I've hacked into the center's surveillance and the hostages are being held in the isolation room. They look uncomfortable in there together. The pirates are living in the main wards of the center. I've drawn a plan of who is where as best as I can make out. I am sending it now."

"All received," Stele said as the document arrived.

"From the cameras it looks as if the pirates are providing their own food and drink. The hostages are being fed by the Healer Center cooks. I'll try and get information on the hostages and how they are once the cooks get home and I can speak to them," Jaz said.

"From our side, we're working on a plan. Kian and I hope to get to speak to the Federation to ask for help at dark tonight. There are a number of Federation councilors that believe the ADF shouldn't have anything to do with it, because Nero has never contributed to the running of the Federation."

Jaz nodded. "I can understand that, but I hope you can convince them. The pirates are violent, and I'm anxious for our women. I haven't seen anything happen yet, but I don't trust any of them."

Stele's stomach dropped. Ariane was one of those women, and she was beautiful. "Our initial plan is to rescue the hostages using ADF marines," she said.

"I've sent you all the information I could find out about the pirates and where they are, where their ships are, and anything else that might be useful."

"Great, thanks," she said.

"I'm still staying out of sight and intend to use the tunnels to keep safe. I'll call you after morn-meal, but if there's any problem, I'll have to contact you at a random time."

"Sure, Jaz. Perhaps you can try and put together a group that could help us. I realize they won't have any training in armed combat. We'll need people who know the local area and can let armed troops in and out of buildings once we're on the ground and perhaps provide us with a diversion near the Square. Be careful though, there will be Neroians looking to ingratiate themselves with Rudd and Sloan, so please don't take any risks," Stele said. "Anything to add, Kian?"

"I don't think so. Jaz, be careful," Kian said.

"I'll be careful. I know we can do this. We'll talk again soon. Time's up," Jaz said.

Stele's Mesh screen momentarily darkened, and there was a brief silence. She looked to Kian who smiled, and she understood that this was going to be a possibility. They had help on Nero now.

***

Stele had learned about the Federation when she was in the Academy but had never visited the HQ or been involved in any of its workings. "Why is this place called the Hive? It's nothing like any vision of a hive I might have had."

"When you look at it from the air, hundreds of workers from the surrounding sectors and buildings swarm into the main building like a cloud of krets every time a meeting of the full Federation is called," said Kian.

"This walkway is magnificent. I suppose it's been designed to impress everyone involved with the Federation." Stele and Kian walked up the magnificent walkway with palisades of colored columns on either side. "Naveh. They've cleverly put the columns to catch the light and interspersed them with these water sculptures as a counterpoint."

Each column was flat and sleek, taking Stele's eyes to the light it captured between it and the next one, the water providing a backdrop of thundering sound that almost deafened her when she got too close. Tears ran down Stele's cheeks as she was enveloped in the moment and the wonder of the light.

"Close your mouth, Stele, you'll catch a stray kret. You're acting like a galaxy tourist," Kian said.

Stele enjoyed her feelings of oneness with her surroundings. "I am just that. I haven't seen much in the galaxy, but I love color and light and how the two are used to create pleasure and well-being. This is so beautiful. I wonder who created and planned it. As much as I hate to admit it, I know I'm the product of my parents. My father used light and color for sculptures with Nero gems, and my mother had a sense of nature and healthiness that she used to make their sculptures speak. Their personalities have melded together in a black-eyed misfit who can feel when something calls out like this."

Kian put an arm around her shoulders. "Perhaps we have it all wrong and instead of a strategic thinker of galaxy missions and would-be leader of an entire world, you're an artist."

"Did I ever tell you about the hours they spent trying to get me to create something, anything? All I could do was enjoy the work and designs of others. My own efforts were a complete mess." She stamped her foot, remembering her anger followed by fear.

Memories. Stele's stomach dropped. She looked at the floor, transported back to Nero and listening to her father berating her for producing art works that were at best mediocre. "How can it be possible that the daughter of the Chief Sculptor produces rubbish? I'm not convinced you were ever created by me." It was one of his favorite barbs.

Kian gave her a gentle shake and brought her back to the wonder that was the Hive.

"But look at you now, about to meet a councilor and present to the Federation. Let's go in and find Elodie."

They sat outside the main chamber in an area reserved for speakers. Councilor Elodie had met up with them, and she radiated charm. Her personal magnetism made Stele want to get close to her and share in it. She could see why Kian was embarrassed when Stele had joked with her. Elodie seemed to delight in having two ADF Officers with her and often put her hand on their arms.

Elodie had let them take a peek inside the vast chamber.

"I don't want you to forget to speak when you see this. It can take your words away the first time, and the councilors have no patience. If you can't speak at the start, they believe you have nothing important to say and will ignore you," Elodie said.

Stele looked at the chamber and could see the magnificence and technological achievements. It was awe-inspiring both in terms of its size and its grandness, with the multi-level tiers stretching into the distance. The one hundred and twenty planets were each represented by an ambassador and a planetary council consisting of some one hundred representatives, meaning that there were over twenty thousand at each full council meeting if the administrators and technicians were included.

"I'm glad we got to see this before the meeting. I'd have been so busy looking that I may have fluffed my lines." Stele wandered to the front of the speaker area and looked below. There were lights blinking far below her, and it appeared to be a bottomless cavern. "Kian, come and look down here. It's endless."

As Kian stepped over, Elodie stood between them. "Councilor, how do they get everyone here? I mean, travel between planets takes time, and although some are close, others are a long way distant. Are meetings set a long way in advance?" Kian asked.

"There are always meetings scheduled in advance, but extra meetings are often called to respond to emergencies, like the one today about Nero. Those people who are not on planet when a meeting is called are able to present using their holograms from wherever they are and thus there's rarely anything other than a full council. It works well, and everyone can take part."

"From my lessons in the Academy, I learned there's no Federation leader, just the Grandcast who's responsible for the matters that the Federation discuss at each meeting and its progress. So where are they?" Stele asked.

"Directly opposite us in the green chamber. They make the announcements and run the meetings along pre-set rules. The meetings are recorded but are rarely shown to the public."

As they sat awaiting their call, Stele could watch the proceedings on a monitor. The Federation could decide that she and Kian added little to what they thought they knew of Nero and were wasting their time. But if they didn't stand up for Nero, no one else would.

A number of worlds had spoken and been clear in their view. Nero had separated itself from the Federation, keeping itself apart, specifically from defense, and therefore deserved nothing from the Federation to help them now.

Elodie made an eloquent and impassioned plea on behalf of Nero citing the problems that Merton, her planet, had had in the past with pirates stealing their stocks of bratta, a shellfish which was considered a delicacy in many of the Allied Nations and hence the pirates' interest in getting hold of the fish to sell at great profit. It was also the mainstay of the Mertonians' diet and without Federation intervention, the Mertonians would have starved. The pirates hadn't returned to Merton since, and there was a strong Federation presence in their shipping lanes.

Elodie's stance was that the pirates would always be looking at worlds just outside the Federation to see which were ripe for picking. It was Nero now, but what happened when another planet had something that the pirates wanted? It was shellfish on Merton, gems on Nero. Who would be next?

"Lieutenant Stele Hosun and Colonel Kian Ray?"

Stele and Kian stood as one at the appearance of a sidesman. The doors to the council chamber opened, and he indicated they should enter. A disembodied voice introduced them. "Colonel Ray and Lieutenant Hosun of the ADF asking you to hear their evidence in defense of Nero."

Kian stood forward into the spotlight and started speaking. Stele listened to Kian but could hardly hear her over the pounding of her heart.

"Representatives and Councilors. I've been living on Alton since I was banished from Nero and have been a member of the ADF since my maturity. If you can see a close up of my eyes, you will see they are purple but covered with a pattern of black we call starburst."

A drone appeared from nowhere and focused on Kian's face.

"I was unable to complete a rite of passage on Nero because of my starburst and was thus banished and no longer considered a part of Neroian society. There are two hundred and thirty-eight other starburst Neroians on Alton, mostly in the ADF or retired from the ADF. I have been empowered to speak for us all; we all want to save our home world." She nodded at Stele.

Stele moved forward into the bright light and was unable to see anything. "I am a Lieutenant in the ADF, but I've not lived on Alton long. I'm the newest-arrived banished. If you can see my eyes, you will see they are black." Stele stared directly into the drone that appeared in front of her. There was a low rumble of noise in the chamber. It started quietly but gained in volume. The drone moved closer. Stele did not turn away or blink. The Federation was obviously interested in her eyes. "I was never going to be able to complete a rite of passage on Nero, because to do that I would need to touch a black shard as part of the rites. There was no black shard on Nero. I was considered an abomination and on reaching maturity, I was banished to Alton." She took a deep breath. "However, a black shard has recently been discovered which we think is related to Nero being in danger, and it will need to be returned there. Testing has shown that the black shard, and even the small gems of it, is immensely powerful. We believe the pirates are there in search of that power and should they get their hands on it, there's no telling how much damage they can do. That alone should require Federation involvement."

Stele took another step forward and looked out into the darkness. She could just make out some faint lights in the distance, and there was a smell in the air reminiscent of the damp moistness of Founders Lake overlaid with glit. "We're here to plead for Nero despite being banished. Most of us still have family on Nero and despite our treatment we believe that they don't deserve slavery or death at the hands of pirates. We need military intervention to remove them." Stele put her hands in together in front of her and looked at the unseen representatives. "I realize that Nero hasn't contributed anything to the Federation in recent generations, but that wasn't always the case. Once, Nero was a thriving port that welcomed trade and visitors. We're asking you to let the ADF play its part in returning Nero to its people and ensuring that Rudd and his pirates are punished for their invasion, and to make sure that the power of the black shard doesn't fall into the wrong hands. Thank you." Stele stood back. Had she said enough? There was a low rumbling noise across the chamber.

"Thank you for your appearance. A decision will be made, and you will be notified," an emotionless voice said.

The door behind them opened and the sidesman reappeared, indicating they should exit.

She and Kian didn't speak as they left the Federation buildings. They walked past the columns and water sculptures, and this time Stele didn't look at them. She worried they hadn't made any impression. It was only when she'd started her speech in the chamber that Stele realized the enormity of the Federation and the smallness of her voice. She was just a kret in an endless chamber, and she was unlikely to enable change. The Federation had to provide the troops to save Ariane and the hostages, and that thought was enough to leave her with a feeling of warmth and a rush of adrenaline as she thought of the rescue.

***

Patience had never been Stele's strong point, and time was passing slowly since she and Kian had given their speeches to the council. There was nothing she could do to change things; they were either going to get help or not. But that didn't mean she had to like it. It had been less than a hundred crons. She'd gone through her plans and maps until she was certain she hadn't forgotten anything. She had talked through the maps with Questa who asked questions that helped her to refine her ideas.

She'd found Kian sitting in the lounge on the Dartington and stood in front of her shifting from foot to foot. She was on edge and desperate to know the Federation's decision.

"I was going to ask how you were, but I can already see that you are impatient," said Kian.

"I assume there's no word yet?" Stele said as she leaned toward Kian.

"I promised I'd tell you as soon as I heard anything. Sit." Kian leaned back in her seat and took a swig of her tak.

Stele stepped back and sat heavily. She had no idea what she was doing. She stood up again and walked across the room and got a tak for herself. People stared and watched her pacing the room as if bothered that their peaceful morning was being interrupted by her impatient steps back and forth.

"It's all right, Stele, I get it. Stay a while. I'll tell you as soon as I have something to tell you." Kian smiled. "Where are we with the plans for getting to the hostages and getting them out?"

Stele appreciated Kian's unsubtle topic subject change. "I think we're about there. We need a diversion to keep the pirates busy when we get to the infirmary, and that's what I hope Jaz will come up with when we next speak. Can you hop on my Mesh call again? I'm being vague with the details because he can't tell anyone what he doesn't know." Her stomach dropped and Stele had that familiar feeling of dread.

"When we talk about things like being captured, I realize just how much everyone has to lose, both on Nero and with us. I know it's what we do, and I shouldn't think like that, but the possibility that ships could be lost worries me. I stop myself from thinking those thoughts because they bring you down," said Kian.

"We can't afford to think about capture and loss. If I start to think about the risk to Ariane, I just turn to chun milk. This has to work. We cannot fail."

Before they could discuss it further her Mesh interrupted them. "Hello, Jaz. I'm in the Dartington lounge with Kian. What news?"

"Hey, Stele. The pirates are struggling to find any black gems. They believe the miners are hiding them, so they're beating them in an attempt to break their resolve. Sloan told me about a legend where black gems were taken from Nero and hidden before this all happened. So I suppose there must be some here, and they think some of the miners must know what they look like."

"If they're looking for the stuff of legends, it's no wonder they're not finding anything." Stele didn't want Jaz to know what they knew about the gems in case he was captured and tortured. The knowledge would be of no value to anyone on Nero. "Kian and I managed to present Nero's case to the Federation, so we're waiting to hear."

"That's good news, because the hostages are apparently struggling too, from endless interrogations by Rudd and Sloan. I assume they're all being asked about the black gems. One or two look as if they've been beaten. Ariane hasn't been touched yet, and she's still with the hostage group," Jaz said.

"Thank you, I know I'm selfish worrying about Ariane, but your words go a long way to keeping my heart warm," said Stele.

"I've managed to get word to a few trusted friends, and we've got a plan worked out to create the diversion. We'll light a fire in the warehouse at the spaceport, not far from the Square. It's not guarded because the pirates are assuming we aren't likely to do anything to it. Everything's planned, just let us know the when and we'll do our best," Jaz said.

"Can you contact us again in fifty crons when we're more likely to know what's happening?" Stele asked.

"Sure. Jaz out."

Stele had barely stood to begin pacing again when Kian held up her hand and engaged her Mesh to take the call from the Federation. Relief at what Kian shared nearly made her knees buckle, and she sank into her chair.

Thirty crons later, Questa and Dash joined them in the lounge at Kian's request.

"The Federation have agreed that the ADF should help and have notified Admiral Heddin," Kian said. "We all need to get back to our stations where we'll be told the plan."

Stele was glowing and brimmed with energy. This was it. She was going to rescue Ariane.

CHAPTER FIFTEEN

STELE WENT STRAIGHT to the bridge and looked around. Every member of staff including Questa had their heads down and were concentrating on their duties. "Hosun reporting for duty, sir," she said, standing to attention and looking straight ahead. She hated being late and not knowing what was going on.

"At ease, Hosun."

Stele relaxed and let out a breath.

"I hear the people of Nero have you and Colonel Ray to thank for our involvement in their rescue."

Stele thought back to the Hive and presenting into what seemed like infinity, and now here she was on the bridge doing her everyday job. The difference was bizarre and too complex to comprehend. "Yes, sir, we managed to present to the Federation. It was terrifying, but we must've said something right." Stele could still feel the camera looking at her eyes and hear the buzz around the Hive afterward.

The admiral smiled. "The Hive is enormous, isn't it? I'm impressed that you got to go there and speak. Who presented you?"

"Councilor Elodie Dann from Merton. Merton had to be rescued—"

"Yes, I know. I was in charge of the task force that went to Merton. That was easier than this because there were no hostages, and the pirate force was small with only a couple of ships." The admiral gestured to the map he'd moved to show his command position. "We have a number of different problems. If you look at this, it's easy to see. Colonel Ray says the hostages are being held here in the Healer Center under heavy guard. The four landing force ships are over here, and they too are heavily guarded. Finally, there are at least six ships of various shapes and sizes bristling with guns in the skies above Nero, keeping a watch on the main shipping routes and jump gates to counteract any possible rescue force."

This was a rare moment in her life. She could help, and she had ideas. When she was younger, she didn't have a voice and even when she spoke, she wasn't trusted, accepted, or heard. That was no longer the case. "I think I can help you with that, sir. So, you know I had trouble on Nero?"

The admiral nodded.

"Nero is riddled with tunnels and caverns. There's a whole world underground, but most Neroians never set foot anywhere near them. I spent most of my time in the tunnels just to keep out of people's way. I know them well." Stele took out her maps as she was talking. "I got into trouble for suggesting that the miners map the tunnels, because each miner has his own favorite spots for getting gems and his own source of gem nests. They don't share." Stele put her maps on the display. "I've produced some tunnel maps that we could use. I think we should land with a marine force to rescue the hostages here, in the shadow of Mount Arrarat. It's a comms blackout area and just a short journey through the tunnels leading to the Coliseum and the Healer Center." She was in the groove, presenting a serious option for the admiral. This was what she was born to do; the strategy and plan she had prepared was sound, she was confident of it. "Questa went through the detail with me and checked the available information in terms of options, tunnel height, and things like that."

"Hosun, if you keep going like this, you'll soon be a captain." The admiral smiled again, and his eyes had a twinkle in them.

The admiral's compliment made her blush. It was a two-way thing though. She enjoyed working for him because he allowed her free rein and gave her room to make mistakes, to work out the why and correct them.

"You should lead the hostage rescue into the tunnels. You also know most of the people involved on the Ruling Council, so that should make rescuing the right people easier," said the admiral.

She hoped that was true. Many were still mired in the distrust of someone with all back eyes. "Yes, sir. Jaz, my contact on Nero, has been helpful. He has a team standing by to create a diversion once we're in place to rescue the hostages. I assume that you'll be planning the sky battle to take place simultaneously."

"I've been trying to convince Command Central to let us have the only mobile jump gate in the ADF. It's being tested by the Future ADF engineers. Future ADF experiments with technology, food, clothing, and well, anything that we may use in the future. I've asked Admiral Heddin to back me up, because I think that it's the only way we're going to get to

Nero without Rudd spotting us."

"I agree, sir. Have you got anything specific you need me to pull out for the Fleet strategy for the mission?"

"Yes, we'll adapt the usual jump gate protocol because the whole Force will need to jump together. I'm working on something like six destroyers including the Dartington, eight frigates, and two troop carriers with additional air defense. I would expect the troop carriers to land the major marine force on Nero who would take out the pirates. I suggest that we use something small like the Oboe for landing the hostage rescue team. Had you any thoughts about what to do with the hostages once we've rescued them?"

Oh yes, once Stele had Ariane in her arms, she didn't intend to let her go. No one would separate them again. "My idea was to take the hostages back into the tunnels and to hide them there until the ADF had taken control of the planet." They discussed the black shard and how to get it into the Coliseum.

"Sounds a good plan. Could you work on the jump protocol? Take Quess and see if you can work it out together. You'll need their communication knowledge. There should be no need to create something completely new, just adapt and mix protocols that already exist. That will make it easier for the fleet to use." The admiral went toward his ready room but turned as he reached the hatch. "I'm here if anyone needs me. I have to talk to Admiral Heddin and Command Central. Wish me luck. Hosun, you have the bridge."

"Yes, sir. Hosun has the bridge." Stele looked for Questa. They were working at the Comms plot with their head in a myriad of interfaces covered with numbers and flashing lights. It was good to see them. The last few days had meant she and her friend had spent much time apart, and Stele missed their calm support. "Questa, the admiral suggested you help me sort out a problem. Have you got a few crons to spare?"

"It will be a pleasure. I am checking, updating, and amending communications wavelengths across the Federation to ensure we have the latest. A different project will be good for my mental health," Questa said, laughing and walking across the bridge toward Stele with their blue skellen waving as if to reflect their delight at being given an enjoyable task.

"Admiral on the bridge," Stele said later when the admiral returned, and she jumped to attention along with the rest of the staff. The admiral nodded and the bridge staff relaxed. She and Questa had put the finishing touches to their new mobile jump gate protocol which they named Fleet Instruction EXP1 as the new protocol for something experimental.

"Will we need the protocol, sir?" Questa said.

Stele hoped that the answer would be yes. It was the crux of their plans to rescue Nero.

"Yes, yes. We've managed to obtain the mobile jump gate," he said. "The experimental team didn't want to let it go. Admiral Heddin and I didn't get anywhere with Admiral Clerk who's in charge of the team despite some pretty powerful pleas and a lot of threats. But we had a secret weapon on our side. Admiral Clerk is from Merton, and all it took was a word from your Councilor Elodie and the jump gate was ours. In addition, we've been given an experimental mobile cloaking device for the Oboe."

Stele grabbed hold of Questa's arms. She wanted this feeling to last. The task force was a real go now. They had all they needed. For the first time, Stele was confident they could do this.

"We will leave in one hundred crons." The Admiral drew a deep breath. "Hosun, make your way to the Oboe. You're to join the Hostage Rescue Task Force under Colonel Ray. She'll be leading the marines."

Stele turned to Questa and took their hand. "I'll see you soon, my friend. Good luck."

"I'll be on your comms throughout the mission, so it's almost like I'm going with you. Everything is going to be fine," Questa said.

***

Stele clipped herself into her seat and struggled to do the belt up. The ADF fleet were on their way at last. It had been a frantic dark but at two moons, the fleet was on the move. Stele was in the depths of the ADF Oboe, their smallest ship and one she'd visited while practicing the Hosun Flip. She looked down at her unfamiliar suit and smiled. She was going to Nero with a squadron of marines alongside Kian, to act as their guide in the tunnels. She looked at the rows of men and women alongside her, who all had their eyes shut in a picture of calm. The pervading smell in the hold was of sweating bodies, which Kian likened to a cavern of snock on heat. They may have looked calm, but there was an undercurrent of tension in the rows. Stele, however, was excited. Her excitement hadn't faltered once since she had got the news that the ADF were being committed by the Federation and they had the mobile jump gate.

"You'll be pumped up as we go to Nero. Expect it and take control of it. Don't let it take control of you," Kian had said.

Stele understood that now. One leg was rattling like an unlatched window in the breeze and even though she kept taking long breaths out, it seemed there was always more air to release to get to that position of calm.

"Know as well as this hyperactive feeling, you're also likely to feel guilty because you're enjoying it, and the people you're rescuing are probably suffering and possibly dying. You'll also have friends who'll be putting their lives at risk and other friends who'll be worrying for your safety. All these thoughts will keep running through your mind. This means your emotional experience before we come into Nero will be different to a day on the bridge."

Kian hadn't been wrong. Stele smiled as she thought of her boss, mentor, and friend and her words of wisdom. She did feel guilty, guilty that she was enjoying the mission. This was why many people served in the ADF, to get the thrill of combat, to put themselves physically in harm's way and to defy the odds. For her it was more about pitting her mind against someone else's, to see who could create the best strategy and win.

"Prepare to jump in twenty crons," a disembodied voice announced on her Mesh.

Stele had been so deep in thought that the announcement surprised her. She sat up straighter and held her breath. She wasn't prepared and yet here she was.

"Jump in five, four, three, two, one."

Stele's heart lurched. She was pushed firmly into her seat, and she closed her eyes. She was slightly nauseous for a moment before her stomach settled. It would be a short journey taking her across the galaxy to see Ariane. Stele's thoughts drifted to her memories of their time together on the Vanguard and their bodies wrapped around each other.

"Lieutenant, wake up."

Stele must have closed her eyes. Had she been asleep? With the amount of adrenaline in her body she expected to be awake for the next three sun cycles. It looked like she had missed the jump into Neroian space too.

"Stele, come," said Kian.

Stele hurried to undo the belt holding her in place as Kian grabbed her arm and hurried her forward.

"We have problems."

Stele had the wooziness of first being awake. That time when the dream world leaks like a fog into real life, until she wasn't sure whether she was awake or asleep.

"We've left half the fleet behind. We need you on the bridge."

Naveh. This wasn't a dream; it was a nightmare. Stele took a hold of reality, and her stomach sank. "Did you just say we've lost half the fleet?" Stele asked.

"Yes. The mobile jump gate was experimental and had never been used for such a large number of ships."

They arrived at the bridge, and Stele nodded to Captain Halt. She had spent a number of cron liaising with him and the ship's crew when they'd been the first ship in the fleet to do the Hosun Flip. Captain Halt had been helpful and understanding. They both had a lot riding on the performance of the Flip. Stele because it was her maneuver and Captain Halt because he was a junior captain with his first command, and a successful flip would ensure his name would be remembered when it came time for promotion.

"Lieutenant Hosun, I asked the colonel to fetch you. I could do with the inside track on what's happening here. I'd hoped to leave you down below with the marines, but Naveh had other plans. I'm pushing hard for the planet surface, and we should be there in about thirty crons. I just wanted your overview to give me a little awareness of what the changes might do to the fleet, as we are working cloaked and in comms blackout."

In some respects, Stele was pleased that he'd asked, and it was likely she could help as she'd been aware of the plans and the protocols and had been working with Admiral Simpkin before coming to the Oboe. "What's actually happened, captain? Did the Dartington make it through?" Stele hoped it had, because with the admiral this side of the jump gates, everyone's lives would be easier.

"Yes, we have the Dartington, one other destroyer, five frigates, and two heavy attack craft left. I'm not sure about troop carriers. With twenty ships plus when we set out, we had a far superior force than the pirates. I'm not sure how we stand now as far as numbers go," Halt said.

"Did we lose any ships? Please tell me everyone is safe." Stele didn't know whether it was the adrenaline or the situation, but she fought down a nauseous feeling in the back of her throat. She was horrified that lives might have been lost before they'd even moved the fleet anywhere. She turned to look at Halt.

"I've had no reports of any loss of ships. There are a number of ships that have damage and one or two minor injuries. The jump gate just didn't work for all of them."

"I can help you with that. Let's have a look." Stele looked at the Oboe's display. "I can see the jump gate has allowed through the forward half of the fleet, the Dartington being the last ship because it was protected at the center of the attacking force. It's going to be difficult. We're almost evenly matched with the pirates now. It'll come down to the battle plans that we have and how the admiral amends them. The ships that made it through will be in the dark behind Nero now and working out their new strategy."

Stele looked at the visual again and superimposed her knowledge of the plans on top of what she could see on the Oboe's display. "I think that the problem is the lack of numbers of ships and firepower. Oh, wait. What happened to the other troop carrier? It was near the back. It won't have made it through." Stele almost stopped breathing. They would only have half the troop numbers on Nero. It would have to be enough. Hopefully Jaz and his friends would stir up enough resistance on the planet.

Stele turned to Halt. "As I see it, the admiral will have a workable number to plan with. We certainly have more flight squadrons which'll give us a lot of flexibility, and we'll have attack supremacy, and I think we'll be able to add some devastating blows to their fleet. I'm certain they don't have many attack flights, so that may be the only place we can dominate. The troop carrier with the main landing force will land on the other side of Mount Arrarat further to the south side of Nero as planned, and it should allow the attack by land to be a surprise. Even if the numbers of troops aren't as many as we planned for," Stele said. "We need to hope that they haven't felt the change in movement to notice our arrival through the jump gate. Once the Oboe lands and the rescue force are in place, we can surprise the pirates."

Captain Halt looked around the bridge. "Open all-around vision. Thank you, Hosun, that's been useful. We'll be landing in ten crons, time for you and the colonel to take your places. We'll wait cloaked close by the landing area in case you need us, but I'm hopeful that you won't. May Naveh be with you and your marines."

Valden Bush

Stele arrived with Kian at the rear unloading platform in time to pick up her gear and ready herself for leaving the Oboe. She took a deep calming breath and thought of Ariane. She was the center of her being, the settling thought in her mind that never stopped, but now Stele needed to concentrate on her duties. She'd never been a part of a ground troop landing and her fellow marines were like a smoothly oiled machine; when one section or brick moved, they all moved. She didn't want to stand out as being a first-timer. She followed Kian, ready to take the lead if needed with the direction of their invasion. Hopefully her map wouldn't lead them astray.

"Ready in your bricks," the sergeant major said.

It was too late to worry. Stele ran down the landing ramp and took her first deep breath of pure Neroian air since her banishment. It was like a moment of rebirth. The adrenaline rushed through her veins, and she inhaled deeply. That wondrous odor of damp black rock. It was pervasive and unbroken across Nero except in the flarnic rock forests.

Stele gestured to Kian and pointed to the spot she'd chosen for them to start their journey to rescue the hostages. It was a rock pathway which became an above-ground cavern alongside a shallow waterway. Stele had always believed that this cavern was the spot where she was closest to Naveh. The high ceilings of rock crossbeams and openings into the sky allowed the sunlight and moonlight to cascade through the gem nests in the rock and create light patterns throughout the cavern. It had always been good for her soul. It was one of those places that she would take from her memories and inhale when she needed a boost. She'd never expected to see it again.

She didn't have time to linger. She was ahead of the bricks of marines, moving forward like machines, bending up and down and turning from side to side, protecting them with their weapons for a full three hundred and sixty degrees. It was a difficult sight in some respects, watching the force in her private world. It was her safe haven and had always been somewhere peaceful and calming especially with the sound of quietly flowing water. In contrast, the cavern was now bristling with armed soldiers. Another memory to tuck away.

The bricks of marines moved forward like a line of decko swaying from side to side, with their weapons reminiscent of decko tails moving out to swat kret. Kian was behind Stele at the front. She could hardly hear any of the marines despite all their movement. In the middle of the force were four bricks with grav-trollies. One brick was the rear party which had a grav-trolley loaded with food, drink, blankets, and first aid supplies for the hostages. The next group of two bricks had the black shard on its grav-trolley. It was silent as it carried the weight of the shard above ground. The troops were in charge of guiding it to the Coliseum and its security. Another brick accompanying them had a grav-trolley of equipment that might be needed to tether the black shard on its base. Stele was particularly nervous about the whole shard enterprise. If she and Kian were wrong and the black shard didn't fit in the Coliseum, all of this would be for naught. Still, it was too late now.

The troops fanning out behind her continued along the side of the shallow waterway. The other side of the water was a mass of tunnel entrances one after the other leading into the maze that were the gem tunnels of Nero. "We cross the water and go in here," she said quietly.

Kian waved her hand, and the instruction was passed back. The troops stopped and waited for their next instruction. From this point the tunnels would be pitch-black, and the floor would slope up and down, the tunnels would get bigger where gem nests had been pulled out and smaller where the darkness would envelop the rescuers in a damp blanket of closeness. The walls, ceiling, and floor could surround a person and shroud them in dark despair with claustrophobic walls as if in a grave. The oppressive black wasn't something to be frivolous about. It was possible to get lost in these tunnels and never reappear. Stele had seen even miners get scared when they had lost their light of clear gems and could no longer see. But the tunnels had always been home, and the darkness had been a comfort to her. The color of her eyes didn't matter here.

Kian switched on the gem light attached to her shoulder and the marines followed suit. Stele stepped through the water, which was about a hand deep, and moved into the tunnel as she switched on her own gem. There was a sound of splashing as the troops followed her through and into the tunnels. They moved forward in the darkness for less than five crons before they arrived at the junction where the team would split.

The rear party brick turned right to take control of a cavern that Stele had identified as a safe place to take the hostages once they were rescued. It had four tunnels leading from it, one that ran eventually to the Coliseum and another that surfaced close to the landing position of the Oboe. The other two led further into the tunnels. If they needed either an emergency evacuation or to lose chasers, that would be the place to do it. As the brick left with their grav-trolley of supplies, she hoped that the directions she had given were adequate.

Despite the coolness of the tunnels, Stele's temperature ramped up, along with her anxiety, as they closer got to the Healer Center. Questa talked through a personal comms system in her Mesh, keeping her grounded and to keep her updated as to the whereabouts of the fleet. "The rear party are moving to their nest," Stele said.

"I have them on my system," said Questa. "I won't speak much now but will follow you and be ready to pass on anything you need. Good luck. Please stay safe, my friend."

The main party picked up their weapons and packs and set off with Kian leading the way, her long legs ensuring a brisk pace with Stele following closely behind her in complete silence. Each of their clear gems cast a small light that showed them the way. When Stele had last spoken to Jaz, he'd been unable to find out where the pirates might be in the tunnels or where the miners were looking for black gems.

The tunnel began to narrow and some of the taller marines had to bend over to avoid knocking themselves out. There was a banging noise up ahead, and the thirty marines stopped, and their lights blacked out as if one. Low ceilings with complete darkness and no light whatsoever were completely disorienting. With no sound or light to act as a guide, it was natural to feel trapped and fear that you might never breathe fresh air again.

The silence stretched, and the tension of the troops behind her almost slid through the air to Stele. It was one thing to have the enemy in front of you and be able to see them. It was another to find yourself having to defend yourself against the unknown. The marines all knew that using their weaponry in these tunnels could prove disastrous with friendly fire a distinct possibility.

Stele touched Kian's arm. "I'll move forward and see what's making the noise and where." She walked ahead slowly, leaning into the wall a little. She was used to moving about the tunnels in the dark, there was some kind of knack to it; she could almost sense the walls and floors to check on her position. The noise was coming from one of the subsidiary lower tunnels though there was no light visible. Once she'd identified the tunnel, she could faintly hear men's voices and a lot of clanging. It was probably miners doing their best to find black gems. As long as they didn't come up a level, they would be fine.

She returned to Kian. "I think we can use our lights again," she said quietly when she was close. "The miners are on a lower level. I can't see their lights, so I assume they won't see ours.".

"Great." Kian switched her light on and motioned for the rest of the marines to do the same.

The tunnel began to incline, and Stele put her hand out to Kian. "This is where we need to be careful; the pirates may stray into the tunnel system from here on in. This one reaches the back of the Coliseum, running close alongside the shards in a couple of crons."

The team reduced their lighting to the minimum and when Stele recognized a junction, she messaged to switch the lights off completely. The group moved forward quickly in the darkness and Stele could smell fresh air. It was dark outside, but it somehow appeared slightly lighter than the darkness of the caves and tunnels.

Stele's heart began to race.

This was the moment of truth. All that had gone before had led to this moment. Whatever it was, be it luck, fate, or Naveh, she was about to take the biggest step of her life. Those left in the team rested in the lower cavern behind the Coliseum. Stele and Kian made their way into the Coliseum toward the shards, careful to stay in the shadows. The three bricks of marines followed on behind, with the two trolleys glinting in the moonlight. There were no guards in the Coliseum, probably because they didn't think there was any reason to watch a big empty space.

Despite the darkness, the moonlight allowed them to see the mighty gems standing like four sentinels in front of them, each one higher and wider than a tall Neroian. The more important thing was in the fifth position, where the sculpture sat. Corporals James and Trollo were experts in artifact restoration, and Stele hoped that they would be able to look at the work and see how to remove it. The two marines moved over to the sculpture, crouched down and looked at the ground below them. Corporal James shone a pencil of light. They stood and moved over to Kian and Stele.

"It can be moved, and we have the right kit. Your information was accurate. Give us five crons, and we'll have the sculpture removed and be ready to put the black shard in place," said Corporal James.

Less than five crons later, the base was clear. The sculpture was placed to the side of the row of sentinels so that it would now look as if there were six, not five.

The team moved the black shard up and held it in place before tipping it over onto its base. The ground below the shard became luminous briefly and the shard did the same, showing a white edging before darkening again. Stele didn't know what she was expecting, but it was more than that.

They didn't have time to linger. Stele put both hands on the rock and at once, it was the shard she'd always needed. It had power she could feel and communicate with. She became part of the rock and yet separate from it. There was so much more information than she'd had the moment before, and she became aware of so many things that she didn't yet understand, about the history of Nero and the rocks themselves. It gave her a depth of thought she wouldn't have believed impossible ten crons ago.

A black color in her mind showed her the whole of Nero and the forces spread out against it. There was an array of different colors: hot red making her angry, white making her clear-thinking, but the purple surprised her because she could feel Ariane, so close. Her mental image of the world was transformed and color-coordinated to her emotions and needs. She shook her head as if to shake off the rainbow of colors. It was a shock, but not an uncomfortable one. She needed some time to assimilate things. Time she didn't have. Stele looked at Kian. "It's everything we thought and more. You need to put your hands on it," she said.

Kian put her hands on the shard. There was a moment's stillness and silence before she looked at Stele. "Naveh! This is amazing. I feel like I could save the whole of Nero singlehanded." She looked elated, strong, and even more confident than she had before. "Better get moving."

Kian rounded up the marines and led them onward. Now came the second test of the night. Could they get the hostages out from under the noses of the pirates?

CHAPTER SIXTEEN

THEY EMERGED FROM the tunnels into a disused alleyway tucked around the back of the Healer Center and Stele held up her hand, stopping everyone as a set of guards strolled past, totally unaware of the troops in the shadows. Once they were out of sight, Stele lowered her hand and moved forward again. The alleyway formed a natural cleft between the Coliseum's seating and the layered rock of the Healer Center. As they came out into the night air, the team stopped to get their bearings and to ensure the way ahead was clear. Stele looked out at her first sight of the town and the alleyway that she'd often used to run away from trouble. The spot where she had said farewell to Ariane was only a short distance from here below ground. She could sense Ariane now, purple in her mind. She was close by and shivering. Stele read it as cold and scared.

The team split, with two bricks going around to the front and the main entrance and the rest with Kian and Stele in the back. "We're all set," she messaged Questa, back on the Dartington.

It was only a few crons before the night sky turned molten with the flames from the fire at the warehouse. Once shouts were raised and they saw guards and pirates running in that direction, Stele led the way through the alleyway and across into the back of the Healer Center, followed closely by Kian and the rest of the team. The door was made of Neroian rock and opened silently. Kian took the lead once inside the building and turned left. She headed quietly and purposefully toward their final goal. The corridor was well lit and smelled of glit interwoven with the unmistakable smell of unwashed bodies.

As they got close to the room where Jaz had told them the hostages were held, Stele could tell that Ariane wasn't there. The new power that she'd been given only crons ago showed her that Ariane was somewhere behind them and in another building. And there were no guards here. Something had gone wrong.

She was already half-turned when Kian moved across the corridor behind her with a speed Stele wouldn't have believed if she hadn't caught a glimpse of it for herself. She didn't have time to do anything as the shot hit Kian in the center of her chest. Kian rocked back into Stele's arms, and they both fell to the ground. Stele was aware of a blue haze enveloping her mind. Kian's armor should protect her. It *had* to protect her. Nothing could happen to Kian; this was just the beginning. Stele needed Kian desperately.

Her thoughts tumbled in a stream and faded to nothing. A dark and blue nothing. Rage filled her, and the blue turned to red as she fired at the two men that emerged from the room. They both fell. Kian still lay motionless where she had fallen, and blood ebbed from her chest wound. Creff. Their weapons were armor piercing. Stele called a medic forward to tend to Kian and waved the team forward. The sound of fighting was coming from further down the corridor toward the front of the Healer Center where the marine team were engaging more of the pirates.

Stele indicated to one brick to continue down the corridor to enter through the second door into the room. They moved forward. Stele led the rest of the marines toward the doorway where the two dead pirates lay. She signaled the team, and they entered the room using both doorways, ready for anything and expecting the hostages to be held at gunpoint.

Stele took in the room at a glance. It was thick with heat and lack of air. A pervasive stale smell invaded her nostrils and there were rank overtones to the ripeness. The group of about eighty hostages were sitting and lying around the room and looked disheveled and rumpled. Many had red and black bruises on visible body parts. There were quite a few children in the room sitting wide-eyed with their parents, some staring at Stele and many looking at the pirates' bodies lying in the doorway. There were two armed pirates by the door furthest from Stele and they were quickly dispatched by the marines that entered that way.

Stele had her weapon in the low-ready position with her finger on the trigger. An armed pirate rushed toward her as she inched farther into the room. She fired and he fell and was quickly grabbed by some of the hostages who removed his weapon and pinned him to the ground.

"Drop your weapon, black-eyes."

Stele spun round to face a pirate holding his weapon to her father's head. She almost smiled. Her father was always outspoken about rules that should not be broken. If her father acted as he used to when she was younger, Stele suspected he'd made a lot of trouble both vocal and otherwise for the pirates. He looked so much older than she remembered him. She hadn't been gone that long, but he'd aged more than she expected. His face, neck, and upper chest looked badly bruised. She recognized the fear in his eyes. Her mother, YahYah, was sitting on the floor at her father's feet dressed in one of Stele's favorite smock suits covered in a floral design. Stele remembered it fondly from those days when her mother still hugged her.

Stele wanted to finish this without bloodshed. The best way would be to convince the pirate to give himself up. He was the last one alive in this group. She looked at him closely. He was tall and towered over everyone in the room.

"Put your weapons down before I kill this annoying old kret that's been buzzin' in my ears the last two sun cycles," he said.

Stele looked at him and said nothing.

"I've heard that there was a black eyed Neroian. Keep those demon eyes off me."

One of the marines shifted position somewhere behind her, and the pirate nervously grabbed her father more tightly. She was too far away to use any body charge and by the time she moved, her father would be dead.

Wait. Ariane. She had to deal with this imbecile while her new powers meant that she was thinking purple, and she could feel Ariane elsewhere. Her fear was growing, as were her thoughts of being cold. Where was she? First no Kian and now no Ariane. A red rage boiled inside her and took over her being. This dirty pirate minion was keeping her from Ariane. She turned on her heels in her fury and made to leave.

"I've got more important things to do than stand here and chit chat with you. Just shoot him," she said to one of the marines turning her head as she spoke. "And hurry up."

She feigned disinterest and began to walk away but quickly turned back again and shot the pirate in the shoulder before he had the chance to move at all. He dropped his weapon and was quickly overcome by a couple of the marines. Her father dropped to his knees and was quickly pulled into her mother's embrace.

"Did Rudd take Ariane away?" she asked, needing to know the answer but not wanting to hear it.

"Yes," said Ariane's father. "He came a few crons ago. He took us all individually over the past sun cycles and interrogated us about the black gems he's looking for. His interest in Ariane had nothing to do with the gems, though. I tried to stop him..."

"He wanted her. He said he liked her spirit when she slapped him, but that didn't stop the guards taking her to wherever he's using as his base." Ariane's mother's fear for her daughter was obvious.

"I have to find her. YahYah, has Rudd been living in our quarters?" Stele clenched her jaw tightly, and the redness within her mind grew more vibrant.

"Yes, and I expect it to be a mess," YahYah said.

"I'll start there. I think I can track her, but I need to get to her before Rudd gets her to one of his ships and they disappear across the galaxy," said Stele. "Where is Sloan?"

"We don't know. The dung heap is probably hiding underground somewhere."

She'd have to deal with him later. The coward wasn't likely to stick around to fight.

"What can we do to help?" her father asked.

Ariane's father moved next to him. "Tell us what you need us to do," he said.

"We can't take a chance on the pirates grabbing you again. We'd be back in the same position," Stele said.

Her father nodded. "You're right, of course. We'll go where you need us," he said.

"The sergeant major and his marines will take you to a safe place underground. There's already a group there ensuring it's secure, and they're waiting for you. We'll bring you back as soon as the pirates have been defeated," Stele said. She turned to the sergeant major. "You have your orders. I'm going to find the missing hostage."

"Yes, ma'am."

Stele ran from the room, down the corridor, and back out into the alleyway. She turned and headed to her parents' quarters. They were behind the Healer Center in a discreet setting alongside a number of open tunnels. As the Chief Healer, YahYah was often called out at night or when off duty in the day and therefore needed to be close. The quarters were spacious, well-lit, and open to the sky as opposed to being half underground, which many homes in Nero City were.

Stele kept out of the way of the groups that were still fighting. She could hear weapons firing and there were noises from above in the half-light, which would be the ships fighting in the skies over her head. Kian should have been here with her. Her stomach lurched and the blueness came again. She dived into an alleyway where she retched. She mustn't think of Kian at this moment. She could mourn her once she had found Ariane.

It was now almost morn as she made her way along the walkway looking at her Mesh.

"Questa," she said.

"Yes, Stele. I have you on my screen. I have tracked you so far and can see the marines are taking the hostages to safety. I have briefed the admiral. A group of marines is coming to you, but I have lost sight of the colonel," Questa said.

"The colonel was shot saving me. I don't think she survived." Stele's stomach lurched again.

"Do not think about it now. You need to keep going and find your girl," Questa said.

Stele forced herself to focus on Ariane. The purple bloomed in her mind followed by a radiant scarlet infusion, and her anger rose to the surface once more. "I'm going to get Ariane from Rudd and make him wish he hadn't crossed me."

Keeping to the shadows, she turned into a short tunnel that would take her to the back of the building that used to be her home. She moved silently toward the mouth of the tunnel and thought of all the times she'd been standing exactly here deciding whether to go home or to stay underground. A noise behind her alerted her to movement in the tunnel. She turned and could see Corporal James and his brick.

"We decided to come and give you a hand. Can't have you up against Rudd and whoever is with him on your own, however fast you might be," James said.

Stele nodded. "Thanks," she said. "I was just working out how I was going to do this. You guys will make it easier." She quickly adjusted her plans and let out a long slow breath to calm herself. "Two of you go back there and around to the front door and knock on it. One of you should try and get in, and one should stay outside. Let us know when you're almost there. Be wary when you go in. I don't know who's in there."

Corporal James detailed two marines off who disappeared silently into the dark shadows. The rest of the brick made their way with Stele, until they were all crouched below the building's sitting area window. She moved forward and carefully tried to open the door, but it was locked.

"Corporal James, can we blow the door? We need surprise on our side," Stele said. He nodded. "I need to work out where Rudd is. I think he's at the back of the house… I can feel Ariane is close to me. I need to concentrate." Stele sent all her thoughts to Ariane in a purple haze. *Where are you in the house, my darling? Think about how the room looks, and I'll come and get you. I'm just outside.* She had no idea if it would work. She hoped that Ariane could feel her. She concentrated again, feeling Ariane with purple warmth and hope where before she had felt fear and anger. She became aware of Weston Green drink, and books, and a small gem sculpture. They were in her father's study. She sent love and warmth back to Ariane.

"Corporal James, are the men at the front yet?"

"Yes, ma'am, they're just getting close. There's still some fighting outside the Coliseum but nothing near here."

"Tell them the hostage is being held on the ground floor at the back," she said. "If they can get in the door, keep going straight, and it's the last door on the right. We'll be coming in from the back. There are no other exits, apart from windows."

"They're knocking now," said Corporal James.

Stele and the men moved up to the door, and she heard movement inside. A marine was already at the door and placing two small metal boxes on it. There was a crack, and he pushed the door inwards. He slid it to the side, and they entered around him. Stele turned left and went straight to her father's study. Pieces of wall splintered, pictures and sculptures exploded, and the firefight lit up the house in an explosion of violence.

She pushed the door open and saw Rudd sitting behind her father's desk. The similarity between Rudd and her father, their belief that women should be quiet, gentle and submissive was not lost on Stele as she moved toward him.

Rudd held a glass of Weston Green in one hand and a small weapon in the other. The weapon was pointed at Ariane who was sitting on the other side of the desk, dressed in a flowing piece of see-though material that barely covered her body and left nothing to the imagination. Stele looked at Ariane and the purple in her mind became a sharp red taking over her thoughts. If Rudd had so much as touched Ariane, he would pay. Ariane shook her head and gave her a small, tired smile.

This linking of their thoughts was something that would need some controlling. Did Ariane know she was thinking of making Rudd pay? Stele couldn't help herself as she thought about Ariane when she was astride her stomach and Stele was about to enter her. Ariane blushed, and Stele knew that they were in tune with each other.

"Hello, black-eyes. I wondered if you'd show up on Nero. Another beautiful woman to add to my bed. Come over here and let me look at you," said Rudd, waving his glass at her. "Put that weapon down, or I'll kill her."

Stele obeyed him, wanting to let him think he had the upper hand. She put the weapon on the front of his desk and moved so that she was standing next to the chair Ariane was in. She stood and brazenly stared at him, daring him to come at her.

"I should have guessed you would try to rescue Nero. You'll only have a tinpot rescue team, nothing the size of my pirate fleet. You can't win. It's the premier fleet in this part of the galaxy except for the Federation." Rudd sat with a wide smile showing his pointed teeth. He took another sip of his drink, never taking his eyes off Stele or wavering in his aim at Ariane. "I'm just thinking of an hour in bed with both of you. I will train you both to give me maximum enjoyment. Something to savor."

The red in Stele's mind became a scarlet explosion, and she was ready to ignite her anger. She concentrated on her thoughts for overcoming Rudd. She was going to tip Ariane's chair and at the same time grab the weapon and fire. She hoped that Ariane could hear her thoughts and not be totally surprised by her movements.

As she pushed the chair over, Rudd fired where Ariane had been as he caught the movement, but Ariane was already moving toward the floor. Stele hoped that her extra speed from her rite of passage was good enough as she grabbed her gun from the front of the desk and fired twice at Rudd, once at the heart and once at the head. He fell forward onto the desk, and the scarlet explosion in Stele's mind faded. He was dead, and he'd never come near Ariane again.

She moved the chair pinning Ariane to the floor and pulled her up and into her arms. *Safe. Home.* She kissed her gently as Ariane wrapped her arms around her. The emotion between them was even more heightened than before, and Stele submitted to the deeper understanding of Ariane. She could feel Ariane's desire for her, a mirror of Stele's own feelings: sharp and wanting. There was happiness and wonder that this was happening. She fell almost headlong into Ariane's thoughts, where a residual of fear over Rudd and emptiness at the thought of losing Stele lingered.

Corporal James stood in the doorway and nodded toward Rudd's body. "You've done it. We'll win now. It's a leaderless band of pirates," he said. "Jaspar Sloan, who I'm told was the betrayer here, was shot and killed as he tried to board a ship to escape."

"I hope so, corporal, but you know what pirates are like. Someone is always ready to take over to become top decko. I suspect that whoever is on Rudd's Command ship will be trying to win the air battle if only to take over control of the pirate space fleet," Stele said. "What's happening outside?"

"I think we've got most of the planet under control. There are still scattered battles, but I don't think they'll last for long. We'll go and help the clear-up," Corporal James said.

Ariane stared after the corporal then looked up at Stele. "He wasn't surprised that we were kissing?"

"No, it's accepted on Alton. You can be whoever you want to be there," said Stele. "We're normal." Stele kept one arm around Ariane. "If we go out of this room together arm in arm like this, you'll be telling everyone that you love a woman. It could be difficult or dangerous for you," she said.

"So? Let them banish me. I'll come with you, wherever you go," Ariane said.

"I need to attend to business and check in with Questa and all the various marine units, and once everything is all clear, we'll get the Ruling Council and our parents back up here," Stele said. "Kian was killed at the beginning of the action in the Healer Center. She saved me by leaping into the path of an armor-piercing weapon stream aimed at me."

The thought was as agonizing as the memory. Stele shivered. "She jumped knowingly into the blast so that I wasn't caught. Naveh! Ariane, she was such an honorable and loving woman." Stele could remember those first conversations with Kian as she thought she was a crakah jack serving drinks when Stele was in a drunken stupor. Kian, who had rescued her from drink a second time and beaten Stele when she didn't realize how angry she was and couldn't lose the rage. "I need to say good-bye. What am I going to tell Dash? Their love is so new I don't think they've shared the words yet. Kian was the slow and dark to Dash's perpetual movement and light," Stele said as her eyes filled with tears.

"I'll come with you. It's weird that I can feel what you're feeling. Clearly you have a lot to tell me. I reckon you'll need me. Let's go out and look at what's happening in the square."

As they stepped out into the morning air, there was a smell of smoke in the air and the distinctive burning smell of the aftermath of weapons fire. A number of Neroians out in the square looked at her with curiosity and no small amount of fear.

"Are you receiving, Stele? Look up. The pirate command ship is after us," Questa's voice came in faintly.

There in the Neroian atmosphere, and so close to the ground, was the Dartington. It looked so majestic, and Stele was proud to be a part of it, but she was sorry not to be there with her friends on the bridge.

The Dartington was being chased by a pirate ship, with all guns blazing. The pirates had ducked down low to get a better aim at the weak spots on the underside of the Dartington which gave access to its engines.

Stele did a double take as the Dartington looked as if it was…was it? Yes, it upended itself, heading upward into the sky before flying upside down. She had imagined this move so many times when she planned it, as the Dartington was moving above her and back towards the pirates.

"The Hosun Flip," she said slowly.

The Dartington fired its rail gun and torpedoes from an unexpected position and protected its soft spots. Ariane jumped up and down, their connection allowing her a front row seat of both the action and Stele's excitement and surprise.

The pirate ship didn't stand a chance. It exploded into a starburst with thousands of pieces loose in the atmosphere above the distant mountains on Nero. Stele wrapped her arms around Ariane. Admiral Simpkin had used the Flip on the Dartington. It had served its purpose.

The Neroians in the Square looked around them with a dazed expression on their faces, and there was absolute silence. Stele wondered if they had any idea what had just happened. They probably didn't realize that the Dartington had beaten the pirate flagship and that the pirate fleet was probably already leaving with its tail between its legs. There was still sporadic fire coming from where the pirates had landed on Nero, and Stele supposed the marines were mopping up the last of the pirates and stopping them from fleeing.

There was a sudden roar in the air. Stele realized that a two-seater attack craft was making its way across the sky toward them at high speed. Stele had no time to shout for everyone to take cover when the craft was so close no one would hear anyway. As it flashed past, Stele read the number on the side and realized it was Dash as the wings waggled. The guns fired into the air, and Stele laughed at Domino getting to do this favorite thing in life, fire guns. As quickly as they were there, they were gone. Questa must have told Dash where they were. Poor Dash. She didn't know. The pain in Stele's heart was devastating. Ariane held her hand tightly.

Stele had to get the Ruling Council out of their hiding place, and her heart sank at the prospect. They had banished her, and she was certain that they would still consider her an abomination. There would be a few difficult conversations, she was sure. Her parents and Ariane's parents would have issues with them being a couple, but that was the least of her worries. The shard was in place, showing that she wasn't the outsider they'd made her out to be. They'd allowed fear to erase their history, and she needed to set things right, if not for herself, then for every other person with starburst eyes who wanted to come home and for those who would come later, so they wouldn't be banished.

She had to remember she was someone now, and they couldn't take away her feelings about herself anymore. She had a beautiful lover, friends and chosen family, and a career, and she was accepted for who she was in another world. But she was Neroian, and she belonged on Nero, didn't she? Banishment hadn't severed her link with her home. The added bonus were the magnificent gem nests containing gems that could be sculpted into wonderous imaginings of shapes, light, and color that changed with the sunlight or the moonlight. This was once a place of light and welcome, and it could be again.

Ariane looked at her and nodded. She understood what Stele had been thinking. Ariane had always understood, even in Stele's darkest moments. Stele remembered when Ariane sang, she could feel those thoughts in the composition and words, a voice that was crystal clear and full of feeling for Nero. Stele kissed her, slowly and gently, and then they walked hand in hand across the Square. Stele refused to acknowledge the look of surprise, and on some faces, anger of the Neroians that were watching them. They'd gone into darkness, and it was time to change that.

CHAPTER SEVENTEEN

THE FAMILIAR STREETS of Nero stretched before her as Stele walked down a small alleyway between two businesses. She stepped into the shade with Ariane at her side.

"I didn't know this alley was here. I've walked past it all my life and never noticed it. I must have had my eyes closed," said Ariane.

They were in the shadows, and the tunnel opened into the black rock ahead of them. "It's not so much having your eyes closed, as not needing to see the tunnels. Most people don't have any contact with anything underground, so they don't even think about it," Stele said. "The hostages in their safety cave are only about five crons' walk from here, but I don't think any of them will know where they are." Her mother had told her before she was banished that the Ruling Council knew little about what was beneath their feet, nor did they care. It was just one more way that they thought Stele was strange for spending her time in places that others didn't even think about.

Stele wrapped her arm around Ariane, and they entered the tunnels. "Don't worry about lighting, I haven't used my gem light as I seem to be able to see in the dark after my rite of passage. I'll keep you close and take us straight there."

Meeting up with the Ruling Council would be hard. She'd seen them earlier, but she had no idea what they thought when their banished, their anomaly who they'd said good-bye to all those moon cycles ago, had reappeared to rescue them.

She had to sort out the black shard and what she'd done in the Coliseum with the council. She'd dug up a sculpture and replaced it. She could see their sneers and looks of derision already. She had to keep pulling herself up and out of the black pit the council had figuratively put her in. She was someone now on Alton. She'd completed a rite of passage on Nero, and she had rescued the Ruling Council; she could survive a few looks of derision.

It was her parents that Stele was more concerned about. They hadn't stood up for her as she got older nor when she was banished. Stele had heard their silent sigh of relief as she left the planet and saved them from having to deal with all the controversy she brought. There were Ariane's parents as well. They had always been more caring toward her, knowing that she and Ariane were friends. But even they, as the girls got older, struggled to deal with her difference.

Ariane turned to her after a few crons. "Stop," she said. She took Stele's face in both her hands and pulled her head down. She kissed her. "I can hear your mind churning and you're worrying about the Ruling Council and our parents. Your new powers seem to go both ways just as clearly. I can feel all that worry, and it's making my stomach churn."

"You should feel my stomach," Stele said.

"I'm with you now, and I refuse to be separated from you. We'll work this out and make sure we stay together. Now hold my hand, and let's do business," Ariane said.

Stele received waves of Ariane's confidence and sureness, and her stomach calmed.

They arrived at the cavern where the council sat around the rocks. It was dark on one side, but the other was lit up by sunshine through gem nests and openings in the roof. The rear party seemed to have distributed much of the food, water, medicine, and assorted items of clothing and blankets to the hostages. Stele looked around for a marine medic so that she could find out what had happened to Kian. She was still processing her loss. Her eyes filled with tears, and she couldn't see clearly.

In the distance, Stele could see her mother talking with a marine medic who'd been part of the rear party, and she and Ariane made their way over to them. They were standing over a patient. As Stele got closer to her mother, she caught sight of the patient who moved their head and looked at her. It was Kian.

Stele stopped mid-stride. She opened her mouth to speak, but no words came. She'd blanked away most of her thoughts of her in shock. She hadn't had space to deal with her loss. But here she was, alive. "Naveh. I thought you were dead," Stele said.

"I think I'm still here, though I'm a bit worse for wear," Kian said.

"I saw you fall, dead. You saved me. I didn't know what to tell people… to tell Dash."

"I'm a survivor." Kian looked from her to Ariane and back again. "You must be the lovely Ariane. Are you going to introduce me?" she asked quietly. She coughed, and her body shook. "Keep talking to me, Stele. Take my mind off the pain."

"Kian, this is my girlfriend, Ariane Guy," she said. She pulled Ariane in front of her and put her arms around her waist. "Ariane, this is Colonel Kian Ray, ADF marines: my mentor, and friend, and the person I'm always talking about."

Kian raised her head a little. "I'm so pleased that you're safe. Stele has been so worried about you." She coughed again. "Without the Federation, I think she would have hitched a ride on any ship coming this way to get to you," she said.

Stele turned to her mother and, after a moment, took her in her arms. She seemed smaller somehow and looked tired and worried. "I've missed you, despite everything with the banishment," Stele said. Her mother almost crumpled in her arms and Stele enjoyed the feel of her in spite of the anger and sorrow. Her mother had never understood her, not like Kian, not like Ariane. But she was her mother, and her love had always been there. Stele's anger had meant she'd ignored it.

Her mother looked up at her. "You and Ariane?" she whispered. "You're together?"

Stele nodded. "You know we've always been together," she said. "The last moon cycles have been difficult, being apart, but we're going to stay together now." And she understood that it was up to her to make that happen. "There've been a number of important events that affect Nero, and we need to get Kian well so that she and I can brief the council about what has happened." She turned, looking for the sergeant. "Any news on how quickly we can evacuate the colonel and any other wounded?"

"Yes, ma'am. The Oboe is about to land at the spaceport and is setting up as a medical center. I've booked a healing tube for Colonel Ray. She should be as good as new in a sun cycle."

Stele's father came over to her as they were getting Kian on a grav-trolley to take her to the surface.

"I don't profess to understand what's happened," he said, looking about Stele with wide eyes. "I see you're in uniform and obviously a leader. I'm going to have to get used to a lot of different things." He turned to Ariane and back. "Give me time; I'll get there. Please give your papa a hug."

Her father reached out, and Stele hugged him so close that she could smell his familiar smokiness, before she turned away to leave with Kian and Ariane. "We'll be back soon, Papa, and we can catch up with what has happened. You'll need to talk to everyone over the next few sun cycles. We're here because we were alerted that you'd been invaded, and the Federation agreed to help Nero as a goodwill gesture," Stele said. "And there's a damn good reason the pirates were here looking for black gems."

"I'm sure the Ruling Council will be meeting to debrief as soon as they can. Will you stay with us when you've finished your business? Will Ariane be with you?" her father asked.

"Yes, she will. We're together. We're not being separated again," she said. Stele was surprised her father was already conceding the point that they were together and being so conciliatory. He'd always been so black and white, so argumentative, and never backed down. Stele recognized more than a few of those traits in herself and knew it was something she'd need to be aware of. She yawned and stretched her back. She wasn't going to mention it now. She couldn't remember when she'd last slept. She'd been living on adrenaline and anger.

The rescued hostages, the injured, and the ADF marines made their way out to the Square. Stele and Ariane continued to the spaceport to get Kian on the Oboe. Captain Halt greeted them as they arrived. By the time they reached the medical bay, Kian's complexion was pasty gray, and she had trouble opening her eyes. She looked to be in pain, judging by the grimace on her face. The medical tech put Kian in a healing tube and closed the top and told Stele to return in the morn.

She was at a loss. The adrenaline had been flowing around in her system ever since she presented to the Federation and while it was only two sun cycles ago, she had hardly stopped since. Her energy store had been getting less and less, and with Kian being settled, Stele was empty.

She looked at Ariane. "Let's go," Stele said.

Ariane nodded. "To your parents?"

"Are you okay with that? I know Rudd took you there, and we need to talk about that, and how you're doing," said Stele.

"Rudd didn't do anything more to me than have hands all over me. I hit him a few times to stop him. You haven't had time to talk to me because you've been busy saving the planet. That's what we'll do when we get somewhere private," said Ariane, grabbing Stele by her arms and almost shaking her, as if it would shake some sense into her and stop her negative thoughts.

"My rooms will be totally private, if Rudd hasn't messed the place too much." Stele was hopeful that Rudd hadn't explored enough to find her rooms along one side of the house. There was only one door, and the rooms were a bedroom which led into a seating area with a desk, a tak dispenser, and a bathroom. "We'll have to speak to my parents. But I won't say much or talk for long. Most of the stuff I need to talk to them about should be when Kian is there too, and we need to say it to the Ruling Council. Otherwise, we'll be saying the same thing over and over." Stele took Ariane's hand as they moved toward the bridge. "I need to speak to Captain Halt to make sure the admirals are aware of what's happening and to request some leave."

Business matters concluded, Stele and Ariane left the Oboe and walked to the Healer's House still hand in hand. Stele felt pride in that, walking along the streets of Nero. There was a long way to go yet but she certainly hadn't seen it in her future. There was no open hostility, but the feelings of the population could become vocal quickly, as they had in her past. She refused to hide this time around. She heard running feet and Ariane was grabbed, lifted, and turned around by a man. She was about to go into attack mode but the feeling coming from Ariane was pleasure after the initial fright. Stele tempered the punch she'd been about to deliver with her free hand and used it to run her hand through her hair. Ariane's eyes twinkled over the man's shoulder, and she smiled. It looked like Ariane had guessed what she had been about to do.

"Put me down. We'll make Stele jealous, and we'll both be in trouble," said Ariane and giggled.

Stele loved that sound, like water running over gems in the mountain.

"Stele, meet the real-life Jaz instead of the communication version."

"It's so good to meet you," she said. Jaz was the sole reason they knew what had been going on. "Without you, Nero would have been in trouble. You got word out. We'd have had a hard job rescuing the hostages without your information and help with the diversion." Stele held out her hand. "Thank you. And a personal thank you from me to you, for both that and for looking out for Ariane," she said. "I expect the ADF will also want to thank you. Nero owes you big time." Stele was going to make sure that Jaz got both recognition and some kind of reward.

Jaz's face went red, and he laughed. "Yep. The hero. Underground and well away from all the trouble," he said.

"It took courage to set up the messaging in the first place, and to use it as you did. There are so many people in your debt." Stele put her arm around Ariane. "Once the dust has settled, can we meet up and have some food with you?" Stele wanted to get to know Jaz better. He appeared to be so much more than the man on the messaging interface.

"Good idea. Let me know when officialdom has stopped bugging you. Ariane knows all my hangouts." Jaz disappeared toward a bar.

"He's been such a good friend, hasn't he?" Ariane smiled.

Their thoughts were definitely in sync. Stele remembered that night when she heard that the pirates had invaded, and Ariane had been taken hostage. He'd been there for her ever since. "Yes, he has. Friends like Jaz are as rare as black gemstones."

They eventually arrived at her old home. It hadn't changed any, even though Rudd had taken it over, there was nothing on the outside that showed there had been any trouble. The house was relatively grand by Neroian standards and created using the natural rock caverns with added constructed rock walls. Natural light was provided by clear gem strips or splinters as the builders called it, both in the walls and the roofs.

Stele stood outside wondering whether to go straight in, or if she should ring the bell or bang on the door like any visitor. She looked at Ariane and was about to explain her thought when she was overtaken by a sudden feeling of sexual need and urgency. She looked at Ariane. "Was that you?" Stele said.

"Uh huh," Ariane said.

Stele stared into her eyes, returning those same feelings. She was falling into the purple and was taken away on a wave of wanton delight.

There was a cough. Her mother stood with the door open. She looked from one to the other. "There you are. I was hoping you'd come back. Come in, come in." She ushered them into the house. "Rudd didn't damage much in the house. And it looks like he slept in the guest room. The major casualty was your father's drink collection, which is about half the size it was. Your rooms are fine. I expect you'll want to go there straight away. You both must be exhausted and will want to have showers and food…and things…" Her mother shook her head. "Creff. I know you've never heard me use the word, Stele, but I'm nervous."

Her mother was nervous? It was something Stele was going to have to understand. Before she'd been banished, her mother had always been strong and calm, ready to fix the broken at a moment's notice, although she had never tried to fix Stele. Stele believed that her mother accepted she was broken. Now, Stele had grown up and was seeing things completely differently. It was one of those crystal-clear moments in life when everything makes sense after years of murky fog and misunderstandings. Stele said nothing but moved toward her mother with Ariane wrapped in one arm. She wrapped her mother in the other and the three of them stood there in silence. Her mother leaned heavily into her, as if taking shelter from a strong wind. "We're all exhausted and nervous. In the morn we can sort out all the details. Let's just take this sun cycle as we have it," Stele said.

Her mother nodded. "There's cold cuts, broth, and fresh pilton fruit in your sitting room." She pulled away from Stele and Ariane. "Welcome home."

Stele thought about that. She pulled Ariane closer and kissed the top of her head. She was home without a doubt. She had Ariane, and Ariane was home. That her mother was thinking about this as her home was unexpected. It reminded Stele of all those times she had come in the house and there was a smell of baking. The smell of freshly baked kokon had to be one of the most enduring things about home on Nero. "Thanks, YahYah. We'll talk in the morn."

CHAPTER EIGHTEEN

THE DOOR CLOSED on the outside world, and there was only them. Ariane was there in Stele's mind, that familiar purple aura. Physically, they had been apart for so long that loneliness came back as soon as Ariane was just a few feet away, the kind that was wrenching and dark, and she needed Ariane in her thoughts. Stele moved closer and kissed Ariane, slowly and gently. She ran her tongue along the inside of Ariane's lips and pulled her close. She was at one with her at last. She loved her totally.

Ariane stopped kissing her. "Did you just think that?"

"What did I think?" She hadn't got used to Ariane hearing her thoughts. What had she said? She'd been thinking about what she thought of Ariane. Panic over. It wasn't a secret. She just hadn't said those words often. She loved Ariane so she should tell her. "Yes, I did think it. Now I'm going to say it out loud and tell you that I love you. I love you with every part of me. I can't get close enough to you."

"That's good. I didn't want my love for you to be a one-way thing," Ariane said. "I love you too. I always have. There's never been anyone else in my mind."

"I haven't heard you say I love you in my mind. I know when you're thinking of me, because there's a purple haze blowing through, and it makes me think I'm home."

Ariane smiled. "Oh Stele, that's me thinking of my love for you. Just as you're my home, I am yours. That home feeling is our love."

Stele knew Ariane had the rightness of it. "I want to get close to your skin and show you how much I love you. But—"

"We need food and drink and a shower. Let's see where our bodies are at the end of that list. My love isn't going to disappear in those few crons. While we eat, you can tell me how you got here and why you can hear my thoughts."

A while later, Stele had showered and eaten, and she'd given Ariane a brief description of all that had happened. Now, she was naked and waiting for Ariane, who was in the bathroom. She couldn't stop thinking about the bitter-sweet moment of saying good-bye after her banishment and the black tear gems that she'd found. Some would say it was serendipity, and some fate must have been in the mix too. She had her tear in her hand and felt the warmth and calmness coming from it. It had given her such a closeness to Ariane over the moon cycles they'd been apart but now she wouldn't need it. She could sense Ariane without it. Ariane was singing in the next room, and at the same time, Stele could feel her happiness and the purple haze pulsing love and home.

She walked to the door and looked at Ariane, naked and drying her luscious black hair. Stele's legs felt unsteady. She must be more tired than she thought and leaned back against the wall. She wanted to feel that hair in her hands, to comb through it with her fingers, to get the sensual feeling as it brushed across her body tempting her to new heights, new places, and new wonders. Oh, how she loved this woman.

Stele could feel Ariane's thoughts overlaying her own. She wanted to love Ariane's body, and she could feel Ariane's longing at the same time.

"I can feel that, Stele. Naveh, my own longing is one thing but to know about yours too is a double blast of need," said Ariane.

She came close to Stele and shook her head, and her hair whispered across Stele's face and neck.

She couldn't take any more, the wait for the passion had been long enough. She swept Ariane into her arms, lifted her up, and carried her over to the bed. She lay Ariane across it and looked at the way the moonlight played across her body from the splinters of gems in the roof. Stele wanted to reaffirm her love for Ariane, to spend time worshipping her body. Her lust and need were reflected in Ariane's thoughts.

She lay down next to Ariane and pulled her gently onto her side towards her. They kissed passionately, and while Stele wanted to make this moment last, the Vanguard had been long ago, and there had been so much waiting since. There was no way this moment was going to play out other than them coming together quickly. Her heart was beating almost in time with her thoughts and getting faster. There would be time to celebrate the joy more slowly later.

Stele slid her hands all over Ariane's curves, breathing in the flarnic and relishing the ache that appeared in her mind from Ariane. She moved her hands lower, and Ariane nibbled on her neck. Stele lowered her head and pressed her lips to the soft curve of Ariane's breasts, before exploring her dark nipples with her tongue. Her hand explored lower and found the heat she'd been looking for. Ariane raised her hips to greet her and a cron later, Stele's mind was filled with Ariane's, a melody of softness and love.

Sometimes passion, lust, and love intermingle, and Stele's frustration must have passed to Ariane who didn't linger on her body but headed straight for the dip between her legs. Stele's body rose to a crescendo and the tension in her arms and over her whole body reached its peak and exploded. The purple haze ran through her in a cacophony of starbursts.

Ariane was in a similar place, and she felt the echo of herself in Ariane's mind as she went over the edge. Stele's thoughts spiraled as she thought of nothing but Ariane. They were each like a set of musical notes that intertwined and played a harmony that was so much more than the notes alone. She blinked to hide the tears, but there were just too many and they ran freely down her face.

Ariane wiped the tears away with her fingers. "I understand. You're home, and I love you."

Stele had come completely undone. Ariane was the only person who would know that.

"To the rest of the world you're a prospective leader and a sound thinker. The morn will tell us what Nero thinks of you. But I know you have a soft middle and are kind and loving. You're allowed to have your moments of vulnerability, and I will always be here for them."

Stele kissed Ariane and found contentment in her arms. There was a quietness and calm that followed their passionate love-making. Stele watched as Ariane closed her eyes, and her thoughts stilled. She closed her eyes and thought about the wonder of their love before she fell sound asleep.

She awoke with the early morn light reflected from the ceiling across her face and an urge to make love. This need was beyond any that she could remember having before. She was already raring to go. Once she'd gathered her thoughts, she realized that Ariane had been practicing her thought communication and was lying snuggled next to her, her face radiant.

"Good morning, lover. How do you feel on this wonderful morn?" Ariane asked.

Stele wouldn't mind being awoken like this every day, with the warmth of her girl and the smell between them of togetherness from a night of sleep and sex. She was so happy, and there was nothing that could take this away. She laughed. "You know exactly how I feel, since you had those wild thoughts and put them into my head." Stele turned so that she lay on top of Ariane and kissed her gently. "So now is payback time. What was it you were thinking about? Oh yes, me between your legs."

Stele slid down Ariane's body and gently opened her legs wider. The anticipation bounced between them. It was sharp like a gem splinter and caused Stele's inner muscles to clench. She wanted this. She leaned into Ariane's body so that she could massage her breasts and play with her hard nipples. She took one of Arian's nipples in her mouth and sucked. The reaction from Ariane was instant and hit her mind like a blast from one of Domino's weapons. Stele almost fell backward. "Was that all you?"

Ariane was so much more passionate than Stele had ever imagined.

"Don't stop." Ariane pulled Stele's head toward her chest.

Stele took the other nipple in her mouth and caressed the first one. She slowly made her way down Ariane's body, planting slow kisses as she went. She lingered in several spots that Ariane found exciting or erotic. She spread Ariane's legs and blew across her clit. Ariane groaned. She followed it with another when Stele took a nipple in each hand.

Stele ducked her head a little and licked between Ariane's folds. She could feel Ariane's pleasure in her thoughts as if it were her own. The feel of Stele in her wetness and the need within Ariane came at Stele in a rush. This was Ariane getting close. The purple haze grew thicker and exploded as she entered Ariane. She moved her fingers and explored the fluted muscles changing as Ariane came. Ariane shook and moved up and down on Stele's fingers, calling her name over and over.

Stele moved up Ariane's body and almost fell into the purple eyes that were wide open and looking at her. She felt Ariane move on her fingers. "I love this, being this close to you," Stele said. This feeling of closeness was more than she'd ever dreamed of. It rushed around her body, making her aware of how much she loved and needed this woman.

Ariane removed herself slowly from Stele's fingers and wrapped her legs around Stele's waist. But they didn't end up in a position that Ariane was obviously aiming for, and Ariane giggled.

"You'll have to put me on top, I can't get there without your help," she said.

Stele laughed and put Ariane on top of her. "You won't need to be there for long. You started me off before I was even awake and with all your thoughts since, I'm ready to pop. That's before I thought about what I wanted," she said.

Ariane put a hand between Stele's legs. She ran her finger up and down and circled around her clit. Stele couldn't wait. She needed Ariane inside her, and she didn't have to say the words. Ariane thrust her fingers between Stele's legs, and she came in a flood. A kaleidoscope of thoughts and emotions flooded through her with an all-encompassing purple hue. *My Ariane.*

They spent some crons snuggled together, crons they'd never had in the moon cycles of their relationship. The smell of flarnic mixed with the smell of their lovemaking comforted Stele. She relished the closeness and wanted to have this kind of morn every sun cycle. The togetherness and love were something she wanted for always. She wanted Ariane to be her life partner, to share in her day-to-day work, home and life. But would Ariane agree if she asked her? Ariane was now someone important on Nero and had her future almost assured. Their being together could prove difficult for her.

"Stele, I can feel your thoughts from over here." Ariane took Stele's face in her hands. "Whatever you're both elated and worried about, please tell me."

Stele couldn't leave it, she needed to know what Ariane thought. She stared into Ariane's eyes as her heart beat loudly and vibrated through her body.

"Yes," said Ariane.

"You'll be my partner for life? My love, my home, my everything?" Stele took Ariane in her arms, her heart thudded in her chest and her face ached with the size of her smile.

"Yes," Ariane said.

Such a small word that had so many meanings for her. It was a commitment to Ariane for the rest of her life, to care for her, to make sure she was happy, to love her unconditionally. It was a commitment to home and creating a life together. The together was the important part for Stele, their future would be as a pair, two halves that made a whole and nothing would separate them again.

"Still, yes." Ariane said. "I want to be all of that for you. Will you be mine?"

Yes. Their connection meant she didn't have to utter a word. This was a perfect morn.

CHAPTER NINETEEN

STELE SAT AT the kitchen table, cradling her tak in her hands. Ariane had gone home to be with her parents, to reassure them she was okay and to talk to them about her relationship with Stele. She took a sip and smiled at the memory of their night together. When her parents came in, she sat back and waited for them to start. She was done cringing and feeling bad about who she was.

They sat at the table with her, and her mother looked at her father expectantly.

"We're sorry." He stared at his clasped hands. "I imagine there are things you want to say to us."

Stele rolled her neck. "I guess my biggest question has been why. Why didn't you fight for me? Stand up for me? Why did you let them banish me?"

"The rules are the rules, Stele. Starburst eyes are banished. And you had no color at all. We've never seen anyone with black eyes. Everyone said you were an abomination."

"And knowing your own child, you thought I was one?"

Her mother flinched. "You were so angry. You lashed out all the time—"

"Wouldn't you, if you were called an abomination? If you saw the disappointment in your parents' eyes every time they looked at you?" She leaned forward, red infusing her view. She took a deep breath and settled back again. "I guess that answers my questions, though."

Her father finally looked up from his hands, and his gaze didn't waver. "We were wrong, Stele. We should have fought to change things, but we took the easy route. We should have raised questions, and even if we didn't understand, we shouldn't have allowed people to treat you so badly." He swallowed hard. "We were wrong, and we're so sorry."

Stele's mother let the tears flow as she took Stele's hand. "Please forgive us. We're so proud of you and all you've become."

Peace stole over her, and she squeezed her mother's hand. "No more anger. We'll move forward. I've missed you."

Her mother gave a quiet sob and held Stele's hand to her face, and her father came around the table to hug her. She let go of the years of rage, of betrayal and abandonment. Those feelings were poison, and she was only hurting herself by holding onto them. She wasn't that person anymore, and it was time to be the person she'd become, in every way.

There was a knock at the door and Stele's mother went to open it. Kian followed her back into the room, looking tired but thankfully, most certainly not dead.

"Sorry to intrude, but I've spoken with a member of the Ruling Council, and they'd like to convene."

Stele stood. "Let's go."

"They want to meet in their chamber." Kian paused, as though letting that thought sink in.

Stele considered the implications. "Bad idea, right?"

Her mother looked confused. "But that's where they meet."

"Big public decisions are made in the Coliseum, where *everyone* gets the same information. And this is information we want to share with everyone all at once. I don't want only a select few to have it who would decide what they want to share based on their own agendas." She smiled when Kian nodded, looking proud. "We'll tell them we'll talk to them in the Coliseum, and they can be there or not, but we'll be talking to everyone who's there."

Her father took a deep breath as though to say something, but then stopped when Stele looked at him. He bowed his head. "I can see what you're saying. It goes against all tradition, but I understand."

She put her hand on his shoulder. "I'm glad. I no longer need your approval or your go-ahead, but I'm glad you support me." She turned back to Kian, but not before noticing the flash of surprise in his eyes. "Let's go."

They made their way to the Chamber, and when they entered, they stopped just inside the door. The council members were already sitting in their respective seats.

"Thank you for coming," Stele said, projecting into the room. "I know we have much to talk about. However, I dislike repeating myself and as many of you know, I'm not a very patient person. So in the interest of time and transparency, Colonel Kian and I will be debriefing everyone at the same time, in the Coliseum. I hope you'll join us there."

She turned and walked out, ignoring the few people who called after her as she and Kian made their way to the Coliseum.

Kian burst out laughing and held her sore side. "I think a few of them may have died of shock before the door closed. I doubt anyone has ever said anything like that to them before."

Stele grinned. "I wanted them to know where they stand." She stopped and put her hand on Kian's shoulder. "Without you, I wouldn't be who I am. I wouldn't be here, putting them in their place. I wouldn't have just spent the most amazing night with Ariane, the woman I love."

Kian punched her shoulder, but the pride in her eyes was clear. "I knew this was the woman you could be even when you were face down in your own vomit. I felt it, and you've proven yourself over and over again."

They made their way into the Coliseum. Stele stood in front of the black shard, and she could feel the thrum of its power course through her very being. People were gathered, and more came, including the crew from the Oboe. Ariane joined her and held her hand.

The crowd parted and the Ruling Council made their way to the podium, most of them looking like they'd eaten something sour.

One of them moved to the front of the group. "Colonel Ray, Nero offers you its deepest gratitude—"

Kian held up her hand and stopped him, to his obvious bewilderment. "Thank you. However, to be clear, it's Stele Hosun who demanded that the Federation help Nero. She's the one who created the attack plan, who led the rescue, and who knew how to help the hostages. Stele is the reason you're not the bedmates or slaves of pirates."

It was blunt, and Stele couldn't help but smile. "Council, we have information you need to know, and that all the people of Nero need to know, in order to be what we once were." She motioned to a crew member, who set up the holograph program showing the information the Pargent had provided. "This is what's missing from Nero's history."

The hologram information played. The true history of Nero, of people with black eyes, of the place Nero used to have in the galaxy. Murmurs of disbelief, of wonder, and sometimes outrage circulated through the crowd.

Once it was over, there was a long moment of silence as the crowd waited for the council to respond. When they didn't, seemingly unable to think of anything to say, Stele stepped forward.

"As you can see, our history has been misused to create a world of division. Fear has forced valued people, friends and family, into banishment. Nero has isolated itself, and that isolation made it vulnerable, as you've experienced." She looked at each of the council members before turning to the crowd. "It is time for Nero to join the rest of the galaxy as a place of beauty and to be welcoming once again. It's time to accept difference, embrace it, and understand that we are all one community."

Cheers and applause broke out, but it was silenced when a council member stood. "And you, Stele Hosun? According to our history, the black-eyed are the leaders of Nero. Will you be seeking to be the leader of all Nero?" His purple eyes flashed a challenge.

"No." She smiled at his look of surprise. "You have the information, and I believe that you'll do what is best for Nero. With my occasional input, maybe." The crowd behind her laughed. "I've made my life with the ADF, and I have love and a chosen family. I have no desire to lead a planet. But the citizens of Nero also know what should be, and what is expected, and I imagine they'll also guide the council in making the right decisions."

It was a challenge, and the crowd's response made it clear. The Ruling Council would no longer have total control. People wouldn't be banished on their say so.

Stele turned when someone touched her shoulder. She smiled when Ariane took her face in her hands and kissed her. Life was so much more than she could have hoped for, and she'd do her best to be worthy of it.

CHAPTER TWENTY

THE CEREMONY WAS held on Nero a moon cycle after the invasion by Rudd and his pirates. The Coliseum was packed full of people. From the back of the stage, Stele could see people she had known all her life. Many of them had never spoken to her or ignored her, as if her black eyes might give them some disease. There were others who had always been hostile and rude.

Stele decided instead to concentrate on the people who *had* been kind to her. The head of the miners and several of his colleagues had looked out for her, knowing that she knew the tunnels and caverns better than they did. It was only because of some outside pressure and her suggestion of mapping the tunnels that meant she didn't get to work for more than a few sun cycles with them. There were several of Ariane's friends like Jaz who had taken her as they found her and never judged her or looked at her as if she was something to be avoided.

Stele stood in her ceremonial ADF uniform along with Kian and Corporal James, looking smart in their bright red uniforms. There were a number of other marines with them, Captain Halt of the Oboe, and Jaz. Music played, and there was an almost party atmosphere in the venue.

There was a fanfare, and Stele's father led the Ruling Council out onto the stage in ceremonial robes and medallions. Stele felt her heart drop; the last time she had seen them on the stage had been at her banishment. The shame would never leave her. She burned inside with it, the shame of never being at one with her home world and the people on it, of being different and a misfit. Stele would do all she could to change that, to make sure that anyone else that was different would be able to live happily on Nero and be accepted for who they were. Her thoughts were all positive.

She could feel Ariane in her mind, her purple haze as if someone were shaking it. It was her fluttering nerves that Stele had calmed a few crons ago while Ariane was warming up. She now stood on the far side of the stage and before she had sung a note the crowd were silent. Like Stele, they waited for the crystal clarity of the large voice that was about to pour out of this small woman. It would roll across the Coliseum and outward across the whole of the town and have everyone mesmerized. She could hear that voice in her mind surrounded by a purple haze, and she was home.

When the last note of the song finished, there was uproar amongst the crowd as they all whistled, clapped, and cheered. Ariane bowed to the different sections of the crowd. She nodded to the gathered council members, blew a kiss to Stele waiting in the wings, and walked off the stage.

Stele's father walked forward and addressed the crowd. "We have gathered to offer Nero's thanks and gratitude to a number of people without whom we would still be under the control of the pirates. All of the recipients are also being thanked by the Federation for their efforts. Councilor Guy has been nominated to do the presentation for Nero, and we welcome Admiral Simpkin, Fleet Admiral in the ADF to do the presentations for the Federation," he said.

Councilor Guy and Admiral Simpkin made their way on to the stage.

"Jaz Zemper, for courage, honesty, and providing information at grave risk to himself. The first person ever to be awarded the newly created Neroian bar made from all the colors of gems on Nero," Stele's father said.

Jaz made his way across the stage and was presented with the Neroian bar.

"And the Founders Bar from the Federation." Admiral Simpkin presented him with the Federation medal.

This was repeated for a number of marines who were mentioned for their various tasks in the rescue, including Corporal James and Captain Halt. Stele stepped forward, expecting the awards to be issued in rank order, but Kian stopped her.

"I'm going first, you'll see why," she said.

Stele's father looked across at Kian. "Colonel Kian Ray for her far thinking, excellent planning, and leadership of the hostage rescue force. For taking fire to protect others. The Neroian bar with the addition of the first award of the newly created Neroian Valor bar."

As Kian made her way across the stage, Stele allowed herself to feel proud of her and all that she'd done. Kian was presented with the Founders Bar with an additional award for valor from Admiral Simpkin, as well.

He raised a hand for silence from the cheers that were ringing out. "Finally, I am also pleased to announce that the ADF has awarded Colonel Ray a field promotion to General."

The crowd roared but were no match for the shouts and whistles of Dash, all of Kian's marines, and her friends.

"Finally, Lieutenant Stele Hosun, who despite being unfairly banished, used her integrity, values, and knowledge of Nero to rescue us both culturally and physically and who put herself in harm's way to save individual hostages. The Neroian bar with the addition of the second ever award of the Neroian Valor bar." He pinned it to her uniform, and when Stele got to Admiral Simpkin, she was presented with the Founders Bar with an additional award for valor.

Admiral Simpkin raised his hand for silence a second time. "I am also pleased to announce that Lieutenant Hosun has been awarded a field promotion to Commander."

Once again, the Coliseum erupted in a loud roar.

"In addition, The Ruling Council on Nero have decided to join the Federation. They have chosen Commander Hosun to consider becoming Nero's first Ambassador. You don't need to make a decision now, but we want the people of Nero to understand how much you have done for them and how important your voice is throughout the galaxy."

Stele was transfixed. The promotion was a surprise. The route to commander was usually based on length of time in service, and Stele was still a junior. Even more of a shock was the suggestion that she be a Neroian Ambassador. That Nero had considered asking her, a banished, to represent them was something she had never expected.

She could hear Ariane in her mind thinking about kret flying into her mouth. She snapped her mouth closed and could feel Ariane's laughter and love blowing through her. She was home, and home was wherever Ariane was.

EPILOGUE

Six moon cycles later, Stele met with her friends in Xin's restaurant in the spaceport on Alton. It was almost empty as it was early, and Stele was glad to have a few moments to herself before everyone arrived. The dark Alton air mixed with the smells of space engineering and the aroma of spicey food would always be one of those memories that she'd have when she thought of Xin's place.

"Is this table good for you, Stele? Or should I say Councilor or Ambassador Hosun?"

"Lai, the table is perfect, and I'm still the Stele I was all those moon cycles ago. So please don't change anything."

"I'll bring you a tak until your friends arrive," Lai said.

"Can you make it two please, Lai, Ariane will be here in a moment." Stele's heart beat faster. Ariane had let her know with her thoughts that she was close, and she accompanied it with shards of lust. Ariane arrived and kissed Stele deeply.

"Hello, Ambassador Hosun. I love saying that. How was your first day?" Ariane asked.

Stele felt the heat rush to her face whilst dealing with a sharp stab of Ariane's lust and working out how to answer that. She inhaled a breath of flarnic. "It was different, that's for sure. I was thrown into the thick of my first Federation meeting with no notice. We were later called to make a vote, and I managed to get here early enough to have a few moments to clear my head. Otherwise, it's been full on," Stele said. "And you, my love?"

"Today has been one of the best yet. I went back to the Federation about that house for us to use as our base here. They will subsidize us, and we can have it. Success. We'll be close to the Federation, close to Kian, and we'll be able to fly in and out quite easily." Ariane still hadn't sat down and as Lai arrived, Ariane danced around the table with her.

Lai laughed. "You people make me feel young and happy."

"Well, we're happy. We've just found out we have somewhere to live now, instead of having to stay with our friends. Our real home is on Nero, but we travel back and forth a lot." Ariane let out a deep breath and sank into a seat next to Stele.

"I hope that Questa can make it. I haven't seen them for a few days. Because they spent their leave with us means that when they went back to work, I missed them. They're just like family," said Stele.

Ariane laughed. "Your family of Questa, Domino, and yourself. The three of you have been joined at the hip ever since you met," she said.

"If I didn't know better, I'd wonder if we had some qualities that made the ADF put us in the same pod." What the three of them had was special. They'd gone through the Academy together and in spite of, or because of, their differences they'd molded into a single entity and that had stayed with them even after leaving. "You knew we were talking about you," Stele said as Questa and Domino arrived together deep in conversation.

Questa looked up. "I was asking Domino about his new friend, Zazu," said Questa.

The way Questa put emphasis on the new and friend made Stele think that they were perhaps a *special* friend. "Who's Zazu? I don't recall anyone on the squadron called Zazu. Is it your new pilot?" Stele asked.

"I wasn't expecting an inquisition before I'd even sat down. And no, Zazu isn't my new pilot. After Dash left, the new Chief Pilot is Tim Sharp and you know I'm not into men, so no need to question me about him. He's okay as a pilot, though no one will ever be as good as Dash. She was professional, but she was fun. Zazu is in charge of the railguns on the Dartington and she's like me: we both love firing weapons. We talk for hours about the relative merits of different torpedoes, and we've gotten close. She has red hair and is so fascinating I find myself staring at her instead of endlessly talking."

"She must be important if she shuts you up," Stele said. Domino's eyes twinkled, and he blushed. Domino's happiness was as important to her as her own and to see him so obviously at one with a woman was good.

"Now all you need is a Pargent in Federation space that Questa takes a shine to, and you'll all end up with partners and your new pod will have six members," said Ariane.

"My parents have messaged to tell me that there is a new team of Pargent coming to Alton to liaise with the Federation. Jonti Jon is part of the team, and I have missed them. So I hope they will be posted close to me," Questa said. "I thought you said that the general and Dash were coming?"

"They are, but Dash is bringing Kian from Nero. This new life we have of moving between Nero and Alton is exciting but tiring. Since Kian was promoted to general, she's been looking after her marines here and dealing with the banished who wanted to go through a rite of passage. She felt like it was her responsibility." Things had moved forward so much. Nearly all the banished had gone through a rite of passage, and several had stayed based on Alton as members of the armed forces. She leaned back and put her arm around Ariane's shoulders.

"Nero has also decided that as well as being in the Federation they want their own security because of the possible value of the black gems. Kian is helping set up the Neroian Security Force, and several of the banished who are moving back to Nero to be with their families will be part of it. Ah, here they are," said Stele.

"Sorry we're late," said Dash, almost running to the table ahead of Kian. "I couldn't get a time to land early enough because Kian was delayed, and I lost my slot." She turned and took hold of Kian's hand.

"All my fault. But blame the Ruling Council on Nero. They got caught up in their discussions and wanted my ideas. I thought I was never going to get out of there. Sometimes it would be nice to be ordinary and not have to make decisions that could be important to what happens in the future." Kian sat down in the empty chair. "You'll get the news eventually but the cases against the pirates, Harlen Sloan, and the others have all been heard. They were all convicted and sentenced to hard labor for life on Clacton, the mining penal planet."

Everyone at the table cheered. Stele grabbed Ariane's hand and held it to her lips. She was so proud of her for those moon cycles of putting up with Jasper Sloan, who would no longer trouble anyone, and having to deal with the pirates. The sentence was what she'd hoped for. "Just desserts, I think," she said quietly between kisses.

"It came out that Harlen Sloan had overheard half a conversation at your graduation, Stele, when you were talking to Weller about black gems and how valuable they could be. He passed the information to Jasper and Rudd via Zentos on the Vanguard," Kian said. "No doubt it will keep us talking for most of the evening. But before we get to chatting." Kian nudged Dash. "Are you going to tell them?"

Dash blushed as she glanced at Kian and stared around the table. "Last night I agreed to be Kian's partner for life. I'm so happy I could burst. I had to keep quiet about it all day, and it's been killing me. I love her. This is a new beginning for us."

Kian looked around the table much as Dash had done. "We wanted you to be the first to know, which is why the day seemed so long with all that waiting to tell you," she said. "The other news, and why I was delayed, is that the Ruling Council have decided that they want to have more than just Dash available for trips around the Federation and further afield for them and the Ambassador's team. They also realized that Ariane is now travelling around the Federation singing, often about Nero and selling it to the galaxy. They asked Dash to set up a Neroian Flight Service with a number of different sized ships for different length journeys," Kian said. "Nero is going to open up to the galaxy again. No one will be banished for being different. People can love as they will."

Stele could see the pride in her face in all that Dash was achieving.

She took her hand and kissed it. "I'm so proud of you, my love," Kian said.

Dash bowed to the table and laughed. "We need to order food and drink, I'm starving. Important people should not have to live on fresh air. Food, please."

Stele waved to Lai and began the important business of ordering food. She took a moment to scan the eclectic bunch of her friends gathered together, and her heart swelled. She'd never imagined she could feel belonging like this.

Ariane squeezed her hand. "I feel you," she said simply.

Stele leaned closer and kissed her, deep and soft. All the years of pain and loneliness melted away as Ariane wrapped her arms around Stele's neck.

She was loved.

And she was home.

What's Your Story?

Global Wordsmiths, CIC, provides an all-encompassing service for all writers, ranging from basic proofreading and cover design to development editing, typesetting, and eBook services. A major part of our work is charity and community focused, delivering writing projects to under-served and under-represented groups across Nottinghamshire, giving voice to the voiceless and visibility to the unseen.

To learn more about what we offer, visit: www.globalwords.co.uk

A selection of books by Global Words Press:
Desire, Love, Identity: with the National Justice Museum
Times Past: with The Workhouse, National Trust
World At War: Farmilo Primary School
Times Past: Young at Heart with AGE UK
In Different Shoes: Stories of Trans Lives

Self-published authors working with Global Wordsmiths:
E.V. Bancroft
Valden Bush
Addison M Conley
Emma Nichols
Dee Griffiths and Ali Holah
Helena Harte
Dani Lovelady Ryan
Karen Klyne
AJ Mason
James Merrick
John Parsons
Ray Martin
Robyn Nyx
Sam Rawlings
Simon Smalley

Other Great Books
by Independent Authors

Music City Dreamers by Robyn Nyx
Does following their dreams mean losing out on their new love?
Available on Amazon (ASIN B08WR5ZMN6)

Scripted Love by Helena Harte
What good is a romance writer who doesn't believe in happy ever after?
Available from Amazon (ASIN B0993QFLNN)

Come Dream with Me by Karen Klyne
When your past and your future collide, who do you become in the present?
Available from Amazon (ASIN B096PB3HMF)

Rock My Heart by Emma Nichols
What will it take for her to stay?
Available from Amazon (ASIN B09G1YNHQC)

Judge Me, Judge Me Not by James Merrick
A memoir of sexual discovery and finding the courage to be true to yourself.
Available from Amazon (ISBN 9781915009074)

The Proud Weed by Sam Rawlings
Children's picture book about discovering your place in the world.
Available from Amazon (ISBN 9798728860617)

The Adventures of Daisy the Boy Sparrow by Dani Lovelady Ryan
Children's illustrated book about chosen family and having the courage to live the life you crave.
Available on Amazon (ISBN 9798730349025)

Warm Pearls and Paper Cranes by E.V. Bancroft
A family torn apart. Love is the only way forward.
Coming October 15, 2021 (ISBN 9781915009029)

That Boy of Yours Wants Looking At by Simon Smalley
A gloriously colourful and heart-rending memoir.
Coming October 31, 2021 (ISBN 9781915009074)

Printed in Great Britain
by Amazon

79256719R00129